"Hank, they'll kill you."

Shadoe's fingers ignited a flame on Hank's skin. Her touch was magic for him, and he knew if he didn't turn away, he'd drag her into his arms. "You've wasted your time coming here," he said. "I won't go back and turn myself in to face a murder charge. I'm innocent."

Shadoe felt her body warm. Hank was a lawman, not a killer. Whatever else he'd done, he deserved a chance to defend himself. If he went after the wolves alone, he wouldn't get that chance. "Let me help you."

"You want to help free the wolves?"

"No, but I want you to live. And if it takes setting the wolves free, then I will."

"Oh, Shadoe." Just as he bent his head to kiss her, the trees behind his head exploded into splinters and the delayed whine of a bullet echoed on the morning air.

Dear Reader,

They're rugged, they're strong and they're *wanted!*
Whether sheriff, undercover cop or officer of the court,
these men are trained to keep the peace, to uphold the
law. But what happens when they meet the one
woman who gets to know the man *behind* the badge?

Twelve of these men are on the loose…and only
Harlequin Intrigue brings them to you—one per month
in the LAWMAN series. This month, meet U.S. Wildlife
Service Agent Hank Emrich, brought to you by
seasoned author Caroline Burnes.

For Caroline Burnes, the Montana wilderness where
this story is set is part dream and part legend. The
release of wolves into the U.S. wilderness captures the
conflict of two life-styles Caroline understands and
sympathizes with. But she firmly believes that the
balance of nature is the key to survival of the planet.
Each species is important—and deserves a chance to
live. In *Midnight Prey*, sexy lawman Hank Emrich and
Shadoe Deerman, with her Lakota heritage, embody
the conflicts being fought in the West today.

Be sure you don't miss Hank and Shadoe's exciting
story—or any of the LAWMAN books coming to you
in the months ahead…because there's nothing sexier
than the strong arms of the law!

Regards,

Debra Matteucci
Senior Editor and Editorial Coordinator
Harlequin Books
300 East 42nd Street
New York, New York 10017

Midnight Prey
Caroline Burnes

Harlequin Books

TORONTO • NEW YORK • LONDON
AMSTERDAM • PARIS • SYDNEY • HAMBURG
STOCKHOLM • ATHENS • TOKYO • MILAN
MADRID • WARSAW • BUDAPEST • AUCKLAND

For Dianna—live the dream

ISBN 0-373-22409-5

MIDNIGHT PREY

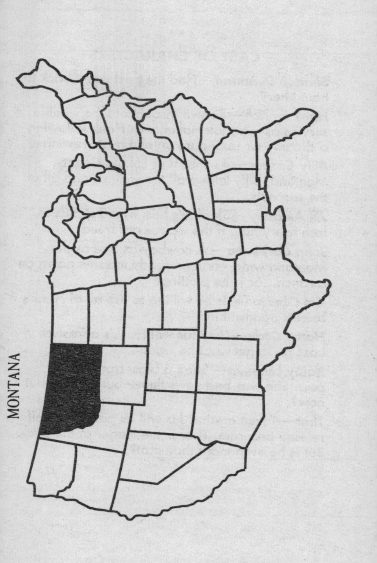
MONTANA

CAST OF CHARACTERS

Shadoe Deerman—Had the past come back to haunt her?

Hank Emrich—Known throughout the wildlife service as a troublemaker, was Hank following a dream—or setting up an elaborate revenge?

Billy Casper—As sheriff of Lakota County, Montana, Billy knows all the victims, and all of the suspects.

Jill Amberly—Shadoe's best friend stands to lose everything if the wolves are freed.

John Carpenter—A cowboy as free as the Montana wind—is John ready to settle down on a ranch...or is he plotting?

Cal Oberton—Is he willing to use all of Hank's secrets against him?

Harry Code—How far will Hank's abrasive boss go to get what he wants?

Kathy Lemmon—She's a blast from Hank's past. She was bad news then—but what about now?

Thor—Taken against his will as part of a wolf-release program, Thor is the leader of the pack. But is he even more than that?

Chapter One

The moon silvered the snow into a long white plain making the dark shadows of the forest even more sinister. Shadoe leaned against the tree, her breath puffing out in sharp gusts in front of her. She could sense the creature behind her, golden eyes able to follow her easily in the night.

Snow scrunched beneath a light step. She looked around, but there was no place to hide. If she tried to escape across the open meadow, she'd be easy prey for the animal. She could almost feel the hot breath on her neck, feel the fangs tearing into her throat. That's how the end would come, she knew. The wolf would get bored with stalking her. When it knew she was tiring, it would suddenly dart out of the trees, catching her in the leg and bringing her down. Savage jaws would close on her throat.

Then the chase would be over.

The heavy snow trapped her feet, and she was amazed to look down and see that she was barefoot. How had she come out into the deadly Montana winter without her boots?

How had she come out without her gun?

In the distance she heard the pitiful whinny of a young, terrified horse. The sound galvanized her into action. That was how she happened to be barefoot and defenseless in the snow. She'd heard something after the foals. Something hungry and predatory. The wolf.

Her breath came in short, flat gasps. She could sense the wolf, watching her, listening to her struggle to get oxygen. In trying to save her horses, she'd made herself the perfect target. Smart, cunning, the wolf had abandoned the stalking of the horse and come for her, sensing that she was the enemy. She was the one who most threatened the predator. But tonight, she was no match for the wolf, not when she was weaponless.

She pushed her weary body away from the tree. If the wolf came for her, she would not die a coward's death clinging to a tree trunk. In the deep snow her bare feet found a limb. She pulled it from beneath the white cover and held it. The wood was stout, better than nothing.

Turning to confront the woods, she held the limb-like club.

"Come on, you demon. Come on and fight." She spat the words into the night, her brown eyes seeking some sign of life from within the woods.

A silvery shadow slinked just within the safety of the trees.

Shadoe's heart tripled its beat, pounding so hard she heard it in her ears, felt it slam against her ribs.

"Come on, you bastard."

She saw the movement almost before she could turn to meet it. The wolf came at her out of the timber. A silvery gray male, he ran with his head low, his golden eyes holding her in a gaze that promised a quick and savage death. The pink tongue flicked in hunger.

Shadoe cried out, a primal sound of war, and dropped into a crouch.

The wolf hit her with full force, knocking her backward in the snow. Her club was thrown from her hand, falling a dozen yards away. Defenseless, she twisted her fingers in the thick, soft fur even as the animal's white fangs glinted in the moonlight.

Shadoe was a strong woman, but she was no match for the power of the wolf. The hungry mouth pressed down, the teeth grazing her throat. The jaws opened wider....

SHADOE DEERMAN SCREAMED and sat up in bed. Totem, her cat, hissed, spat, and leaped to the foot of the bed, frightened and annoyed with the rude awakening.

For the first few seconds, Shadoe could see nothing but the silvery snow and the black images of the trees, heard nothing except the thumping of her heart, but as the dream began to fade, she realized she was safe in her own room, in her home. Outside the bright April moon glinted through her window. Just to make sure, she got out of bed, slipped into her robe, and went out on the small porch that gave her a long, uninterrupted view of the range land that she'd claimed as her own. New spring grass gave a silvery wave in the moonlight. The snow was all but gone from her land, just lingering in some of the higher reaches.

Standing on the wooden deck, Shadoe started the litany of self-assurances she'd come to rely on whenever she was awakened by one of the terrible nightmares that had begun to plague her sleep ever since she'd learned that Canadian timber wolves were going to be set free in the Montana mountains.

"It's only a dream. The horses are safe. I'm safe. The wolves haven't been released yet. The horses are safe. The horses are safe."

The words calmed her fears, but she knew she would have to get dressed and make a check of her stock before she could consider returning to bed. If there was any reason to go back to bed. If the pattern of nightmare and anxiety repeated itself, she'd not sleep another wink the entire night.

A low sigh escaped Shadoe as she leaned on the porch railing and stared out across the land. The velvet sky was filled with the sparkle of stars, and a quirky breeze teased the new spring grass into foolish dances across the range. She listened to the stillness of the night, a solitude that had driven some to madness during the long isolated winters. But it wasn't winter now. It was spring in Big Sky Country.

This was a land she both loved and hated. As a child, she'd dreamed of spending the rest of her life here. She and her father had talked and planned, imagining the horses they'd raise, the competitions they'd win. She had been a different person then, a child with no understanding of the terrible price a wild land could extract. A child who believed that she was bound to nature by bonds of love and understanding. A naive child.

Had she been wrong to come back to her family ranch and try to make a living? In truth, had she a choice? Her father's people would say she had been called back. That she had come to finish her father's dream. A faint smile tugged up the corners of Shadoe's lips. When she'd first come back to the ranch, she'd see her father in the darkened hallway of the barn, or standing in a copse of trees at the edge of a meadow. She'd catch him out of the corner of her eye, a watchful presence, a spirit happy to see his daughter back on the land that they had both loved. In her mind she knew he was not there. But in her heart…that was another matter. Perhaps she didn't have a choice, and with spring greening the meadows, she could only pray that she had made a wise decision to walk so close to old scars.

She was smiling when she caught sight of a movement along the south side of her barn. From her vantage point on the deck, she had a clear view down to the barn through the still leafless branches of a birch tree. For a second she calmed herself by saying it was only a shadow, the shifting of a cloud across the moon. But the night was cloudless, perfectly clear. She wrapped her arms around her body, feeling too vulnerable in her nightgown, and stared at the barn. Waiting, watching, as her father had taught her. The movement came again and she knew it for what it was, a person edging toward the main barn door.

The horses!

Shadoe eased back into her bedroom and picked up the bedside phone. Sheriff Billy Casper was a family friend and she dialed the number from memory. ''Helen, this is Shadoe up at the Double S. There's a prowler in my barn. You'd better send someone out here.'' Before the dispatcher could give advice or warning, Shadoe replaced the phone. She found her jeans, a sleeveless T-shirt, a green flannel shirt, socks and insulated boots. With her jacket bunched under her arm she picked up her gun and flashlight before she went out the front door.

She felt the panic squeeze against her lungs, and she fought it back by taking long, measured breaths. This was one of the moments she'd dreaded, the idea of confronting a rustler. It was 1997, but outlaws still rode the range, only this time in tractor trailer rigs with the goal of stealing horses and cows for butcher. The outlaws usually weren't brazen enough to raid a barn, but the county had been torn wide open by the controversy of releasing a dozen Canadian wolves into the wild. Many of the ranchers were in Washington, protesting. In fact, Shadoe had been scheduled to go but had stayed home at the last minute with a pregnant mare. Had the intruder expected her to be gone? It was a question that would bear lots of thought, later.

The shotgun was loaded and she had shells in her jacket pocket. She was ready for anything as she sprinted the last distance across the open barnyard to the barn door. Her heartbeat accelerated as she found the lock snapped in half and the door open a crack.

Remembering her father's teachings, she cleared her

mind of panic. She could see his lean features, the brown eyes that never flinched but often smiled. Breathe slowly, shut out the fear. Shadoe could remember the things he'd taught her, but that was a long time ago. A dream.

This was real. This was not some flight of imagination, some situation made up to test her skills. Someone had entered her barn, and the safety of her horses was now in her hands. Look, listen, think, then act. Four clearly defined steps. Four steps of a warrior.

Slipping in through the crack in the door, Shadoe held the shotgun at the ready, but she stopped long enough to let her eyes adjust to the deeper darkness of the barn. To let her ears pinpoint the slight differences in the sounds of her animals. In the middle of the barn, Geronimo was pawing in his stall. Dillon was also fidgeting. The intruder was somewhere near the middle area. She calculated the angle she would have to shoot to make certain she didn't hit one of her horses. Look, listen, think.

Then act.

Sliding along the aisle, she started to move to a place where she had a better shot, if she got the opportunity. The horses began to fidget, destroying her ability to hear. At the far end in his stall with the iron bars, her stallion, Scrapiron, gave a snort of unrest.

Shadoe sought the darkest hiding place beside the rolled-up water hoses, praying that the intruder would make a movement or sound that would give his location away. Could she shoot him?

The answer to that was yes. If she had to, she could. To save her horses, her future, she would do whatever was necessary.

The smooth stock of the shotgun was pressed into her shoulder, her fingers on the trigger as she left her hiding place and advanced into the center of the barn. She had a flashlight, but she wanted to pinpoint the trespasser before she turned it on. She would have only a few seconds to sight him and shoot. She had to be close, too, so the pellet pattern of the bullets wouldn't spread out in too wide an area. It was a tricky situation, and where the hell was Sheriff Billy and the other ranchers?

A noise at the end of the barn gave Shadoe her first clue to the intruder's location. Someone was down at the end, near Scrapiron's stall. She heard metal on metal, the sound of the stall door sliding on its rollers. He was opening the stallion's stall, hoping either to injure him or set him free. She had to move fast.

Dropping to a crouch, she started forward. Behind her, the barn door swung open wide. Damn! There were two of them and she was caught between them! She heard the tattoo of powerful hooves and knew that Scrapiron was whirling in his stall, excited by the stranger who approached him. It was now or never.

She lifted the gun to sight but she never got a shot off. Scrapiron lunged from his stall and raced toward her. The horse saw her, but too late for him to swerve, and his muscled chest caught her shoulder with such force that she nearly went down under his hooves. She kept her feet under her, but the impact spun her, knocking her to the left as her finger slipped on the trigger. The shotgun discharged into the dirt floor of the barn with a violence that lifted and then dropped her in a crumpled heap in the middle of the barn. Stunned, she heard the sound of running feet and soft cursing. In the distance was the wild cry of a stallion and the pounding of his hooves as he headed for the upper pastures.

Shadoe fought the desire to close her eyes and escape from the pain that tore through her right shoulder and exploded in her chest. Her stomach felt as if a mule had kicked her, but she was still alive, and the intruder was still on her property.

Moaning, she forced herself to roll over and she reached into her pocket to get more shells. The motion gave her a moment's dizziness, and in the confusion she saw the clear Montana sky through the wide open barn door—and the tall silhouette of a man walking toward her.

The shells fumbled in her fingers and she couldn't get them free of her pocket. Fighting the panic she tried to sit up and drag the gun into position, but before she could manage it a strong hand grasped the barrel and pulled it out of her grip.

In the darkness of the barn she couldn't see the man's features, but he was big, a tall, broad-shouldered man who bent down to her and held her to the ground with one hand.

"Easy," he said, his voice a tense command.

She struggled against him, fear sending a surge of strength to her limbs. He wasn't afraid of her at all, not even scared that she would see him. That probably meant he didn't intend to leave her alive. That thought made her struggle against the hand on her shoulder.

"Hold still, dammit." He pinned her to the barn floor, exerting enough pressure to make her cry out.

"Get away from me." She fought to keep her head, to think. The pain in her stomach and chest was almost unbearable as she fought against the punishing hold he had on her.

"Hold still," he ordered again. While he held her with one hand the other moved down her body, sliding over her right shoulder and down to her breast. At her sharp intake of breath, the hand moved on, down to her ribs. The sudden, excruciating pain made her cry out.

"What damn fool thing were you doing out here with a shotgun?" His voice conveyed disgust—and something else, a trace of relief.

The question was more effective than his grip on her shoulder. Shadoe stopped struggling and forced her mind to think. Who was this man and what was he doing in her barn in the middle of the night? If she wanted to survive, she was going to have to use her brain. She swallowed before she spoke.

"You'd better get out of here now. The sheriff is on the way. Get out of here while you can. I haven't seen your face. I won't tell them which way you went." She forced herself to speak in a low, steady voice. If he wasn't after the horses, what did he want? The very possibility made her stomach roll.

"For a lady with some cracked ribs, you aren't in much of a position to bargain."

The dry, amused tone of his voice frightened her even more than his touch. He was one cool customer. Either he didn't believe she'd called the sheriff or he knew how long it would take the law to get out to her isolated ranch.

"Sheriff Billy Casper is an old friend of mine." She tried to catch a glimpse of his features in the moonlight that poured in through the open door, but it was useless. His face was in total shadow. "He *is* on the way, and he'll break all speed limits getting here."

"I hope he brings a doctor. You're going to need those ribs taped." The man rocked back on his heels. "Now I'll let you go if you promise not to try to shoot me or get up. That horse smacked you pretty good, and I don't think squatting over that shotgun blast was real healthy for you."

Shadoe started to protest, but she felt the pressure on her shoulder ease as he removed his hand. "Take it easy, now," he cautioned her. "I'm not certain how much damage you've done to yourself."

"Who are you?" She started to sit up, but the sudden pain in her chest convinced her to give up the thought.

Instead of answering her question, he said, "Lady, I can stand here and gab with you, or I can go after that stud of yours. I figure he's halfway up the mountain by now."

"Scrapiron!" For a moment she'd forgotten that the stallion was loose. And the other intruder was somewhere on the premises. She put one hand beneath her and tried to lever herself up, favoring her injured side.

"Stubborn, as well as stupid. I can see you haven't changed a bit." Even as he spoke he put his hand on her, pressing her back into the dirt.

For a split second, the meaning of his words didn't register. That he was insulting her was clear, but that the insult also implied that he knew her was a little slower in coming. "Do I know you?" she asked. There was nothing familiar about the man who was either her jailer or rescuer. She wasn't certain which yet. There was a trace of a soft accent, but not one that was familiar.

"Shadoe, your stud is gone. The guy who turned him loose is gone. Now, I can waste my time making sure you stay still, or I can go after the horse and see if I can find any evidence of the intruder. I'd say he wasn't exactly a stranger to this place."

The urgency in the man's voice struck Shadoe. "Did you see the other man?"

"No, but I would have caught him if you hadn't gotten yourself run down by a stallion and then discharged your own gun into the dirt."

Condescension, arrogance and aggravation were all evident in his tone of voice. And the truth of his words scalded Shadoe. She'd never done such a stupid thing in her life. She still wasn't certain how it had happened, but she could have killed herself, her horses, or any innocent bystander. It didn't matter that Scrapiron had come out of the darkness in an unexpected move. What mattered was that she could have killed someone or something. She had been careless, and stupid. But she didn't need the man hovering over her to point that out.

"Just exactly what are you doing in my barn?" she

asked, turning the tables. "As far as I'm concerned, if you hadn't appeared at my back like you did, I would have been able to corner the man."

"Did you see him clearly?"

Shadoe started to answer, and then thought better. This man acted as if he knew her, as if he had some right to be on her property. "Who are you? What are you doing at the Double S?"

The man eased back. One hand, lifted as if he meant to touch her face, hovered between them for a moment and then fell back into the darkness at his side. "It's Hank. Hank Emrich."

As painful as the shotgun blast had been, the name spoken by the man who now eased his hold on her was far more devastating. Shadoe couldn't think of a single thing to say.

Hank sighed. "I'm going after your horse, if you'll loan me one to ride." He withdrew his hand from her shoulder completely. "I trust you won't try to jump up and attack me."

"What are you doing here?" Shadoe's question was softly put, but there was an edge of steel to it.

"It's a long story. Did you really call the sheriff? I can't chase the horse and the trespasser at the same time, and I think I'll stand a better chance of getting the horse. At least tonight."

"Billy'll be here in less than ten minutes."

There was the promise of warmth and humor in his voice as he spoke again, and just a touch of sadness. "Billy will make it here in less than five. He'd give his right arm to protect you. You were the daughter he always wanted." Hank rocked back on his heels and stood up.

In the moonlight that came in through the open barn door, Shadoe could clearly see the gun that rested on his hip. "You never said what you were doing on my prop-

erty...Hank.'' She added the name at the last, her voic
hesitating, then turning slightly rough as she managed t
get it out.

"I was following the man who came here. I've bee
following him for a while now.''

"You know him?'' Shadoe felt another pulse of unde
finable emotion. She might as well be hog-tied. Every tim
she tried to sit up or move, her ribs screamed a warning
The last thing she needed was a rib through a lung, so sh
made herself hold as steady as possible.

"No, but I was tracking him, hoping to catch him doin
something illegal. He's been over a lot of our property to
night.''

"Your property?'' Shadoe knew she sounded just like
parrot, mimicking everything he said. "I thought you le
here. I heard you sold out.'' What she'd really heard wa
that Hank had been forced to sell. That hard times and rocl
bottom beef prices had finally run the Copperwood Ranc
into bankruptcy. She couldn't be certain, but in the moon
light she thought she saw the hint of a smile.

"I did, Shadoe, but just like you, I couldn't stay away.''
The tiny smile, if it had ever been there, was gone. "Yo
might as well know, I'm here with the wildlife agents t
make sure the release of the wolves goes without a hitch.''

Shadoe let the air out of her lungs slowly. She had t
breathe, to accept. Long ago, when she was only a littl
girl, she'd fallen from her pony and broken her arm. He
father had held her then, as they waited for help to come
and he had taught her how to let the pain out with he
breath, to relax her muscles and bones and not fight th
pain. She thought she'd forgotten that lesson, but as sh
absorbed Hank Emrich's words, she forced herself to relax
Moving very carefully she got up to a sitting position an
managed to lean against the barn.

"I'm sorry to hear that, Hank,'' she said, perfectly calm

"Maybe, when you get used to the idea, you won't be so sorry," he said. He shifted his weight. "You want me to go look for Scrapiron, or you want me to stay here with you and wait for Billy?"

The one thing Shadoe knew she wanted was for him to be as far away from her as possible. "Take the buckskin in the first stall. Chester. He's steady but fast."

Whatever else Hank Emrich was, he was an excellent tracker and horseman. If anyone could find Scrapiron, it was him, and Shadoe knew that as soon as the shock of seeing Hank wore away, she'd be frantic about her stallion.

"Are you sure you'll be okay?"

"Billy will be here any minute. Go for Scrapiron," she said. "But before you leave, would you load the shotgun and hand it to me?"

Hank got the gun from beside her leg, broke it open and took out the shells and replaced them with two fresh ones that she handed him. He snapped the breech shut and handed it back to her.

"I'll find the horse and be back."

Shadoe took the gun and eased it down beside her leg. "Bring Scrapiron back. After that, you're not welcome on Double S property."

Hank Emrich walked to the barn door and stood as if he were intently counting the stars in the brilliant Montana sky.

His dark silhouette was the body of a mature man, not the slender youthfulness of the young man Shadoe remembered with a pang she couldn't suppress. He was tall, muscular, well made. She'd heard he'd moved to Virginia. Richmond if she remembered right. Well, he should have stayed there, or Timbuktu for all she cared. Any place but Montana and her ranch.

Hank stood there for a while before he turned back

around. "The wolves are here, Shadoe. Here to stay. There's nothing you and the other ranchers can do to stop this. Don't try, or you'll be sorry."

Chapter Two

"Shadoe! Shadoe!" At the sight of the open barn door Billy Casper had pulled the patrol car into the barnyard and aimed the lights into the black depths of the huge building. In the glare of the high beams he saw her propped against the barn wall. Fear almost made his heart stop.

"I'm okay, Billy."

Her voice came to him, strong and a tiny bit frustrated, which was the clearest sign that she really was okay. He was beside her in a moment, taking in her stillness as she leaned against the wooden wall, the gun resting beside her leg.

"I think I've cracked a couple of ribs, but nothing serious. Would you help me up?" She gave a rueful shake of her head and forced a smile up at her old friend. Billy Casper had been sheriff of Lakota County for more than six terms, and he had also been her father's best friend. His lined face showed the hardships he'd endured, but his blue eyes showed his love of life, and his work.

Billy slipped his hands under her arms and lifted her up, making the motion quick and clean even as she cried out in a tiny gasp of pain.

Once on her feet, Shadoe gave a sigh of relief. "Someone was in the barn and I came down to check it out, after

I called you." She forestalled his lecture. "Got down here to the horses and found a nasty surprise."

Billy dropped into step beside her as she made her way down to Scrapiron's empty stall.

"The stud's out?" Billy felt a niggle of concern. Scrapiron was Shadoe's only hope of bringing the Double S back. If that fool stallion broke his leg running around in the dark, or if he jumped into some rancher's field and started trouble, he might be shot. And she would certainly lose the ranch. Billy took the big flashlight from his belt and pinpointed the light at the floor. Large male footprints were clearly visible in the dirt. "Someone let the stud out, deliberately. He went north and the intruder went south." He could read the evidence.

"Scrapiron knocked me down in the aisle." Shadoe took a deep breath.

"I'll radio in to the office and round up some volunteers to find the stud. We'll have him back by daybreak." He put his hand on Shadoe's shoulder and gave the lightest squeeze. Her back was still straight, but he could feel the tension in her. She'd put up everything she had left to re-open her family's old ranch, but it was more than that. By coming back to the Montana wilderness, Shadoe was confronting her demons. It was a rocky road she had chosen to travel.

"Well…" She hesitated. "It gets worse."

Billy heard the tremor in her voice. "Are you hurt worse than you said?"

"No." The word was spoken quietly, her control back. "It's Hank Emrich. He's back here. He's with the team bringing in the wolves."

"You've got to be kidding." Billy spoke before he thought.

"I wish I were." Shadoe turned to her old friend. "He's gone after Scrapiron. If anyone can catch him, Hank can."

"Best tracker in these parts, except for your daddy."

"Yeah, Hank was the eldest son my father always wanted." Shadoe allowed the bitterness to show.

Billy put his arm around her shoulders and gently began to guide her toward the house. "Shadoe, honey, if things had worked out differently, you and Hank would have married and been happy here."

"Yes, Billy, if my father had lived, my marriage to Hank would have been the thing that pleased him most." Shadoe felt a surge of emotion so strong, so raw that she wasn't certain whether it was anger, hurt, loss, or the need for revenge. "But Dad died, and I ran away."

"Things didn't go easy for Hank after you left here. He tried to hang on to his family's ranch, but he couldn't make a go of it." Billy remembered those long-ago days. He'd been sheriff, and he vividly recalled the painful foreclosure on Copperwood Ranch. It wasn't something he was likely to forget. "You and Hank, that was all twenty years ago, Shadoe. To be truthful, though, after the sale of Copperwood, I never thought Hank would come back to this part of the world. Did he say when he'd come back?"

"I didn't exactly have a cozy chat with him." Shadoe felt the sting of jealousy at the note of sympathy in Billy's voice. It was almost as if Billy felt sorry for Hank. "If you want to have a reunion with him, he'll be back with Scrapiron. You two can relive the good old days then." She stepped out a little ahead of him even though the extra effort caused her ribs to burn with pain.

Billy let her go, walking slightly behind her as she led the way up to the big cedar house. He couldn't help but admire her arrow straight back, the discipline she used in walking perfectly erect, even though he knew she was in great pain. Shadoe Deerman had left Montana with a deep, abiding hatred for the land that she felt had killed her father and her younger brother. But she was like the land. And more like her father than she would ever know.

Hurrying his pace to catch up, Billy sighed with a sense of sadness and foreboding. It was an ugly twist of fate that Shadoe and Hank should both return to the tiny town of Athens, Montana in the same spring. And both end up on opposite sides of what was shaping up to be one of the biggest range wars of the west.

"YOU CAN LET ME tape those ribs or you can let Billy take you to the hospital." Doc Adams waved the Ace bandage in Shadoe's face, his own red from arguing.

"One or the other," Billy said, coming to the veterinarian's rescue. Shadoe wouldn't hear of going to the hospital, but she had allowed Billy to call her next door neighbor, Dr. Franklin Adams, one of the best veterinarians in the universe. But Doc was having a hard time managing the headstrong woman. "Look, Doc, if she won't cooperate, we'll give her a shot of Rompum and put her down for an hour or two. When she wakes up, we'll have her wrapped, tied and up in a sling where she'll have to behave."

"I've seen wild boars with more sense," Doc snorted as he moved in on Shadoe to wrap her ribs. "Now take off your shirt and sit up there like a...like a grown-up."

Shadoe sighed and gave up. Billy and the crusty old vet weren't going to leave her alone until they'd bound and taped her into submission. It wasn't that she didn't trust Doc Adams's judgment, but all of that bandaging and tape were going to be a royal pain.

"I'll go take a look-see for Hank," Billy said as he discreetly left the room. He'd already scouted the barn and surrounding property but had found few clues of the intruder who'd set Scrapiron free.

Shadoe dropped her shirt and held her arms up for the doctor to bandage her ribs.

"I hope you know I would be censured by the vet association for doing this. A little appreciation would go a long way, little missy."

Shadoe couldn't resist the smile that crooked up the corners of her mouth. Doc Adams had called her little missy since she was first born. Like Billy, he was always there when she called him. She had a sudden, terrible thought. What would she do without her old friends, these men who were her father's age or older?

"Thank you, Doc," she said, her voice soft. "Thank you and Billy both."

Something in her voice made him look up from his bandages and catch her eye. "You're not hurt someplace else, are you?"

She shook her head, blinking away tears that came on her so suddenly they almost escaped. "No, but I was just thinking what I would do without you two. You've both been good friends to me."

"Behave like a young woman and you wouldn't have to be calling on us," he admonished. "Find you some man to marry and let him chase the horse thieves in the barn."

From anyone else, the words would have infuriated Shadoe. From Doc or Billy, she knew that it was their concern for her. In their world, women married men who could protect them. For Shadoe, none of that was true. She was on her own. And she liked it that way. She had to fend for herself, but she also knew exactly who she could count on.

She felt the last of the tape smoothed into place and Doc nodded for her to stand. She buttoned her shirt as he lectured her.

"Rest, Shadoe. Give those ribs a chance to heal or you're going to be sorry."

"Is that what you tell all the young cows you tend?"

"I tell them all that, but most of them listen about as

good as I expect you will. They'll go on off and do what they want anyway.''

Shadoe laughed and kissed him on the cheek. ''Thanks, Doc.''

''Don't thank me,'' he said, ''Just give those ribs a little time to heal. That shotgun blast could have killed you.''

''I know.'' She walked to the front door and gazed out into the night. It took her a moment to adjust to the darkness, but in a few seconds she saw Billy standing at the barn. And he was waving and calling out. Hank was back!

As if on cue she heard the scream of her stallion as he called to the mares. There was an answering chorus from the barn, and Shadoe couldn't help the smile on her face as she reached for her coat.

''I said rest.'' Doc Adams snatched the coat from her hand. ''I think you can trust Billy to stable that stud for you.''

''I want to make sure—''

''I think I'm a little more qualified to make sure he's in good shape than you are.'' Doc slipped into his own coat. ''Now make us some coffee if you must do something.'' He slammed the door behind him.

Shadoe hesitated at the door, but then turned and walked into the large old kitchen. It was her favorite room in the ranch house, a place where she'd spent many happy hours as a child. Lifting the pot of water, she felt her ribs complain, but she poured the water and waited. Doc's command had not kept her in the house. It was more that she hoped Hank would leave without coming in. She'd made her desire to have him off her property very clear.

The coffee was almost made when she heard the clump of boots on the front porch and the whisper of the door as it opened. Peering around the kitchen door she caught sight of the three men as they removed their coats.

Damn! Hank had come inside with them. Billy's doing,

probably, since he felt such sympathy for him. Well, sure, Hank had loved Copperwood, but she'd lost more than a ranch, and now Hank was in a position to make sure that every rancher in the Montana area paid for his own personal loss.

Footsteps approached the kitchen and she heard Billy clear his throat. He shut the door for a moment's privacy with her.

"Scrapiron's fine, Shadoe. Hank caught him up in Ryland's pasture. You'll have to get together with Kyle and check his mares. I don't think he'll be too upset if Scrapiron bred a few of them."

"Tell Mr. Emrich he has my thanks. Then ask him to leave." Shadoe couldn't help the anger in her voice.

"I couldn't walk in and leave him standing in the barnyard." Billy tried to lift her chin but she jerked her head away.

Shadoe knew her feelings of betrayal were stupid. Worse than dumb, they were inaccurate. Billy hadn't chosen Hank over her, he was just being a reasonable, warm man. Like he always had been. But every issue around Hank was fraught with emotion. Shadoe had deceived herself that she'd put him behind her long ago.

"How about that coffee?" Billy got mugs out of the cabinet and began pouring them full. "We could all use a cup. Doc and I have to get back to town and I don't want to fall asleep on the drive."

Shadoe twitched with guilt at his words. He'd driven halfway up the mountain to come to her rescue and now she was treating him as if she were angry with him. She walked up behind him and gave him a quick hug. "Sorry, Billy. I guess I'm acting like a fool."

He didn't turn around, but kept preparing the coffee tray. "Not at all, honey. You're acting like someone who's been hurt. Sometimes a wound doesn't always heal clean. Sad to say, but there are some things that will always give you a twitch or a twinge. The trick is to keep going forward. You can't let those little twinges stop your life.''

She hugged him again and let him go. ''Well, I'm going to keep going. I think I owe Hank at least a thank you for finding my horse.''

Billy picked up the tray. ''And I want to ask him some questions about the intruder. You said Hank had been following him?''

''That's what he said.'' Shadoe disappeared through the door, going to the den where Hank and Doc stood before the fire.

The sight of Hank, standing with his back to the flames, was so natural that past and present were momentarily confused and she stopped. It took only a few seconds for her to see the differences, and they were significant. Hank had been seventeen when he'd been as much a part of her life as her father or brother Joey. He'd spent almost every evening of his senior year in high school sitting in the den with the family or standing in front of that same fireplace, warming his back, as he and her father had talked about the mountains, about the vast wilderness land that bordered the Double S. About life and history and a way of believing. About a future where Hank and Shadoe would be a team.

Billy put down the tray and left, and Shadoe walked forward and offered coffee to Doc, then Hank. She looked down as he put the one spoon of sugar in his cup, unable to meet his gaze.

''Hank's turned into a man,'' Doc said to break the silence that filled the room with an electric tension.

At last Shadoe looked up and met Hank's dark blue gaze. ''Yes, he has.'' She could say that truthfully. He was very much a man. She hadn't caught a clear look at him in the barn, but she could see him now, and he was strikingly handsome. She turned to put the tray on a table and lifted her own coffee cup.

Tall, blond, broad-shouldered with a quiet confidence, he was everything she had once dreamed he would be. Gone was the lanky, awkward boy with the sincere brown eyes and the hesitant smile. Twenty years had given Hank his maturity, and an abundance of poise. She swallowed.

"Shadoe has grown up, too."

Hank's words brought her back around to face him. His voice was deeper, his words slower, but it was a voice she now recognized. She felt as if she were standing nude before him and his voice was a touch.

Hank spoke again. "She's every inch a woman, though she could use some training in how to handle a shotgun."

His remark was like a slap, and it effectively startled her out of the past. "You never did tell me why you were following the man who turned Scrapiron loose." She lifted her chin and held her gaze steady with his. She wouldn't back down. He couldn't make her. Not this time.

"In case you haven't heard, not everyone in these parts is real excited about the prospect of those wolves." Hank's brown eyes drilled into her as he spoke. "We've established our camp up on the mountain, and we've been having a little unwanted company."

Hank let the words hang in the air. When he'd first returned to Athens, he'd heard that someone had moved into the Double S ranch. He hadn't believed the rumors that it was Shadoe Deerman. Even when his initial investigation showed that a thirty-six-year-old female named Shadoe Deerman was involved in the movement to stop the release of the timber wolves, he hadn't acknowledged it. He actually hadn't believed it until he'd seen her in the barn this very night. And then he hadn't wanted to believe it because every instinct he had told him Shadoe and the man he'd been following were somehow involved.

The fact that her prized stallion had been turned loose hadn't changed his mind about that, either.

Hank's unspoken accusation was like gasoline on a fire. "Are you insinuating that some of the ranchers have been fooling around your camp?" Shadoe took a deep breath to calm herself and felt her wound react with a painful jab.

"I'm not insinuating anything. I'm stating it as a clear fact." Hank met her challenge. This was not the young girl he'd fallen in love with twenty years before. He had to remember that single fact. This was a woman, a capable female who had been tempered by loss and regret and anger. The girl he remembered was tender, innocent—erased by tragedy. His gaze fell on the rise and fall of her chest, the movements shallow because of her ribs, but deep enough to show her outrage, her anger.

"The ranchers are opposed to the release of the wolves. That's not a secret. But we have no reason to sneak around your camp. What good would that do?"

"None," Hank said. "Unless you intended to try to sabotage the release. As a wildlife agent, I can promise you that won't happen."

Shadoe felt the stab in her ribs, but she drew in the breath and held it until she could speak without shouting. "I think you should leave."

Billy and Doc moved toward Hank simultaneously. "Listen, Hank, I know you federal boys are all tied in a knot over this wolf business, but to go around accusing the people here of sabotage, that's a little extreme."

Hank reached into his pocket and pulled out a small red capsule. "Is it, Billy?" He handed it to the sheriff.

"What is it?"

"Arsenic. We found it in some ground beef that someone left in one of the cages. Lucky for the wolves that we checked the empty cages thoroughly before we turned them loose in the pens."

Billy held the capsule. Out of the corner of his eye he watched Shadoe. Her olive complexion had paled. He noted that Hank saw it, too.

"Do you think someone who really meant to kill the wolves would have been stupid enough to bait an empty cage?" Shadoe had finally found her ability to speak. Hank's accusation was so low, so disturbing.

"I think desperate people will do just about anything."

Before Shadoe could respond, Billy stepped between them. "That's enough, Hank. As sheriff of Lakota County, I resent what you're saying. You have no proof that any citizen here was involved. There are other factions in this mess, not just the ranchers. Those wolves are a political issue now. It isn't just the ranchers against the animals."

"Then you tell me how come I was able to track someone all the way from our campsite to this farm. The tracks came here by the easiest paths. The man I was following knew his way around these parts, and he made a beeline for Shadoe's barn."

"Get out." Shadoe didn't wait to think through what he said. She pointed at the door. "Get out now before I have Billy arrest you. How dare you..." Her voice trembled and she stopped.

Billy put a hand on Hank's shoulder. "I think it's time for you to go, Hank. I can only say that I sure do hate to see things come to this. You and Shadoe have known each other a long time. A real long time. There's a lot between you two and even though things didn't work out in the past, you're making some serious charges here."

Hank let Billy move him toward the door without protest. But as Billy swung the door open, Hank turned to face everyone in the room. "You can tell the other ranchers that those wolves are going to be set free. They have a right to the wilderness. As much right as the ranchers. And Shadoe, if you could ever get past your personal loss, you'd know it for the truth it is. Your daddy taught you that much.''

Billy pushed Hank through the door. Before the lawman could close it behind him, Shadoe heard him speak, his normally easygoing voice roughened with anger.

"I don't know who the hell you think you are, Emrich, coming in here and saying things like that to Shadoe. I'm filing a report tomorrow with the Fish and Wildlife Service. If anyone is out of line, it's you.''

"Right." Hank's response was followed by the sound of his angry footsteps going across the porch and down the steps.

"Shadoe, girl, I'm sorry about that." Doc Adams picked up his bag and walked over to pat her arm. "Seems to me that Hank isn't the boy he used to be. But then I guess none of us are. Time has a way of making all of us pay.''

Shadoe nodded. She was still in shock from Hank's verbal attack.

Billy cracked open the door and stuck his head inside. "I'm going to take Hank back up to the site. He came down on foot and I think it would be best for everyone if I made sure he got back to the camp safely. Tomorrow morning I'll be back and check out the tracks he said he found. Whoever let Scrapiron free is the man we need to find to resolve all of this.''

"Thanks, Billy." Shadoe forced a smile for Billy and Doc. "You two go on now. I'm perfectly fine. In fact, I'm going straight up to bed and finish out the night.''

"You're going to have to rest, Shadoe. No riding. No lifting. No fence building. None of the usual activities, you hear?''

"I promise, Doc." Shadoe didn't see how she could obey, but now wasn't the time to argue. The work had to be done, and she wasn't funded to hire a crew.

"I'll be by tomorrow to check.''

"There's no need for that." She saw the futility of her protests in the set of his jaw. "Okay. I'll see you tomorrow." She gave him a light kiss on the cheek and then went to kiss Billy, too. "Thanks, both of you."

"Shadoe, honey, don't pay any attention—"

She shook her head. "There's a lot of scar tissue between me and Hank. You said it earlier, Billy. Not all wounds heal clean. When I left here, I hurt both of us. Hank hasn't forgiven me." She tried for a smile and settled for a shake of her head.

As she closed the door behind them, Shadoe felt the pressure of the tears in her eyes.

ON THE ROUGH RIDE up the mountain, Hank maintained a stoic silence. After the first ten minutes, Billy felt the first rush of his anger begin to dissipate and he turned to the wildlife agent.

"Those things you said to Shadoe were pretty harsh, Hank. Don't you think you're carrying an old hurt a little too far?"

"The past has nothing to do with this." Even as he spoke the words, Hank knew they weren't completely true. The past had everything to do with what had happened tonight. Everything...and nothing. He had come down the mountain, tracking the man who had always stayed just two hundred yards ahead of him. Every time Hank took a shortcut, he found that his quarry also knew the same tricks. It didn't take a brain surgeon to figure out that the man he was chasing was as familiar with Saddleback Mountain as Hank himself was. It wasn't a stretch to put two and two together and come up with the fact that the man he was chasing had gone to the Double S intentionally.

But if Hank had been completely honest with Billy—or himself—he would have admitted that with each turn in the path, each shift in direction toward the Double S, Hank had felt a number of emotions, the most prevalent being anticipation. He'd heard Shadoe was back at the Double S. Heard and doubted. Heard and hoped.

The simple truth was that he'd wanted to see her.

Hank cast a glance at the sheriff, and saw that Billy was content to let him stew in his own juices as Billy drove the old Jeep higher and higher up Saddleback.

"The facts don't lie, Billy. You know that as well as I do."

"I also know there are a lot of ways to interpret facts. Tell me, Hank, do you honestly believe Shadoe would have risked that stallion? For any reason?"

When Hank didn't answer, Billy continued. "If anything happens to that horse, she'll lose the Double S. She put everything she had into fixing up that ranch and bringing that stallion here. She's got some nice mares and a show gelding out of Scrapiron that she's going to campaign in the competitions. The gelding's valuable, but it's the stud that will make or break her."

Hank stared straight ahead.

"You federal agents have college degrees. You figure it out," Billy added, a touch of anger in his voice.

Hank saw Billy's point, but he also knew that people didn't act rationally when their emotions were aroused, and the prospect of releasing a pack of timber wolves had ignited some powerful fears in the entire wilderness area. Folks were afraid their herds of cattle, sheep or horses would be destroyed. They were scared their children would be attacked and dragged off into the woods. They were simply afraid of nature. They wanted to subdivide, pave and neon everything in reach. What they really wanted was to destroy the wilderness, to bring every single element of it under their destructive control the way they had the rest of the country.

"I want your word that you're going to stay clear of

Shadoe.'' Billy put the Jeep in lower gear to make a steep incline.

"You have my word I'll protect those wolves."

Billy slammed on the brakes, holding the vehicle in the middle of the road. "If I have to take it to your boss, Hank, I will. If I thought any of the ranchers were involved in poisoning the wolves, I'd tell you. But I know Shadoe Deerman wouldn't do such a thing. If you look into your heart, you'd know it, too."

"I know that when Shadoe's security is threatened, she's capable of anything, Billy." He turned to look at the sheriff, a hard, angry look. "I probably know that better than anyone alive."

Chapter Three

"I'll get out here," Hank said when Billy pulled into the narrow timber trail he indicated. "I can walk the rest of the way. It isn't far."

"Afraid I'll find your camp and go back and report to the ranchers?" Billy spoke with anger. It took only a few seconds for him to apologize. "I'm sorry, Hank. The chip you're carrying on your shoulder is beginning to rub off on me."

"If I act suspicious of everyone, it's because I am." For the first time there was more regret than anger in Hank's tone. "Billy, I need to tell you this anyway. We've gotten threats against the wolves and the agents up here. Serious threats."

"How serious?" Billy felt the skin along his neck tighten. For all the ways Hank Emrich had changed, Billy didn't believe he'd lie about something this important.

"The arsenic was the most overt. One of the other agents, Cal Oberton—someone drained the brake fluid out of his truck. Luckily he was able to drive into a tree and stop it without too much damage."

Billy nodded as he stared over the steering wheel into the total blackness of Saddleback Mountain. They had driven up to the highest part of the mountain, the area that looked, from a distance, exactly like the horn of a western saddle. Locally it was known as Stag's Horn because of the abundance of wildlife. The federal agents had picked well when they'd chosen the release site for the wolves. "Any suspects?" he finally asked.

"No one specifically." Hank cleared his throat. "That's the trouble. Whoever is doing this is smart and knows this area like the back of his hand. Or her hand." He didn't flinch when Billy turned to glare at him.

"Why are you so determined to point the finger at Shadoe?"

"Maybe because I'm so determined not to let the past get in the way of my job now." Hank was surprised by the truth of his words. "And there are things about Shadoe you don't know."

"I know her pretty well. And I knew her dad better than anyone in the world. That girl's a lot like her father, Hank. You should know that. Jimmy Deerman might not have cared for wolves in his backyard but the man respected the right of nature. Hell, he taught you to respect it. And Shadoe, too, for that matter."

Hank felt an old familiar stab of pain. He'd thought it was long gone but he should have been smarter than that. It had merely hidden, waiting for a new opportunity to attack. Jimmy Deerman's death had been a terrible tragedy. A double tragedy along with little Joey's. Shadoe had been devastated. Had blamed herself. And finally, because she couldn't bring herself to blame her father, she'd blamed the very wilderness she'd once loved. She had lost her father, her brother, her home, her beliefs. Eventually, even her mother. She had lost everything. But Hank had lost, too. A lot more than most people knew. More than he'd ever let on to anyone.

"Billy, we've got files on all the area ranchers. It's a standard workup in a case like this. We feel it's better to be prepared and try to avert a tragedy than wait for something to happen and then enforce the law. We want this release to go smoothly, without either side suffering losses.''

''Hell, Hank, you sound like you're geared up for a war.'' Billy was chilled by the dispassionate note in Hank's voice. ''These people were your neighbors once. You went to school with Kyle Ryland and Andy West and Jill Amberly. Don't you remember them?''

Before he did, Hank dropped the curtain on his memories. He could remember them, but he didn't want to recall the feelings he'd had back then. Emotions got in the way of his job. ''That's the past, Billy. Folks change.''

''I can see that, Hank. I can certainly see that looking at you.'' Billy cranked up his truck. ''I've got to get back to town.''

''I'll come in later today and make a full report with you on the incidents that have happened up here. The arsenic and the brake fluid were the worst, but things have been stolen—small, personal items as well as equipment—trees have been chopped down along the paths. It's a consistent effort to thwart this release. I want to catch the *people* responsible before someone gets hurt.''

''That's one thing we can agree on, Hank. Stop by and we'll talk.'' Billy waited until Hank slammed his door and then swung the vehicle around in a tight circle and headed down the mountain.

WITH THE MEN GONE, Shadoe found herself pacing back and forth inside the rambling cedar house that her father had designed and built. Sleep was out of the question. From out of her distant past, Hank Emrich had emerged to reopen painful wounds. She silently cursed her luck that he would be the agent to work this case. It was almost as if the gods were playing some nasty trick on them both—to bring them back together on the very land that had torn them apart.

Ironically, once again the land was the issue that stood between them. The land and who, or what, would rule it.

She walked to the window and saw the first pinkening of the sky. Dawn was on the way, thank goodness. She returned to the kitchen and made a fresh pot of coffee. If she did drift back to sleep, she knew she would face only nightmares. Worse nightmares than the wolf that stalked her.

The pot had not even stopped dripping when the shrill ring of the telephone almost made her jump. Who would be calling her at this hour? She lifted the receiver.

"Shadoe, it's Jill. I just got a call. They're bringing the rest of the wolves today. Up near Stag's Horn."

Shadoe took the news in silence. "All twenty?" she finally asked.

"Hoss saw them, but he couldn't tell exactly how many. The agents with them were heavily armed. I guess they're going to stay with them until they take off on their own."

Shadoe crooked the telephone into her neck and held it with a shoulder as she poured herself a cup of coffee. "They think some of us ranchers are trying to kill the wolves."

"Well, they aren't far wrong on that." It took Jill a moment to register Shadoe's odd tone of voice. "Are you okay?"

"I had a run-in last night with one of the federal agents." Shadoe took a deep breath and felt her ribs complain. But Doc was right, the tight wrapping was helping.

"What happened?" Jill was eager for the details.

"Someone was prowling around down at the barn—"

Before she could finish, Jill interrupted. "Did you see him?"

"No such luck. Too dark. But I went down to catch him and ended up in the barn aisle with broken ribs and Hank Emrich towering over me."

There was silence. "Hank's back? Here in Lakota County?"

"He's a U.S. Fish and Wildlife agent. He's taking the return of the wolves very personally. Someone let Scrapiron out and Hank caught him and brought him home."

"Ah, sh—" Jill bit back the word. "What are you going to do?"

"What can I do?" Shadoe asked.

"You know, after you took off, Hank ran Copperwood for a year and then started night classes. He got his degree in biology, or maybe it was forestry. I can't remember. He must have gone into law enforcement after Copperwood was sold at auction."

"Well, however it happened, he's a federal agent now."

"I can't believe Hank would do this. I mean, he used to be a rancher. Surely he must understand how we feel." Jill's voice rose.

"Did it ever cross your mind that he understands? Maybe that's exactly why he's in this wolf project."

"Shadoe!" Jill drew a sharp breath. "You're not saying you believe he's doing this as some sort of revenge? As if ranchers were to blame that he lost his place?"

Even as Jill said it, Shadoe didn't want to believe it. "I don't know. Maybe it's just..." She let the sentence fade.

"You know Hank was really influenced by your dad. I can remember myself feeling this real connection with Saddleback Mountain and with the creatures in the woods when your dad took us camping."

Shadoe blocked out the memory before it could hurt too much. "Yeah, but that's over. That was for children. We've got cattle and horses to protect, Jill. The last thing we need is a wolf population."

Jill heard the distress in her friend's voice. "If we had a congressman who was a rancher, this wouldn't be happening. To most folks a few cows or horses is the cost of doing business. They don't understand that for some of us, that's the profit by which we live or die. I'm barely hanging on." Her voice turned bitter.

"Well, the wolves are a fact now. We'll just have to guard our stock more carefully."

"As if there's not enough natural disaster in the cattle business, or horses. I lost a heifer yesterday. Got her head hung in the fence." Jill's voice shook. "It's getting to where I can't sleep nights now, worrying. Anyway, I didn't call to tell you about my insomnia. Want to ride up and take a look at the wolves?"

Jill's question startled Shadoe. She hadn't considered such a thing. "I don't think so." What was the point of meeting her enemy face-to-face? Shadoe had never killed a living creature for sport or survival. But the wolves imported from Canada might be a different story. If they came for her horses, or anything else she loved, she'd do whatever she had to.

"Oh, come on. Go throw some feed, turn out your horses and let's ride over. Curly said he'd feed and then check your barn. Maybe if we go up there and personally take our concerns they'll understand."

Something in Shadoe wanted to go. "I suppose it couldn't hurt." She could hear herself talking herself into going, and she was confused about her reasons why.

"Make up your mind," Jill prompted. "I have to do some things before we set out."

"Okay. But we can't stay all day. I have to be back by two. Mark's coming to shoe Luster."

"Gotta get those shoes set for the big competition this weekend." Jill's voice held a teasing note. "I know you deny it, but I do believe you're a rodeo queen."

"Never a queen, just damn good at picking a smart horse. The talent is Luster's."

"False modesty is just vanity turned inside out," Jill

said, suppressing her laughter. "I'll pick you up in an hour."

"I'll be ready."

THE SITE THE United States Fish and Wildlife Service had selected for the release of twenty Canadian timber wolves was isolated, and very beautiful. It was the best Montana had to offer by way of mountains and forests. The blue spruces clung to the hard, rocky ground while snow was still deep in the upper elevations. There were granite out croppings that gave a view of green meadows and wood lands sweeping up to distant purple mountains. As Jill drove, Shadoe tried to shield her heart against the beauty of the wilderness.

Jill pulled the four-wheel drive truck off the road and sat, her hands clutching the wheel. Her reddish blond curls were in their usual disarray, a contrast to Shadoe's straight black hair, a shining sheet that hung to her shoulder blades.

"They aren't going to be happy to see us." Jill tightened her grip on the steering wheel.

"It's a free country," Shadoe answered. She picked up both pair of binoculars from the truck seat. "They won't let us close, but maybe we can catch a glimpse of them."

Jill slid out of the truck and waited for Shadoe to join her before they took a barely noticeable path back into the woods.

They walked in silence, both of them more than a little anxious about the wolves. Jill ran a beef cattle operation that had been her father's dream. There'd been no son to inherit, so Jill had taken over when her father decided that Florida winters were more compatible with the crippling arthritis that had made his legs almost useless.

"I think you've gone far enough."

Both Jill and Shadoe stopped dead in their tracks. Stand ing in the path before them was a tall, lean man that Shadoe recognized instantly. It took Jill a moment longer. The rifle at his side was held casually, but with great familiarity. He wasn't threatening them, but he clearly wasn't going to let them pass.

"Hank! Hank Emrich!" Jill stared at him, then dropped her gaze to the gun.

"Jill." He remembered her as the head cheerleader who'd always had a kind word for everyone in school.

"Shadoe said you're a fed." Jill's irrepressible personality showed through in her smile. "I never thought the boy who hated authority would turn out to be a law officer."

Hank's smile was slow in arriving and lasted only a few seconds. "How are you, Jill? I can see you haven't changed much."

"I'd be a lot better if you'd take those wolves back to Canada where they belong."

The warmth that had shown briefly disappeared from Hank's face. "You don't own the whole mountain range, Jill. You nor any of the ranchers. The wolves were here long before man."

"Times have changed," Jill said. "Or maybe you haven't noticed." Her sarcasm was hard to miss. "We came up to talk to your boss."

"My *boss* isn't here, and this area is closed to everyone but the wildlife agents." He looked beyond Jill and Shadoe down to the place where they'd parked their vehicle.

"We came up here to make a reasonable attempt to explain our position. We have a right to do that." Shadoe spoke up. The sun was behind Hank, haloing his light hair, softening the years that had passed. For all the illusion of the lighting, though, Hank could have been made from stone.

"There's nothing you can say that will change the course of events." He didn't even look at Shadoe as he spoke.

"I can see it was a mistake." Why had she let Jill talk her into such a stupid idea? Knowing she was likely to run into Hank, knowing his attitude toward her and the other ranchers, she'd come on a fool's mission anyway. In fact, it was Hank's very presence that had drawn her up the mountain, and that fact made her angry with herself.

"Well, Shadoe said you'd changed. I guess I didn't believe her. Until now." Jill shook her head at the lawman. "Whatever happened to the Hank Emrich I went to high school with?" she asked.

"I think you should turn around and head back home. I can make that an order if you really push me."

Jill shifted her weight. "Come on, Shadoe, there's no point starting trouble now. We'll see the wolves soon enough. And you can tell Mr. Harry Code that if they're on my property, they're dead."

"What is the problem with you people?" Hank's voice was harsh. "There are thousands of miles of open mountain range. We're releasing twenty wolves. Under the best of circumstances they'll remain a very small element of the natural order here."

Shadoe spoke in a low, emotionless voice. "Maybe the problem is that I've seen firsthand what a wolf can do to a young, defenseless creature. Maybe it's because I saw what one did to my eight-year-old brother." She spun on the path and ran after Jill.

Hank felt as if he'd been gut-kicked by both back legs of an angry mule. Shadoe's last retort had been a direct hit, and he cursed his own stupidity. He listened to the sound of rocks being dislodged as the two women hurried down the path to their vehicle.

Hefting the gun in his firm grip, he turned to go back to the area where the cages had been unloaded from the trucks. The wolves would be held in the cages until they'd had a chance to sniff out their surroundings, and then the cage doors would be opened onto larger pens. The final step would be total freedom. An animal that had been wiped out by man would once again roam the Rocky Mountains. The natural order would be restored. He had to hang on to that thought and not allow himself to be diverted by the human complaints.

He fixed his mind on a mental image of the huge silvery gray animals running through the patchy snow and reality was replaced with a movie he'd seen in his mind over and over again. In the distance was a tall, arrow-straight man with long dark hair. As the wolves ran past him, he gave Hank a slow, easy smile.

But superimposed in Hank's mind came the tight, anxious features of Shadoe Deerman. Her heavy black hair trapped the sunlight in dazzles. She would be a beautiful woman, if she wasn't such an angry one. She had been a gorgeous young girl.

"Damn!" he said out loud. "Damn!" He had no one to blame but himself. He picked up his pace, stretching his long legs, but he couldn't walk fast enough to leave behind the image of Shadoe's tense face.

As he rounded a bend in the path, he came within sight of the cages, and his pulse increased at the magnificence of the animals behind the heavy wire. Untamed. Extremely smart. Perfect specimens. He nodded at a huge male as if the animal had spoken to him.

"Communing with the animals again?"

He turned to find the teasing smile of his friend Cal Oberton not ten feet away.

"He's a handsome rascal," Hank said, glad for any subject to erase Shadoe's face from his mind. Why hadn't he invited the two women up to see the wolves? Maybe he could have talked with them, reasoned with them, made them understand. There had once been a time when Shadoe believed as he did. Cal's voice broke through those hurtful thoughts.

"Handsome, and deadly. Don't you think it's sort of ee-rie the way he stares at you? I mean his gaze follows you around the camp. And none of the other wolves will make any eye contact with the rest of us."

"That's for the best." Hank slapped his friend on the shoulder. "They don't trust you, and if half the women in Washington had been one third as smart, you wouldn't have left so many broken hearts behind."

Cal laughed good-naturedly in return. "That was a long time ago, when we were young and foolish."

"And you haven't changed. If I remember correctly, I was too busy studying and holding down a job to do much romancing. I suppose you had to take care of my share for me." That wasn't exactly true, and Hank knew it. But studying and working were acceptable male reasons for not pursuing women. The truth wasn't acceptable. To him or his friends.

"And that hasn't changed, either." Cal motioned toward a waiting vehicle. "We're supposed to go into town and check some facts for the boss man, and then hang around and have dinner, remember? Maybe we can find one of those famous Montana dance halls or saloons. If we're go-ing to be stuck up here in this forsaken country for weeks, we might as well learn about the local culture."

Hank had completely forgotten. He'd been absorbed in the events of the night before—and the wolves. Since they'd been captured in Canada and brought into the United States he'd barely left their sides.

"Let me change shirts and I'll be ready."

The driver blasted the horn, a sign of impatience.

"I'll tell them to give you three minutes," Cal said. "They're about to bust a gut to get to town."

Hank smiled at his friend. "Sounds like something that

will do all of us some good. Just as long as someone stays here to take care of the wolves.''

"Gordy and Jim.''

"Good enough.'' Hank hurried toward his tent where he put away his gun and grabbed a clean shirt. A night on the town, if Athens, Montana could be termed a town in the kindest definition. The population was less than five thousand. There were a few restaurants, some bars, a barber shop, which he badly needed to visit but hadn't had time, and a few businesses. He wondered how many, if any, of the residents would remember him. And how they would remember him? As the young man who'd lost his family ranch?

Even though the others were waiting, Hank made one last pass by the cages. The biggest male wolf stood up and pinned him with a gaze.

"Hey, Thor.'' Against all common sense he'd named the animal. He'd given him the name of a god, a small protection against the many odds facing the animal's survival.

"That wolf's got you in his sights.'' Jim Larson walked up beside Hank. "He watches every move you make, and he doesn't pay the least attention to any of the rest of us.''

"I doubt that.'' Hank looked over at Jim. It wasn't like a field biologist to start personalizing the behavior of an animal.

"I'm not kidding, Hank. It's eerie. Ask the others. I'd be careful when we turn these guys loose. I wouldn't be a bit surprised if old—what was it you called him?—old Thor doesn't hunt you down and kill you. I think he's developed a personal grudge against you for moving him down here from Canada.''

Hank gave the biologist a hard look, but Jim only adjusted his glasses and went back to his tent.

Feeling the skin along his neck prickle, Hank turned back to the wolf. The animal was staring at him again. Thor came up to the wire and stopped. Still holding his gaze steady, he opened his mouth to reveal long, deadly teeth, and slowly licked his lips.

Chapter Four

"Hey!" Shadoe chided the big gelding as she knelt at his front leg and tried to wind a bright red transport wrap around his shin. Staring at some horses in a nearby pasture, Luster whinnied to them and stomped his foot again in impatience.

Shadoe rocked back on her heels, the safety wrap held tightly in her hand and her sore ribs still aggravating her. "Cut it out, buster. I can't do this if you're going to stomp." She bent back to her task, securing the bandage with the Velcro closings that would hold it firmly in place.

She stood up and took a step back to admire her handiwork. Luster's dappled gray coat gleamed in the April sun. His black mane and tail were immaculately groomed, and the red wraps gave him a flashy look. It fit his personality perfectly. Luster was one horse that liked the limelight—and her best chance of showing the Montana area the type of baby her stud could throw.

There was nothing left to do but load him in the trailer and head out on the road to Billings, where the competition was being held. But Shadoe delayed, dawdling by rechecking to make sure she'd loaded water buckets, hay, feed, lariat, her competition saddle. All things she'd checked once before. The truth was, ever since the night of the intruder, she was damned uncomfortable leaving the Double

S Ranch. Four days had passed and there had been no more trouble at the ranch—and no trace of the trespasser. His tracks had vanished in the grass behind the barn.

Jill and her hired hand, Curly, had assured her they would check on the horses four times a day. At that thought Shadoe couldn't help but smile. She had good friends and neighbors. Ranchers knew the importance of sticking together. Normally solemn, Shadoe's entire face lit up with her smile. The corners of her eyes crinkled, emphasizing her high cheekbones. Her mother had often told her not to smile "so hard or you'll wrinkle before your time." But Shadoe's olive skin seemed to drink the sun that Connie Deerman had so avidly avoided. And the truth was, it didn't matter so much now if she smiled hard, because she didn't smile all that often.

"Okay, Luster. We've got to load up if we're going. And we have to go if I'm ever going to sell Scrapiron's babies. Remember, the reputation of this place is resting on you. You're the son of Scrapiron, and it's up to you to show everyone what kind of performance horse he produces."

Leading the horse around to the trailer, she clucked to him and he walked in. Shadoe lifted the ramp, secured it in place, and climbed in the truck. She headed south down the narrow road that would connect with the highway to Billings. Even as she drove away, she watched her home disappearing in the side view mirror of her truck. Everything would be fine. She had to believe that.

THE FIRST FEW HOURS in Billings were frantic with settling Luster into his stall, paying her entry fees, making sure her show clothes were neat and ready, polishing a few extra silver sparkles on her saddle and chatting with the other riders she'd been competing against for the past eight months. There was an easy camaraderie among the riders who came from all over the west, and she enjoyed the bustle and nervous energy of the show.

Luster was a standout among the horses. His gleaming gray coat glistened beneath her brush, and she was glad to see his easy adaptation to the new stall and excitement. With each passing hour, her own show jitters heightened, but this was one type of anxiety she knew how to put to her advantage. The jitters gave her that little bit of an edge that made her do her best. By five o'clock, she had saddled and was ready. Hanging at the gate she watched ten other riders as their horses maneuvered among the cattle, herding and cutting out the designated cow for the exercise. She was both delighted and anxious that the other riders and horses had performed so well. Luster would have to be on his very best to win the competition, but she knew he could do it.

The crowd was enormous, the perfect spring weather drawing spectators from all over the area for the big show. Along with the cutting event there were a multitude of crowd-pleasing activities. The cutting circuit was different from that of professional rodeo life, but there were points in common—and people. Shadoe had been on the rodeo circuit for a while, but she hadn't been able to tolerate some of the treatment of the animals. Still, it was an experience that had changed her life, and given her the desire to return to the Double S.

Looking around she spotted several riders she knew and gave them a wave. Her gaze stopped short on a cluster of men who stood at ringside. A tall, lean man with blond hair and a way of standing, that made her heart hesitate before the next beat, was staring at her. Across the crowded ring she met Hank Emrich's gaze and felt as if they'd spoken. There was the jolt of unexpected recognition, then the pain and hurt, the challenge, and finally the anger. Once upon a time, such communication with him would have given pleasure rather than pain.

Shaken by the power of his gaze, and the hurt it could generate, she turned back to Luster's stall. Her hands were trembling as she checked her appearance one last time, mounted and got ready for the anxious moments before she entered the ring. She took her place and waited for her number to be called, studiously avoiding looking at the place where she'd seen Hank.

Hank rested his hand on the showring fence before the next rider entered. He needed the support of the fence to steady himself. The cattle ran in the enclosure, kicking up a small cloud of dust that blocked the opposite side of the ring, and when it cleared, Shadoe was gone. He searched the crowd for her, wanting another glimpse of her in her tight black jeans and black hat with the silver band. As disturbing as she was, he couldn't get enough of looking at her. Why had he ever let Cal talk him into taking a day off and attending the competition? He'd never expected to see her here. When he'd known her she hadn't been a competitor.

"Hey, Hank. Want a beer?" Cal asked, nudging him to get his attention.

"Sure."

"I'll be back." Cal and the three other agents moved through the crowd toward the concession, leaving Hank at ringside where he watched a flashy chestnut swirl and cut through the herd of cattle, singling out a darting steer.

Horse and rider worked well together, and Hank joined the whistles and applause of the audience when the cowboy had cornered his quarry. The announcer called out the time and the score, and the crowd applauded again.

"Our next contestant is Shadoe Deerman on her gelding Luster," the announcer called out. "Number 159, you're in the ring."

Shadoe entered the ring at a dead run, her chin low in the horse's mane as the big gray aimed straight into the herd of cattle and began to cut and wheel with a grace and finesse that made the audience gasp. Riding close and low, she was a blur of black clothes and gleaming black hair.

The event was over in what seemed like a few seconds, and with the steer cornered, the audience rose to its feet with thunderous applause. Hank was too engrossed in watching Shadoe to hear the wild whistles and clapping. Without even thinking what he was doing, he abandoned his position by the rail and began to walk around to the stable area. He'd been around competitions all his life, but he'd never seen a horse and rider work with such unity of spirit. In the years that had separated them, Shadoe had become a professional rider. What Billy Casper had told him about Shadoe and her horses hadn't sunk in—until now. If the big bay stallion he'd chased across half of Lakota County could consistently produce horses like Luster, Shadoe was going to have herself a thriving business in a few years. She'd always been horse crazy, but he'd never realized how much talent she had. He felt pride, and pleasure, in her accomplishment, and he meant to tell her so.

"Hank! Hank!" Cal held up his friend's beer, but Hank gave him a wave that signaled he'd meet him later and lost himself in the milling throngs of people coming and going from the barns. There was something else eating at him, too. He'd spent the last four days going over his two meetings with Shadoe. The conclusion he'd come to was that he owed her an apology. And he meant to give it to her. Now. Whether she wanted to hear it or not. Shadoe also had to understand something.

He knew what had happened better than twenty years ago. He knew because he was there. The Deerman family had been camping in the Canadian wilderness when Joey Deerman had stumbled onto a den of young wolf pups. The eight-year-old had been beside himself with delight at the playful pups, until the mother wolf had come home. Fearing for her young, she'd attacked the boy, killing him. In a red rage, Jimmy Deerman had gone out to track down the wolf and had taken a fall in a snow-covered ravine. Tragic.

But not the fault of the wolves.

That's what Hank wanted to tell Shadoe, to force her to admit. Shadoe knew as well as he that the mother wolf was acting on instinct to protect her young. If Shadoe would only accept what had happened as a freak accident, maybe it would give her some peace of mind about the wolves that were being released. He and Shadoe could never put the past behind them, but they could quit treating each other as antagonists.

He wove through the throngs of people and horses, intent on his mission, oblivious to the laughter and calls, the smells of popcorn and beer.

Nothing could undo the suffering, or make right what had gone terribly, terribly wrong in Shadoe's young life. Nothing could repair the losses in his own life. But if Shadoe was going to make her way in Montana, then she'd best learn that the forces of nature—bigger and grander in Montana than anywhere else—had to be reckoned with. Wolves were going to be a small part of that natural setting now.

That grim thought was in his mind when he rounded a corner in the show barn and slammed smack into a firm black figure with a bucket of water.

Cold water sloshed all over Shadoe, shocking her far more than injuring her. She looked up into startled brown eyes and for an instant, twenty years vanished. Hank's expression was unguarded, and in it she read surprise, concern, embarrassment, and finally, a touch of humor. He looked so much like the seventeen-year-old Hank that Shadoe felt as if a giant hand squeezed her heart.

Anger was the defense she chose against the feelings he aroused in her. "What are you doing here?" she demanded.

The tone of her voice was like a slap, and Hank was brought up sharp. Still, his eyes couldn't avoid looking at the black silk Western shirt, now wet and clinging to her full breasts. The material was molded to her skin, leaving little to the imagination.

Shadoe felt his gaze and was shocked by her body's reaction to it. She lifted a hand instinctively to cover her breasts.

The action was not lost on Hank, and he felt a sudden burning embarrassment at his behavior.

"I owe you an apology," he said, quickly looking away from her.

Shadoe didn't speak. Her heart was pounding, and she was off balance by her own reaction. Slowly she lowered her hand and set the half-empty water bucket down. "I'll dry," she said.

"Shadoe..." Hank hesitated. "I'm sorry about the water, but that's not what I'm apologizing about. Watching you ride, I saw something I hadn't seen before. Or maybe I should say I saw something I wasn't willing to look at. Whatever happened out at the Double S a few nights ago, I know you weren't involved in letting your stud out. I was wrong to accuse you."

She swallowed. Her anger, her only weapon against the wave of regret that threatened to knock her off her feet, was powerless against an apology. "I'm sorry, too, Hank. Sorry for the way we had to meet again."

Picking up the bucket, he gave it a rueful smile. "Would I be too far out of line if I said that you've grown up to be a beautiful woman?"

It was sadness that tempered Shadoe's smile. "Not out of line. Thanks." She felt the wave grow higher, just hanging back in the distance and waiting for her to be alone so that it would sweep over her, drowning her in what-might-have-beens. If her life hadn't changed under her, she might have grown up with Hank. They wouldn't be standing here, awkward in a way they never had been before.

"I know we're not on the same side with the wolf thing, but maybe we could talk." Hank turned the bucket slowly in his hands. "I admire what you've done with that horse. I've never seen a horse and rider work like that." He tried for a smile and finally found one. "What I'm trying to say is that I admire what you're doing." He looked into her eyes and for a moment neither of them spoke. "I admire your dream, Shadoe. We found out a long time ago we didn't have the same dream anymore, but maybe we're both grown-up enough now that we can learn to respect each other's dream."

Shadoe wanted to run as hard and fast as she could in the opposite direction. For twenty years she'd tried to out-distance the past. Now it was standing in front of her, asking her to make friends with it. But wasn't that why she'd come back to Montana?

"Maybe we can try, Hank." Her doubts were in her voice. "We can't ever go back, but maybe we can go forward. As friends. But I won't ever accept the need for those wolves."

It was more than he'd hoped for. He handed her the bucket. "That may be true. Then again, I might be able to change your mind." He smiled, and the secrets of a clear Montana stream seemed captured in the amber of his eyes.

"Shadoe!" She turned with surprise to see a lean, dusty cowboy coming up to her with a long stride. "Great ride! You were superb! Like some Indian princess riding the wind."

Shadoe smiled a big welcome to the cowboy and then rushed into his arms, exclaiming only a little as he squeezed her tightly bound ribs. "John Carpenter! Where've you been? I got your letter and I was expecting you last month!''

''Oh, riding the broncs.'' He eased back from her and rubbed his elbow. ''Spent a few days in the hospital, which kind of slowed me down.''

Shadoe stepped back. ''Are you hurt?'' She ran her hands down his arms, stopping at his left elbow. ''Still bandaged.''

''It'll heal.'' The cowboy looked up into the heated brown gaze of the man who stood at Luster's stall door. ''I didn't mean to interrupt anything.'' Even before he finished speaking his gaze drifted over to the wet shirt clinging to Shadoe's breasts. He didn't have to say a word to show his approval.

''John Carpenter, this is Hank Emrich, an old...we grew up together.'' Shadoe's introductions were as awkward as she felt.

''Another broken heart in the Shadoe Deerman graveyard?'' John extended his hand. ''Shadoe joined up with me to ride the rodeo circuit, and when she learned all my secrets she left me flat.'' John's grin was as smooth as Kentucky bourbon. ''Thought she could sneak away, but I've come to reclaim my Indian love.''

Shadoe felt the flush heat her cheeks. ''Don't be such a fool, John.'' She avoided looking at Hank.

''Yeah, Shadoe took it into her head to leave the rodeo and come back home to make her fortune. If anyone can do it, she can. I've never met a more determined woman in my life. All I can say is, don't get in her way.'' He grinned at both of them. ''Hell, she broke my heart and both of my legs before she left me eating her dust.''

''John!'' Shadoe shook her head. ''You broke your legs after I moved up here. And I didn't...'' She hesitated at the dark look in Hank's eyes. Had she imagined that she'd shared a moment of warmth with him only seconds before?

The look he was giving her was an indictment. She'd be damned before she tried to explain John's comments. Besides, she didn't owe Hank any explanation. None at all.

"If you've finished with the lady, I'd like to take her to dinner," John said to Hank. "We've got a lot of territory to cover, and Shadoe's one unbroken filly I'm ready to try to saddle. Yeah, and I stopped by your place. Old Curly told me where you were and he said for you to call him as soon as you could." At the look in her eyes, he held up a hand. "No, no, it wasn't anything to do with your horses. They're all fine. It was something else. He acted like it was a government secret." John chuckled. "You know how old Curly likes to go for the dramatic."

Shadoe knew, but she could see that Hank didn't. All warmth was gone from him. Whatever emotions were left were all negative.

"I've said everything I came to say, and more." Hank gave the cowboy a long look, then turned away. "Later, Shadoe," he said as he walked back to the arena.

He didn't realize his hands were clenched into fists until he was ten minutes into the thick crowds. How was it possible that even after all that had transpired between him and Shadoe Deerman, the sight of her in the cowboy's arms had given him a jolt of pure jealousy?

THE LONG RIDE from Billings back to Stag's Horn had been made with most of the agents sleeping. Hank had remained awake, sitting beside a window, staring into the night. Once they'd reached the camp, the other agents had wearily climbed out of the vehicle and stumbled to their beds. Hank had taken a seat on a tree stump where he could stare out through a break in the trees at the night sky. A million stars twinkled down at him, and that fact only made him feel sadder.

"What's eating at you?" Cal came up to stand at his

friend's shoulder. "You act like a mule with a lip full of briars. You must have heard Harry Code's been in Athens a few days, 'checking out the mood of the locals.' No wonder they're so hostile."

"Damn." Hank hadn't heard, and it did nothing to improve his mood. "I've got a lot on my mind already. I don't need Code here to mess things up more. We've got to let the wolves loose this week."

"Afraid that gray devil will come back to get you?" Cal laughed. "He does keep his eye on you, no matter how much you deny it."

"He'll be okay." Hank was determined to slip out of his bad mood. "Look, there's Harry's car. He's finally come up to the camp. No whirlpools, no room service. There must be a camera crew nearby, though, or he wouldn't be here."

Cal shook his head. "It's like him to show up just before the wolves are freed. If there's any press coverage, he wants to be in front of the cameras."

Cal's comments made Hank smile. "Well, someone has to take all the credit."

"And Harry Code wants it to be himself." Cal put his hand on his friend's arm. "Be careful around Harry. He knows you're smarter than he is, and he doesn't like to have his nose rubbed in it, Hank. You've got a way of getting under his skin."

"I do my job."

"Better than anyone else. But you're a pain in Harry's butt. You make his life hard because you don't kiss up to him the way he wants you to." Cal rubbed his stubbled chin with his hand. "You've got a problem with authority figures, you know."

"I don't have a problem accepting the authority of someone who actually knows what they're doing."

"Competent or not, Harry's the boss. Try to live with that, Hank. For your own sake."

Along with everything else, Hank didn't need Harry Code at Stag's Horn screwing everything up. He knew Cal's words were spoken in friendship—and concern. One more charge of insubordination, and Hank could be fired. "I think I'll take a walk around the perimeter before I turn in."

"It's three o'clock in the morning. Are you nuts?"

Hank smiled again. "Probably, but it makes me sleep better to check on them. We're almost at the end of this, and I don't want anything to go wrong now. The wolves have the odds stacked against them as it is."

"Whatever." Cal shrugged his shoulders and headed toward his tent. "See you in the morning."

Hank zipped his jacket up closer around his neck. It was spring, technically, but when the early morning hours settled over the mountains, the wind had a biting edge to it. Maybe the cold would help him think clearly. He sure needed some help where Shadoe was concerned. In one brief encounter he'd opened the door on a past that held nothing but pain. For a few seconds, he thought he'd seen something of the girl he'd once loved with all his heart. And the chance that she still existed had given him a rush of pleasure and hope so strong that he was still unbalanced by it. And then another man had walked up and presented another side of Shadoe. John Carpenter had painted a picture of an ambitious woman who went over, under or through anything that got in her way. A woman who had used him and left him behind when she was done. The very idea chilled him colder than the mountain wind. He stood up, too cold and too disturbed to sit still any longer.

The wolves were half a mile from the camp, an attempt to keep them as free of contact with man as possible and yet keep them safe. It was an uphill climb, and Hank needed the exertion to calm his thoughts. Shadoe Deerman and his reaction to her wasn't going to go away. Hell, she'd been in his subconscious more than twenty years, and he'd been so stupid, or so stubborn, he hadn't been willing to accept it. Seeing her, though, he could no longer bury the truth. He'd never gotten over her. And if his encounter with her in Billings was any clue, he probably never would. He just had to make damn certain that he didn't let her interfere with his job.

He climbed the trail, checking the two females that had been caged together. They were smaller than Thor by about thirty pounds each. Instead of meeting his gaze, they turned away, moving to the far end of their space. He moved on, checking several young males and finally coming to the male and female couple they'd captured together. The female was pregnant, and the birth of the pups would help cement the pack's territorial shift to Montana.

He knew immediately that something was wrong with the female. She was stretched full-length on the ground, her breathing too shallow and too fast. The male paced around her whining. Sitting back on his haunches, he pointed his nose toward the sky and let out a terrible howl.

Chapter Five

Hank stood at the veterinarian's elbow as he increased the intravenous drip that pumped nutrients and sedative into the veins of the wolf. Her breathing was slower, steadier, but no one had to tell Hank that it was touch-and-go. What the vet couldn't tell him was the exact poison she had eaten. Not for absolute certain—until the tests had been run.

Doc Adams turned to Hank and shook his head. "I can't be certain until the blood work is complete, but I'd say arsenic."

Hank had trained himself not to react, not to show anger. He nodded. He'd known it from looking at her. "The pups?"

"Stabilized for the moment. I can't guarantee anything, though. Spontaneous abortion would be a natural thing, even if the mother lives. And that's a big if."

Hank nodded again to show that he understood. His gaze drifted to the helpless animal on the makeshift examination table that had been hurriedly erected in a large tent. She was a predator, a creature capable of bringing down a sheep or cow, yet against the forces of man, she was helpless. And poison was the most cowardly of all the tactics used against animals.

Doc Adams had been a vet in Lakota County for over forty years. Hank had known him since he was a small boy.

Doc wasn't inclined to discuss the motives of the ranchers and citizens of the area, particularly not with him. But Hank had seen the disgust on his face. Adams wasn't a man who held with poisoning an animal. Not even a wolf.

"Any ideas who might be capable of this?" It was Hank's job to ask the question.

Doc turned back to the IV. "I've got some thoughts, but I don't have any evidence. It could be one of at least a dozen folks not all that happy about the wolves coming in here. And it could be some outsider trying to fight their fight on my home ground."

"Whoever did this needs to be brought to justice."

Doc picked up his equipment. "I couldn't agree with you more. If I knew who did this, I wouldn't hesitate to tell you. But I'm not going to ruin a man's name based on speculation."

"Can you tell me how they got it to her?"

"Ground meat. That's what she ate."

"We haven't fed the wolves any beef. But I found another arsenic capsule in some beef in an empty cage."

"Your lab showed it was arsenic?" Doc looked interested.

"Yes. No doubt at all."

"Then I'd say this is arsenic, too. Ground meat is the easiest medium to insure a fatal dose. She's just lucky you went up to check her. Another hour and she would have died for sure." Doc shrugged into his coat. Though it was April, the nights were cold, and this had been a long one. "I'll be back in six hours to check her. I've got to go to the Double S and make sure Shadoe's mare is getting along. She's due any minute now, and I promised I'd check her every day."

The mention of Shadoe and the Double S stopped Hank in his tracks. Not that he suspected her of the poisoning. He knew better than most that she was in Billings. With an old cowboy flame. But maybe Doc was just the person to ask about Shadoe and John Carpenter.

"Doc, can I ask you a question?"

"I've told you everything I know about the wolf. If she's a fighter, she might make it."

Hank shook his head. "It's about Shadoe."

Doc's eyes narrowed slightly. "What about her?"

"Do you know anything about a guy named John Carpenter?"

Surprise was evident on Doc's face, and then a twinge of regret. "I know John, a little." The old vet took a breath. "Is this official or personal, Hank?"

It was hard for him to say, but he managed. "It's personal."

"Okay, then, I'll tell you. Shadoe and John met at a rodeo. She was working for an advertising agency and John rekindled her interest in horses. He taught her to rodeo, and she was good, but she didn't like the calf roping business or the bucking animals. Said it was cruel to the animals and even though she wanted to compete, she wanted a sport that didn't rely on mistreatment of animals. I think she and John had played out, and so she went back to work to earn enough money to reopen the Double S. Took a shine to cutting horses."

"End of story?" Hank asked.

"Not quite." Doc shook his head. "I hate to be the one to tell you this, Hank. John Carpenter just bought Copperwood last month. Says he's going to raise horses. If I understood correctly, he intends to use Shadoe's stud."

Hank walked over to the wolf. He stroked her muzzle with the back of his hand. "Thanks for telling me, Doc. What should I do when the wolf comes around?" Hank's question stopped the vet with his hand on the tent flap.

"The best thing for her, *if* she regains consciousness before I get back, would be to somehow let her know her mate is here. Wolves mate for life, you know. I can't help but think that's about the only thing you can offer her.'' He walked out of the tent, closing the flap behind him.

Hank was left with his worries, his anger and a sense of terrible loss. He'd known intuitively that John and Shadoe shared some common past. He just hadn't wanted to accept it. Now he knew it was true. And John Carpenter had bought his old family place. Well, he'd never intended to go back there.

He focused on the wolf, willing her to fight, to try to live for the cubs she carried, for the future of the pack. As he looked at her, he felt a terrible anger. Someone had selected the most vulnerable of the wolves and tried to kill her. Why just one? Since they'd gotten close enough to poison one, why not all of them? These were the questions he should be answering, not mooning over a lost woman and a ruined ranch.

He pushed Shadoe and his family ranch out of his mind and concentrated on the wolf. She was heavily sedated, and would be for hours. How had this happened? How had the men he'd left behind to guard the camp been so careless? He couldn't help the wolf, but he could do his job. He checked the small generator to make sure there was enough gas in it to keep the lights going in the makeshift clinic, and studied the wolf one more time. She hadn't moved at all.

Feeling completely helpless, he found his jacket and started to pick up a flashlight. As he stepped outside the tent flap he found that dawn was creeping over the horizon, and there was no need for the light. It would be smarter to wait until full sunup, but he didn't have the patience. He was compelled to take some action, to begin the process of bringing the criminal to justice. If there were tracks, he might be able to follow them. The poisoner was long gone, no doubt, but judging from the size and depth of the prints he'd left, Hank would at least have an idea of the body type.

The wolves were restless as he approached. They prowled their cages, all except Thor. The biggest male sat and stared at him, as if he'd been waiting for Hank to arrive.

Maybe it was the poisoning, or maybe it was all the teasing he'd been getting lately from the other agents, but Hank felt a ripple of uneasiness move through him at the wolf's unrelenting stare. It was almost as if the animal blamed him for what had happened.

Ignoring Thor, he started around the other pens when he heard something in the underbrush. His hand went to his gun and he eased it out of the holster, holding it in his right hand as he dropped to a lower position and began to move forward. The noise was coming from the area near the pen where the male, agitated by the loss of his mate, paced the enclosure in rapid, worried measure.

As hard as he listened, Hank could hear only the sounds of the wolves and the movement of a brisk wind through the spruce trees. Holding himself perfectly still, he scanned the area to the left of the cage. Was it possible the poisoner was coming back to try to kill another? Even as he thought it, it didn't make sense. Why not kill them all at once? Why risk another trip?

He heard voices, low voices speaking urgently. Two men, whispering in what seemed like anger. They were coming toward him, he could tell, because the voices grew louder, more clear with each second. When he finally saw them, he was ready to launch himself at them.

"Hank?" Cal Oberton looked directly at him. "Is that you?"

Hank caught himself just before he catapulted his body at them. His plan had been to try battering them to the ground with his weight and then holding them there with his gun.

"Hank?" Cal sounded worried.

Hank rose from behind the shrub where he'd thought to set up an ambush. "What are you doing out here, Cal?" He was more than a little annoyed. "Harry?" He looked his boss dead in the eye.

"Harry asked me to take a look with him." Cal sounded apologetic, and a little weary. "Jim Larson came and woke us up when you called for the vet. Harry wanted to start the investigation right away."

Hank grew even more annoyed. Harry Code wouldn't know where to begin investigating the attempted poisoning of an endangered species. As far as Hank had been able to discern since coming to Code's territory, all his boss knew was how to dress for success and how to brownnose. He fought to keep his cool. "Find anything?" he tried to keep the sarcasm out of his voice. Cal was a good friend, and he was caught in a bad situation. If Harry had asked to see the place, Cal had no choice but to show him.

"We didn't find anything." Cal shrugged, more than aware of his friend's displeasure.

"No footprints?" Hank felt a great disappointment. The ground was rocky, but there were places where it was still soft from the melting snow. There should have been some prints, or at least something.

"We didn't find a thing." Harry motioned for the two agents to follow him. "I think we need to make an appeal to the public on this. I was thinking about calling the television crews up here. They've been hounding me to see the wolves before they're released, and I was thinking this would be a good time to use the media's interest—"

"And draw every maniac with a hunting rifle into the area." Hank cut him off. He gave his employer a hard look, and realized for the first time that Code wore a new pinstriped suit and wing tip shoes, now caked with mud and debris.

"The wolves are no secret." Harry slowed his pace long enough to glare at Hank. "You don't like the media, Emrich. I understand why. I remember the stink about that television reporter. That woman almost pinned your ears." Satisfaction edged his voice. "I heard you almost lost your badge. If the media hadn't gotten in the way, you'd have nailed those bird importers. And I suppose you're still smarting over that little romantic encounter. Well, that's the past, this is the present. You have to play the media game by their rules, but we can use them, if we're smart."

Hank ground his teeth together to clamp down the angry remark that wanted to fly out of his mouth. Harry Code was an idiot. An idiot with an ego as big as the Rocky Mountains.

Code continued, running a hand down the side of his head to make sure his salt-and-pepper sweep of hair was still in place. "I think a press conference is an excellent idea. Once we present the wolves as vulnerable, maybe some of the people who are so afraid of them will champion their cause. You know, underdogs and all. Get some of those environmentalists up here to say how wolves round out the natural balance, etcetera, etcetera." He waved his hand at Cal. "Make a note of that, and we'll take care of it as soon as the newspapers and television stations open for business. With some luck we could have them here by noon." He was nodding to himself. "Now come with me, Oberton, I need you to take care of some things."

Code started down the side of the mountain, towing Cal along in his wake, issuing orders and making lists. "Maybe we could call a florist, get a few potted plants up here for color. You know, something for the cameras to focus on," Code said.

Cal threw a helpless glance over his shoulder at Hank

who'd stopped in his tracks. Hank gave his friend a look of sympathy, then a shrug. Cal had been victimized, and there was nothing Hank could do to help him.

It wasn't a good thing that Hank had been left standing, uninvited to attend Code's little media preparation party. It wasn't a good sign for his career. Cal wasn't a brownnoser, but he wasn't as abrasive as Hank knew himself to be. If Cal was willing to put up with the neck-deep bull, then he would get the better positions and the better paying jobs. Trouble was, Hank, personally, would rather do without the money and the titles than deal with Code's insufferable ego.

He watched Cal and Harry disappear and then turned back to the wolves. It always made him feel better to see them and count down the days until they would be free. Whatever else, he was involved in a project that was a good thing. The wolves belonged in the mountains. They were a part of the natural order. No matter what the area ranchers thought.

Thor greeted him with a long, examining look, then paced to the back of his cage and sat down, his back turned to Hank. The agent had grown so used to the wolf's hard appraisal, that for a second or two he feared Thor might be sick. But the big wolf turned, casting a look over his shoulder, watching him from the portion of the cage that had been constructed to protect the animal against the weather.

Moving up to the last cage, Hank slowed. The sun had broken over the humpbacked ridge of a small mountain to the east. The hazy, golden light of morning touched everything with a warm hand, chasing away the chill of the night. At least his encounter with Code, as annoying as it was, had given the sun time to arrive. Now he could look for evidence.

At first he couldn't believe his eyes when he looked at the area beside the cage. Then he looked with growing anger and rage. If there had been a footprint with the owner's name written in DNA certifiable blood, it wouldn't have mattered. The entire area had been stomped and battered. Hank couldn't believe that Cal would have been so careless, but Code wouldn't have a bit more sense. Had the culprit left a map, Code's big feet and little brain would have rendered it useless.

"*Damn.*" The word was explosive on Hank's lips. "Damn it all to hell." He moved beyond the immediate area only to find that someone had trampled everything. And that someone had feet exactly the size of Harry Code's new wing tips. There wasn't a trace of Cal's running shoes. "A herd of buffalo couldn't have done more damage," Hank muttered.

As if he agreed, the lonely male wolf let out a howl.

SHADOE WENT THROUGH her barns a final time. All the horses were settled, even Luster, who'd been worn out from his competition and trailer ride home. He'd done beautifully, and Shadoe had the ribbons to prove it. Three people had come to offer to buy him, and those same customers had been glad to hear that she was standing his sire at stud at the Double S. It was a slow, hard way to build business, but it was finally working. Maybe in a year, by next breeding season, she'd have a respectable list of mares for Scrap-iron to service.

It was her first taste of victory, and it was sweet as she walked into her house, noticing with pride that some of the flowers she'd planted in the beds had bloomed while she was gone. Spring was calling in Montana, and not a minute too soon for her.

She wanted nothing but a hot bath and bed, but she listened to her messages. There were several from her neighbors who'd stopped by to check on things. And one from Doc, who assured her the horses were fine and that Totem, the cat, was eager to come home from the kennel. He also congratulated her on her ride.

News traveled fast in Athens. She grinned at Doc's warm message. He'd been a stalwart supporter of her dream, promising her that it wasn't impossible, and also letting her know that her father would have been proud of her.

The final call was the one that blasted all notions of sleep from her. It was from Jill, and it was short, sweet and concerned.

"Just heard the news. Someone poisoned one of the wolves. They called Doc up there to tend to her. I'll let you know when I hear something else."

Shadoe played the message again. No matter how much she hated the idea of the wolves, she didn't hold with poisoning them. It was worse than cowardly. It was despicable, the act of a person who was totally unscrupulous.

Although her body ached from weariness, Shadoe found that not even a hot bath could relax her. The poisoning of the wolf would lead to repercussions among the ranchers. They would all be prime suspects.

She checked the time of the message and discovered that Jill had telephoned earlier that morning. Surely by now there was additional news about the wolf. And it was only seven o'clock. Plenty early for a meeting of the area ranchers. Maybe it was time they organized—to protect themselves against the accusations that would soon be raining down on their heads.

It took fifteen minutes to arrange for an impromptu meeting at the Double S. Jill and Hoss Kemper, one of the longest residents of the valley, had agreed to come, along with Sheriff Billy, Doc and a half dozen others. Shadoe wanted the sheriff present so there could be no possibility that they could be accused of hatching another plot to injure the wolves. If there was going to be a range war between the ranchers and the wolves, it was going to be fought in Wash-

ington D.C., where the laws were made. The wolves were
as much innocent victims of the government as the ranchers
were.

With that point firmly in mind, and her brain whirling
with ways to **get** that across to Hank Emrich and his gang
of agents, she set about making coffee and putting out the
glasses, ice and mixers for those who wanted something
with more jolt than caffeine.

JOHN LOADED THE last glass in the dishwasher and leaned
back against the counter, watching Shadoe as she wiped up
the final crumbs of the meeting. "Are you still mad at me
for buying Copperwood and not telling you? I wanted it to
be a surprise."

When John had appeared at the ranchers' meeting, Shadoe had been surprised. When she'd found out he'd bought
Copperwood, she'd been shocked. And angered. When
Hank heard about the sale, he'd think she'd known it all
along. Not that it mattered what he thought. She just didn'
like the idea of hurting him, and she knew the sale of the
ranch to John would.

"You put me in an awkward position, John," she said
softly. "That was Hank's family's place."

"I didn't know him from Adam's house cat," John said
"You forget, I'm not from Lakota County. I don't know
the history of all these people like you do."

"I know." That was true. John didn't have a malicious
bone in his body. It had just been bad timing. Like everything else associated with Hank and her.

"About this little trip up the mountain, you think it'll
really do any good for you to go up there and talk to those
guys? They *want* to believe we'd poison a wolf." John had
turned back to the subject of the meeting.

"I want to say we didn't poison her. At least she's still
fighting for her life. And the life of her pups." Shadoe had

been upset by Doc's report on the wolf's condition, but his hopes for her recovery were stronger than they'd been twelve hours earlier. She sank down on a stool by the counter, looking over at the lean cowboy who was so much at home in her kitchen.

John hung the dish towel so it would dry. "You want me to go with Billy?"

Shadoe shook her head. She hadn't wanted to be the one elected to pay a visit back to the wolf site. Having been run off once was plenty for her, but she and the sheriff had been chosen to make an "official" visit. They might eject Shadoe, but they couldn't run off the sheriff of Lakota County. Or at least not as easily.

"I'll go with Billy. I want those agent people to clearly understand that none of us, no matter how opposed we are, would feed an animal arsenic."

John's face darkened. "The very idea." His lips thinned. "I wouldn't put it past *them* to do something like this, then save the wolf in the nick of time, just to make us look bad. Next thing you know they'll be calling a press conference to tell the country about the evil Montana ranchers."

Shadoe didn't comment. Hank wasn't the kind of man who would hurt a defenseless animal, not for any reason. But politics made strange bedfellows, and Hank wasn't the only agent on Stag's Horn with access to the wolves. One thing she'd come away with after the two-hour meeting in her home—the knowledge that the wolves were a political hand grenade. An explosion could damage a lot of people, not just the ranchers.

She was startled by the feel of John's hand on her shoulder.

"Easy there, Shadoe." He grinned down at her. "I just wanted to say how good it is to see you. Watching you ride yesterday." His grin widened. "Well, it brought back a lot of old times. Remember when we used to—"

"I remember, John." She stepped out from under his hand, then softened the rejection by giving him a smile. "Those were good times. Some of the best of my life."

"Mine, too." His grin turned rueful. "Seems like the longer I live the better the past looks."

She laughed at that. "Sort of like the grass being greener?" She brushed a strand of silken hair from her face. "I know what you mean."

"You do?"

"I do, but that doesn't mean I intend to go backward. We made our choices, and when we did, it pointed out exactly how different we are."

"I've changed, Shadoe. I'm ready to..." He hesitated, clearly rattled by what he was going to say. "I'm ready to put the rodeo circuit behind me. I bought that ranch to prove to you that I mean business about this. Hell, I came damn close to breaking my neck, and I don't have that endless faith any more that all my bones are going to mend back properly."

Shadoe couldn't help the soft chuckle. "It's hard to believe, John, but that sounds like a little bit of wisdom coming from those cowboy lips."

"Lips that would like to taste yours."

Shadoe pushed the stool up under the counter, using the motion as an excuse to put even more distance between them. "I've changed too, John. I'm not the twenty-six-year-old girl who spent a wild and reckless summer with you."

"Maybe we've changed together?"

"Maybe." She found she couldn't meet his eyes. "Maybe not."

"Would you at least give me a chance? I've spent the last few years thinking I may have thrown away the best thing that ever happened to me."

"I doubt that." Now it was her turn to be rueful. "There are some who'd say you escaped a terrible fate."

"Just a chance. That's all I'm asking."

She finally met his gaze. Her dark eyes were filled with the shadows of the past. "I can't make any promises. You know I think the world of you, but I can't promise you anything."

"But you won't run me off with that shotgun of yours?"

She smiled. "No, I enjoy your company, just as long as you don't push it. I'm not the kind who likes to feel cornered."

"That I remember." He picked up his hat. "I'll take that warning to heart and skedaddle out of here. I'm already developing my strategy. I'm going to make you beg for me." He grinned again, dispelling his arrogant words. "You'll see. Old John Carpenter is going to become an itch you've just got to scratch."

Shadoe tossed the wet dishcloth at his head, knocking his hat to the floor. "I can see how much you've changed. You're still the same old arrogant fool."

"That's me, baby." He picked up his hat and set it at a jaunty angle. "I shall return."

Shadoe was still smiling as she locked the door behind him. John Carpenter was a man with a lot of grace and charm, and it was flattering that he wanted to spend time with her. But... She slid the dead bolt home. But what?

That was one thought she could finish after a good night's sleep. She had to be up bright and early to ride with Billy up to the wolf site. And she wanted to be rested and on her toes for the confrontation with Hank Emrich.

SHADOE FELT THE GRIP of Billy Casper's gnarled hand on her shoulder as she started up the mountain trail, her tanned face infused with the red of explosive anger.

"Check back, Shadoe," Billy said calmly.

"Check back my ass." She tried to jerk away from him,

but Billy was a tough guy for all of his sixty years. His fingers dug into her shoulders and held her in one place.

"Don't go off half-cocked."

"Look!" She pointed at the camera crews that were busy hauling lights, wires and cameras up the steep trail. "Those bastards have called a press conference, and you can bet who's going to turn out to be the villain."

"Going up there and starting a fight won't help matters any."

"I'm not going to start a fight." Shadoe tried to wiggle free, but he held her.

"Don't forget I've known you since you were born, and I knew your dad. Fact is, I never saw such a split in a family. You and Jimmy, both so dark and explosive, and then your ma and little Joey, as blond and sunny as a June day."

The memories struck Shadoe like a wall, stopping her tug against Billy's hand. She gave him a sidelong glance, taking in the waxed moustache that matched his solid silver hair. He was an old-time sheriff, a real lawman, not one of those pseudo federal agents. Billy knew his territory, and he knew his people, and he cared about them—enough to go on a wild-goose chase up a mountain with her. She owed it to him not to make a jackass out of herself.

"Have you got a grip on yourself?" He gave her a knowing look.

"Yeah, thanks," she added grudgingly.

"Your dad always thanked me when I stopped him from charging off like a maddened buffalo. Wish I'd a been there to stop him the day he went after that wolf."

"I wish you had, too, Billy." That took the final steam out of her boiler and she walked along beside him as they made their way up to the point where the cameramen had congregated.

Shadoe saw Hank immediately. It was almost as if she

sensed him, realizing by instinct where he stood at the edge
of the crowd of reporters and federal bureaucrats that had
turned out for the circus of a press conference. To her complete amazement, she saw that huge pots of daisies and
some other pink flower that wasn't even native to the area
had been brought up the mountain. For the cameras, no
doubt. Hank stood with feet planted apart, his arms crossed
over his chest. She mentally dubbed him The Guardian. He
acted as if he were guarding the entry to the pearly gates.
And judging by his scowl, no one was going to get admitted
on this particular day.

Her attention was drawn to a sleekly dressed man in an
immaculate gray suit that contrasted nicely with a head of
salt-and-pepper hair that looked like a wave cresting. He
was stepping up to the microphones.

Shadoe hadn't come prepared to listen to a speech, but
she did with mounting anger. Even Billy, usually as laconic
as the day was long, was tensing up as the man who iden-
tified himself as Harry Code spoke of the poisoning of the
wolf and how an innocent animal had become the victim
of some ''misguided rancher.''

It was use of the word *rancher* that Shadoe couldn't tolerate. Before Billy could nab her, she pushed her way to
the front of the crowd.

''I'm one of those misguided ranchers, and I demand to
know what evidence you have to say such a thing.''

The television cameras swung to her, an eager ripple
running through the crowd of reporters. They'd come up to
get some footage of the wolves and the obligatory press
conference. Now they had something really interesting to
shoot.

''Who is this woman?'' Harry Code snapped, looking
toward Cal with displeasure. He glared down at Shadoe.
''Who authorized you to be up here?''

''This is Montana, Mr. Code. I authorized myself. As far

as I know, this is still federal property here. I have as much right to be here as you do. Probably more." Shadoe hadn't been so angry in years. In fact, she'd thought herself beyond such disastrous surges of emotion.

"Hank, get this woman out of here." Harry Code was truly irked that his moment in front of the cameras had been upstaged by the angry woman with the flashing eyes. She looked decidedly dangerous.

"I want to know what evidence you have that a rancher tried to injure that wolf. You've made an accusation. I want the evidence. In front of these cameras. *Now!*" The final word cracked out like a whip.

Hank remained on the edge of the crowd, making no effort to jump to his boss's defense. He'd warned Harry Code about accusing the ranchers or anyone else when they had no evidence. But Code, always one for the dramatic gesture whenever a television camera was trained his way, had stepped in it. And Shadoe had caught him at it. Good for her.

Besides, she was something to watch with her eyes flashing and her cheeks whipped pink with anger. Those firm breasts, which he remembered in full detail, were heaving up and down with her strong emotion.

"Emrich!" Code yelled at him. "Remove this woman."

Hank took his time walking over to the platform that Harry had ordered erected just for the press conference. Hank saw the cameras swivel and found himself an unwitting third party to the little drama that was playing out.

"The press conference is open to the public. That's what you said." Hank's tone bordered on insolent, but he couldn't help it. He felt her surprised gaze swing to him, but he ignored her.

"Remove her now."

"And open the agency up to a lawsuit?" Hank forced his voice to sound puzzled, apprehensive. "If that's what you want, Harry.'' He reached for Shadoe, but slowly, and with the faintest grin.

''I haven't broken any laws. And I want to know what evidence you have to say that a rancher hurt that wolf.'' Shadoe sidestepped his unambitious grasp and turned to the television cameras. What was good for the goose was good for the gander. ''He has *no* evidence. If he did, he'd spit it out,'' she said. ''Ask him. I'm done here.''

Pushing through the crowd, she made her way back to a smiling Billy Casper.

''Emrich...'' Code's tone held disaster.

''I'll make sure she leaves the premises.'' Hank walked away leaving the cameras no option but to return to Harry Code, who looked decidedly as if he wished he'd never hatched the press conference idea.

''What *is* the evidence, Mr. Code?'' one reporter asked. ''Is an arrest imminent?''

''Very possibly.'' Code's eyes were narrowed with fury. ''I'll keep you all informed. At this time I can't reveal any more information. Now Cal Oberton, one of our top agents, will escort you up to get some footage of the wolves before they're released.''

Chapter Six

Jill dropped Shadoe in the driveway of the barn and pulled out for home, eager to tend to her cattle before the last hours of daylight faded. Shadoe called to the yellow tabby sunning himself in the branches of a silver birch tree just budding into bright green leaf. "Come on, Totem. Give the birds a rest and help me at the barn." The cat leaped to the ground and ran to her, crying. As she turned toward the open barn door, she talked to the cat, telling him her adventures for the day.

Jimmy Deerman had made his young daughter believe that animals had the capacity to understand humans. It was something Shadoe wasn't certain she believed now—although sometimes she felt that her ability to communicate with Scrapiron or Luster or even Totem was eerily acute. Her father had also taught her that man and wild animal could coexist, if they both respected each other. That had been totally untrue.

But Jimmy had gotten her into the habit of talking to the animals, explaining events to them. Now she didn't stop to think whether they really understood; the talk was habit. She found that it soothed her, and maybe that was the point after all. She could be completely honest with Totem about the chaos of emotions Hank Emrich generated. How was it possible that twenty years after she had put him behind her, he was now an obstacle in her path? It wasn't that she still felt real emotion for him, it was simply that he had gotten out of the place in her path where he should have been and climbed ahead of her into the future. He was out of order, and his big, muscular body was blocking her way. That was what was bothering her. That was all it could be.

Totem watched her with complete interest as she tidied her tack and talked. Though her house was mostly organized, she kept the barn meticulously clean, especially the tack room where she kept tools and medication. In an emergency, she didn't have time to hunt for wire cutters or bandages. Running the ranch alone, she didn't have precious minutes to waste. She had to be able to put her hands on things instantly. She checked the medicine cabinet to make sure she'd put up the emergency supplies she always took with her when she went on the road with a horse. The vials of medicine, syringes, wound salves and powders, bandages and tape were in perfect order.

The horses had been turned out, except for Scrapiron who had a paddock adjoining his stall. As she picked up the broom and began to sweep, she could hear the stallion coming in and out of the stall, waiting on her to bring his dinner. It was almost time to feed.

Shadoe shook her head and looked at the cat. "So why do I let Hank bother me? He's doing his job. I'm trying to run my ranch. None of the other agents get under my skin like he does. Not even that pretentious boss of his."

Meow. Totem's tone was wise.

"Oh, so you think I'm making a mountain out of a mole-hill?"

Meow! Totem flicked his yellow tail and yawned.

"I think you're right. It's me, not Hank." She put the broom back and reached down to stroke the cat. "Thanks for the advice. Now let's feed up and go see about our own dinner." As she started to stand, her eye caught the edge of material hanging from her tack truck. She'd been in a hurry when she unloaded from the competition in Billings, but she didn't think she'd been in that big a rush. Opening the truck she saw her transport wraps had been hastily stowed. The end of one hung out, just enough to show when the trunk was shut. She picked it up, rewrapped it, and put it back, closing the lid.

Totem waited patiently at the door, scooting out into the barn as Shadoe followed. Together, they distributed the feed for the horses and Shadoe went up to the pasture gate to call them in. She gave two long whistles, one short, opened the gate and walked back to the barn. They'd be along in a few minutes, eager for food and a clean stall. Curly had been as good as his word about taking care of things while she and Jill were gone.

Shadoe stopped to stroke Scrapiron's white blaze a minute before she went in the house to make her own meals. The stallion nuzzled her hand, then danced away at the sound of approaching hooves. He snorted with excitement, whirling around, eager to be with the herd as they came into the barn and ran straight into their stalls.

Scrapiron's dancing feet kicked back the clean straw and Shadoe thought for a moment she was imagining something. She unlatched his door and went inside, pushing him over to the opposite side of the stall as she booted back the hay and bent to pick up the carved bone pocketknife. She remembered the day her father had given it to Hank. His eighteenth birthday.

Shadoe felt cold, then hot.

She latched the door behind her as she exited the stall and stood, knife in her hand, heart racing.   There was only one conclusion to draw. Hank had been in her barn. But when? And why? He'd shown up the night some intruder had turned Scrapiron free, but he never went near the stall. Had he come back? To investigate further? But she'd told him not to set foot on her property. Her fingers curled around the knife that was closed. None of it made sense.

"We'd better call Billy," she said, and the sound of her own voice, talking to the cat, made her feel better.

Totem didn't bother answering. He ran down the barn aisle toward the house and his can of savory seafood.

Shadoe hurried up to the house, headed straight to the phone. Before she could pick it up to check with Jill and Curly to be certain Hank hadn't stopped to see the horses while Curly was there, it rang beneath her fingers.

"Get ready, Shadoe, there's a television crew headed your way." Jill's voice tingled with excitement. "After your scene up on Stag's Horn, the television station got my tag number and looked me up. But it's you they want to talk to. I think we ranchers have got ourselves a spokesperson."

"Jill, someone was in my barn while we were gone. Did Curly see anyone?"

"I'll ask him." Jill heard Shadoe's anxiety but didn't press. "I'll call you back when I see him." She hesitated a moment. "This probably isn't the best time for you, but the camera crew really is on the way." She sounded less certain of Shadoe's reaction. "You will talk to them, won't you? I told you on the way home that you were awfully impressive. You looked like a warrior taking on the cavalry."

"I'm not sure that's flattering," Shadoe said. She didn't like the idea of television cameras. "I don't mind being part of the movement to stop the release, but no one elected me spokesperson. I think Billy would make a better on-camera person."

"He can't, he's an elected official."

"Then you, or maybe John. He's a landowner here now."

Something in Shadoe's tone revealed her difficulty with

that fact. "Are you angry that John bought Copperwood? I thought you'd be pleased." Jill was clearly puzzled.

"I'm angry he didn't tell me and...well, the timing could have been better."

"Oh." That word told Jill understood a lot more than Shadoe had said.

"It's not that. It's just that Hank had come back to Lakota County, and he lost the ranch because of money, not because he wanted to give it up. When I left here, I had enough money from the insurance...it's just hard."

"Yeah." Jill sounded reserved. "Look, I see Curly. Let me ask him about visitors. You talk to the news people and at the next ranchers' meeting we'll decide on an official spokes*woman*."

"Call me," Shadoe said. She put down the phone and hesitated about calling Billy and reporting the intruder. Maybe it would be better to wait until Jill had checked with Curly.

The decision was taken out of her hands when she heard the sound of a car coming up the rocky driveway. Looking out her front window she saw that the television crew had lost no time tracking her down.

HANK KNEW he was in trouble by the expression on Harry Code's face. A blue vein pulsed in his forehead, and his gray eyes were flint hard beneath his perfectly styled hair. For a split second, Hank was tempted to tell him how good he looked on television, but common sense prevailed. It was the television debacle that Harry was so mad about, and not even the three hours Hank had taken to check the perimeter of the camp had cooled Harry off. Shadoe had completely upstaged him, and he wasn't about to forgive or forget.

"How did that woman get up here?" Harry snapped the question.

Hank watched his superior as he paced the tent area he'd taken over as his office-home. Two biologists had been pushed out of the tent to accommodate Harry's decision to spend a few days on location. The arrogant ass made it sound like a film shoot, which he probably thought it was.

"Best I could tell, she walked." Hank almost regretted his answer. Almost—until he saw the red flush across Harry's face. Then he was glad.

"Emrich, your attitude has kept you from advancing in the service, and I can see why. You had the reputation of a troublemaker and I took you on anyway because of your knowledge of the locale. But I won't put up with your attitude. This time it's going to cost you more than a promotion."

Hank kept his mouth shut by smiling, which infuriated Code even more.

"You think I'm making a joke?"

"No, sir." Hank made it flat, toneless.

"Good." Code sent him a piercing look. "That woman is a known troublemaker. How did she get up here?"

"She came with the Lakota County Sheriff, as a spokesperson for the county ranchers." Hank kept his tone flat. The interview would end sooner if he didn't provoke Code.

"Billy Casper," Code said, sounding the name as if it would tell him secrets. "You know the man, don't you?"

"I do."

Code waited. "Well?"

"Billy's a stand-up guy. He's been sheriffing for nearly a quarter of a century."

"Then you're vouching for him?"

Hank felt the trap, but he couldn't see it. He could only tell the truth. "Given everything I know about Billy, and it's a considerable amount, I'd say he was a good man and a good sheriff."

"He wouldn't lie to protect someone?"

Hank felt his temper rise. Code was having too much fun, and he couldn't see why. "I don't think Billy bends the law. He's devoted his life to it." He couldn't resist. "In fact, when he was younger, he turned down a job working on a movie with Clint Eastwood. He didn't want to abandon his elected duties." Hank saw his jab had hit the target, but then Code's giant ego would have been hard to miss.

"You're old friends with Billy, right?"

Hank had had enough. He sighed as he put his hat back on his head. "I've got work to do, Harry. If there's a point to these questions, get to it. If not, it's been a pleasure talking with you."

Code stepped across the tent and blocked the exit. "Oh, there's a point." He pulled a slip of paper from his pocket. "Do you know who signs your check, Emrich?"

"Is that a rhetorical question?" Hank glanced at the paper but wouldn't give Code the satisfaction of showing interest.

"No, it isn't rhetorical. It seems strange to me to see the names of Billy Casper, Shadoe Deerman and one of my agents in a written report on the same day I see the three of them at a press conference. It might make a man wonder who's involved with whom, and what the benefits of such a liaison might be. The last time your name was on a report with a woman's you were almost fired."

Now it was Hank's turn to feel the blood rush to his face. He was angry enough to do something rash, but he wouldn't. Long, long ago Shadoe's father had taught him the lesson of self-control. A lesson that had cost him dearly, but one he had not forgotten. "Is there a point to this, Harry?" He spoke softly, as Jimmy Deerman had taught him.

"What's your relationship with Shadoe Deerman?" Code's question was whiplash quick.

"We went to high school together. I knew her family."

"That's it?" Code pressed. "It's all in the past?"

"In a nutshell. That's it." Hank stepped to Code's side. "Now is there anything else?"

"Cal got a report from the sheriff's office. Shows you were at the Double S Ranch a few nights back." Code tapped the paper against his jaw as he smiled at Hank. "That doesn't sound too much like the past to me."

Hank started to respond with an angry retort, but stopped himself. Now wasn't the place for anger. Now was the time for brains. He hadn't told anyone about the intruder he'd been following that night, and his lack of a report was a serious breach of procedure. But reports had a tendency to get leaked, as the one in Code's hand showed. And Hank had always felt better when he worked alone. His investigation was his. Not even Cal knew anything about it. Now he was going to pay for his solitary ways. Again.

"I was following a lead."

"Not very specific," Code said. He continued to tap the paper, his smile widening. "We've had a wolf poisoned, and then I find my top field agent has been visiting down the mountain with the leader of the rancher insurrection." Code paused dramatically. "That action might be viewed by some as treasonous."

"And by others as solid police work." Hank wasn't budging.

"I want a full report of the incident, typed and on my desk by tomorrow."

It wasn't a request, it was an order, and one Hank couldn't disobey. "Yes, sir."

"Good." Code waved his hand, dismissing Hank. As Hank turned he felt the other man's hand on his arm, holding him. "She's pretty, Hank, but she's not worth your badge." He dropped Hank's sleeve as if it were hot.

Hank stepped into the cool afternoon, the touch of the wind a comfort against his overheated face. Code was insufferable, but at the moment he held the upper hand. Hank set off up the steep path to where the wolves were. He fel as trapped and confined as he thought they must.

"Hank?"

He was so busy thinking that he almost knocked Do Adams down. The vet caught his arm.

"Sorry." Hank looked down at the shorter man. "How is she?"

"Better than I expected. I'd like to move her into a cage beside her mate."

"Beside him?"

"So she can know he's there, but I may need to get to her for the delivery of the pups. I don't want to have to sedate him to do it. You never know how much sedative a wild animal can take before it will react negatively."

"You mean before it kills them."

"Before they quit struggling against it and give up completely."

It wasn't an image that helped Hank's mood. "We'l move her now."

"Good." Doc fell into step beside him, going back up the way he'd come. "About Copperwood..."

"There's nothing to say." Even at the name of the ranch Hank felt longing, betrayal and a lingering sense of em barrassment that he had let the land slip away from him.

"Hank, you did everything one human could do to hold that place."

"And it wasn't enough." Hank increased his pace. He didn't want to talk about this. Why was everyone he me digging into the past?

"I heard Shadoe was up here." Doc grinned. "She makes quite an impact, doesn't she?"

Hank couldn't resist the vet's obvious pride in Shadoe He was another one of the Lakota County old-timers who viewed Shadoe as a surrogate daughter. "She got unde

Harry's skin.'' Hank's grin widened. ''Worse than a prickly pear.''

''That's our girl.'' Doc chuckled. ''It's been hard on her, coming back here, Hank. She's come back to settle something inside herself. To prove something, or else to accept it. I'm not certain which. But she's afraid. She may not show it, but she is.''

''Is that a professional diagnosis?'' Hank tried to take Doc's talk lightly, but he was discovering that anything involving Shadoe was hard for him to take, lightly or otherwise.

''It's an old man's diagnosis, looking back at how hard it was to be her age. A lot of time has passed, but surely you remember how much Shadoe loved that ranch and all the country around here. Jimmy raised her up as close to a wild thing as a human child could be. They were a part of the mountains. I've never seen anything like it.''

Hank didn't say a word. He remembered, and the memory cut at him. Since he'd returned to the area, there wasn't a place that didn't remind him of the Deerman family. In fact, Stag's Horn, where the wolf camp was located, had been a place where he and Shadoe's father had once thought they saw a wolf during a camp out. That was why Hank had picked the location—a tribute to Jimmy. The release of the wolves, though it distressed his daughter, would have greatly pleased Jimmy Deerman.

Doc watched the play of memories across Hank's face. Those past moments were painful, and deep. ''You were often a part of that picture, Hank. You and Jimmy and Shadoe. We thought when she went off to school you'd go with her.''

Hank felt the pressure of anger rising again. Twenty years had not cooled it. He had only deceived himself into thinking he was over it. ''Things didn't work out that way, Doc. Shadoe took a different course. I still had Copperwood, and I had to put everything into trying to save it. As it turned out, it was wasted effort."

"Jimmy's death brought a lot of dreams tumbling down."

"Well, I don't think I was cut out to be a rancher anyway. Things happen for the best." Hank motioned the vet up to the holding pen where they'd put the female wolf. She looked even gaunter than usual, except for her belly, swollen with the cubs that were due any day. Hank watched her with a critical eye. The poison had taken a toll, but Doc Adams had done wonders. She was up, alert, pacing. Waiting to see what her human captors had in store for her next. "It's okay, girl. You're on the road to freedom." Hank spoke to her softly. At the sound of his voice she stopped pacing and turned toward him, but she refused to meet him eye to eye.

"She's listening." Doc nodded approval. "I think she understands the intent of your words."

"Jimmy always thought animals understood a lot more than they were willing to let on. He said it was part of their intelligence to trick us humans." Hank couldn't stop the smile that played across his face, giving him for a moment the look of an eager young boy. "Jimmy filled my head with a lot of foolishness, I guess."

"Foolishness?" Doc's probe was gentle. "There's no scientific data to show they understand. Then again, there's nothing to prove positively they don't." He looked at Hank. "Now, how are we going to make the transfer?"

Hank approached the cage. "I think we can carry her up to the pen beside her mate and just open the gate."

"Good idea. The less trauma the better." Doc stepped up. Together the two men lifted the cage and started out of the area up the trail to the rest of the wolves.

Both men were breathless when they finally maneuvered the pen against the door of the cage. Hank opened the release latch, and the female shot into the larger enclosure, going straight to the heavy wire that separated her from her mate. She made a low sound in her throat, a sound of eagerness and relief.

The male wolf put his nose to the wire and tried to lick her.

Hank watched the sight in fascination, while the old veterinarian watched him. Doc's expression was thoughtful.

"If she'd died, he probably wouldn't have adjusted," Doc said. "Some creatures, like wolves, mate for life."

Hank was silent, but his hands were clenched in fists at his side. When he finally spoke, his voice was soft. "So much has been written about the power of love. It's funny that no one acknowledges that it has the power to kill."

"Not kill, Hank. But with some species, the mating bond is more powerful than the will to live." Doc hesitated. "I'm an old man, but I've seen a lot, with my animal clients and their owners. Some animals are simply meant to be together. Some people, too."

Hank turned away from him. "Let's head back." But he stopped short. Coming up the trail was Harry Code, his face red with anger. "Uh-oh, here comes trouble."

"Emrich," Code halted ten feet away. "I just got an interesting call from an anonymous source." He waved a sheet of white paper at Hank. "This woman called to ask me if I knew that you've got a personal score to settle here in Montana."

Hank didn't say anything, he simply looked at his boss.

"Well?" Harry was furious.

"Well what?" Hank said.

"Is it true?"

Hank swallowed the angry reply that came to him. "You knew I was from this area. That's why you asked for me."

"I didn't know that you'd lost your ranch up here."

"That was a long time ago, and it has nothing to do with

what's happening now." Hank's dark eyes narrowed. "I don't see where that's any of your concern."

"Everything that affects this project is my concern." Code stepped closer. "Let me warn you right now that you'd better not have a personal stake in this issue. You've been in trouble before, but this time it will be your badge, and maybe your freedom."

Chapter Seven

Shadoe cinched the girth on Scrapiron with a sense of overwhelming relief. Ever since her interview with the television station the day before, her phone had not stopped ringing. Even her mother in West Palm Beach had somehow heard about her appearance on the six o'clock news and called her—with all the dire warnings and predictions of disaster because of Shadoe's return to Montana. The mention of Shadoe in the same breath with the word *wolf* had sent her mother into a three-martini breakdown.

A surge of guilt washed over Shadoe at her own thoughts. Her mother had learned to handle the anxieties of life in her own way. Connie Deerman had loved her husband and son, and it was the loss of them that had made her change so completely. For a period of time, Shadoe herself had been tempted by the idea of using prescription medications, parties and a highball to ease her down the road to life.

"Steady, boy." Shadoe settled the stud as he fidgeted while she adjusted her stirrups. The horse was definitely picking up on her internal conflict, no matter that her hands were steady and her voice calm. Horses were a lot smarter than anyone gave them credit for being.

She swung up into the saddle and felt a measure of comfort at the power of the horse beneath her. He was a fine animal, and she had trained him well. He wasn't the show horse that Luster was, but his talents lay in a pleasurable ride and the ability to produce foals that shared his athletic ability and laid-back disposition.

Once out of the barn and down the drive, she gave him the signal to canter. But not even Scrapiron's eager plunge into the ride or the sweet smell of mountain laurel could push out the sound of Connie Deerman Frazier's worried voice. Shadoe's mother had been violently opposed to Shadoe's return to Montana. But then Connie had not been pleased by any of her daughter's actions lately. Not since her interest in horses had been reignited by John Carpenter. With Jimmy and Joey's deaths, Connie had reinvented herself. She had carved a new life for herself with a new marriage and the high-class society whirl of West Palm Beach, Florida. She couldn't understand Shadoe's desire to return to the place that had broken her dreams into a million pieces.

Shadoe didn't really understand it herself. She only knew it was something she had to do. Or else she'd drift through the rest of her life never fully giving herself to anything, or anyone.

Scrapiron flexed his powerful neck and tugged at the reins, and Shadoe gave him the freedom to gallop. He needed the exercise, and she wanted the wind to whip her thoughts out of her head.

No matter how hard she rode, the past years spun before her in grim truth. Her adult life had been a series of evasive maneuvers. She'd gone into advertising, hoping the glitz and excitement of that career could erase what she had lost. For a few years she'd enjoyed her job in Dallas at one of the biggest advertising firms in the Southeast. She'd lived high on the hog with a red Porsche and a beautifully furnished house where she gave parties for the firm's clients that made the society pages of the Dallas papers. She'd spent every penny she made, which was considerable, and most of the money she'd gotten from her father's insurance policy. She'd dated bankers, lawyers, business executives—anyone who wore a suit. And then she'd run across John Carpenter and the wall she'd built around herself had begun to crumble.

She'd squandered her money and years of her life, and worse than that, she'd been running the whole time. Well, she was through running, and her mother would just have to trust her to be smart and strong enough to survive.

Feeling the challenge of the future rather than the regrets of the past, Shadoe focused on the beauty of the landscape. She'd taken the trail that crossed Silver Flash Creek, and as the incline steepened, Scrapiron slowed his wide-open pace and dropped to an easy jog. This was a part of the ranch she hadn't visited since her return the previous fall. She found that she had to make her reacquaintance with the land in tiny increments. There was the beauty itself that could sometimes be painful, and then the layers upon layers of memories.

Every acre of the ranch echoed with her father's laughter, a bit of legend or folklore. A lot of Montana newcomers thought Silver Flash Creek had been named for a mineral find, but Jimmy Deerman had told her the truth. The small creek, which was clear amber and cold even on the hottest summer day, was the place where a spirit dream had touched Crazy Horse. In the swirl of the crystal current, the legendary Indian warrior had heard the thunder of calvary hooves and had seen the flash of the sun on the metal bores of the long rifles that were to be the death of his people, and he had urged the Sioux nation to war.

Shadoe topped the rise and looked down on the narrow band of water that snaked over rocks and rugged terrain until it disappeared behind a jutting crag of rock. She listened for a moment, a half smile on her face. She and her father had camped along the creek many times, listening for the sound of hooves mingled with a bugle and the cries of the Indians. Scrapiron stood perfectly still, as if he, too, listened for the ghost of horses long departed.

The sun was hot on her shoulders and she nudged Scrapiron down the rough slope to the water. He was hot and eager to drink, but she allowed him only a swallow or two as he stood, hock deep in the cold stream. During a heavy rain, or when the snows were melting higher up, the little creek would be very dangerous. So much of the beauty of her home hid sudden dangers.

That made her think of the wolves. In a week or so, they would be roaming the timberland north of her. The furious anger that had first gripped her was gone. In its place was a far more complicated array of emotions. In the middle of it all was Hank Emrich. He confused everything.

His behavior up at the wolf site had confounded her. Instead of going to Harry Code's aid, Hank had seemed to protect her. He'd always had a problem with authority, but he also had a major problem with her. Yet she'd seen the amusement in his eyes. She could have sworn she also saw pleasure, and congratulations.

But why?

She'd gone to speak out against something he believed in. Or at least it was something he said he believed in. That was one thing that troubled her. Hank had always dreamed of being a rancher. They'd spent all their high school years planning a life together that involved cattle and horses. Hank knew the devastation a wolf pack could cause, and yet...and yet he was cramming it down the throats of the ranchers he'd grown up among.

Wolves. The very creatures that had taken the man who'd loved Hank like a son.

It didn't make a bit of sense. Unless it was personal.

Scrapiron snorted and swung around as if he sensed

someone behind him. Shadoe, too, looked into the line of heavy timber that grew along one side of the stream. She'd learned never to underestimate her horses. Their sense of hearing was extremely keen.

The woods were dark, the limbs of the blue spruce meeting overhead to create a dark haven of trunks. Beneath her legs, Scrapiron trembled.

Gathering the reins, Shadoe angled toward home but kept the line of trees in her vision. She wasn't spooked, not exactly, but something was in the woods. Maybe a bear. Maybe one of the big cats. There were predators other than wolves, but they hardly ever came as close to the settled areas, and more importantly, they didn't run in packs.

A coyote was the more likely candidate, and they were harmless to a person. Coyotes preyed on smaller animals and were basically cowards. The threat they offered to livestock or humans did not compare to wolves.

"Easy, Scrap," she whispered as she tightened her legs on him to let him know she was there, that she was in charge.

Something moved in the woods. There was the crackle of a limb, a shift in the gloom of the trees. She felt her heart pump harder. Her ribs were almost healed, but she felt the tenderness as she sucked in a lung full of air and prepared to ride. The little clearing beside Silver Flash wasn't the place to stage a standoff. The animal had the distinct advantage. The trail out was the perfect place for a predator to attack.

Just as Shadoe was weighing her options, the creature in the woods bolted. Instead of coming at her, it went north, deeper into the woods. Survival instinct made Shadoe prompt Scrapiron forward, toward the trees. If the animal was running, she wanted to really make it think she intended to pursue. A bitter spike of remorse made her clamp her lips tight at the thought she'd left her rifle back at the house. One day she'd learn not to take anything for granted. Not in Montana.

Scrapiron caught a glimpse of the quarry, and though she'd never seriously trained him in cutting, he knew enough to head on a diagonal to cut off the escape path. She urged him on, thinking perhaps she'd gotten herself worked up over a deer coming down to the stream to drink.

The animal was on the run now, and Shadoe felt her tension ease up. She'd let Scrapiron play a minute more, then pull him up. If it was a deer, she didn't want to give the animal a heart attack, and it was thrashing deep in the woods, so afraid now that it didn't bother to try to move silently. She wanted a glimpse of it, just to satisfy her curiosity. Then she'd call it quits.

Scrapiron had chosen an opening through the trees that angled into the woods. As soon as horse and rider entered, Shadoe felt the temperature drop a good ten degrees. The blue needles of the spruce trees met overhead and seemed to drink the April sunlight. A shiver of apprehension marched along her skin. About fifty yards to the northeast, the animal was running, but in the gloom and thickness of the trunks, she couldn't get a clear view.

She leaned forward and let Scrapiron plunge ahead, picking up speed as he followed what once had been a neatly maintained trail that her father had cut for them to ride on.

They were drawing closer to the quarry, and Shadoe stood in the stirrups to try for a better view. She wasn't certain what happened next. There was a terrible pain just below her neck, a searing line of fire that struck her with such force she was propelled backward off the horse. She hit the ground with full force, losing all of the wind in her lungs.

Startled by the loss of his rider, Scrapiron stopped a few yards ahead.

At first Shadoe could only try to find enough oxygen to

breathe. She lay on the ground like a fish pulled from water, gasping and unable to sit up or do anything to help herself. Bright red lights swam in front of her eyes, but she forced herself to think only of breathing, of filling her lungs with air.

There was the sound of someone, or something, scrabbling rocks on the trail up ahead, but she was helpless. If some wild animal was coming after her, she'd be an easy victim. And Scrapiron, too. He stood, reins dangling to the ground, waiting for her command.

Just when she thought she was going to faint, Shadoe got air into her lungs. The sound of something approaching was louder, eager sounding, and she forced herself to her hands and knees. Her entire chest felt as if she'd been slammed with a board, and she finally realized what *had* happened. She'd been clotheslined. She forced her head up and searched the area across the trail. The gray wire was detectable only because she knew where to look. Had she not been standing in her stirrups, the height of the wire would have struck her neck, possibly killing her.

Fury powered her to her feet, and she was standing when the lone figure stepped out of the woods. He was a big man and he held a hunting rifle in his hand, his face shadowed by a cowboy hat. He paused only a second before he continued toward her. Shadoe reached for Scrapiron's reins, fully intending to get at least one foot in a stirrup and riding for her life. She didn't know who the man was, but she didn't like the idea of being caught helpless and alone in the woods with him. At the very least he was trespassing. At the worst he was responsible for nearly killing her.

Still pulling hard for oxygen, she found that her fingers were clumsy as she reached for the horse. Her foot refused to obey her. When she looked over the saddle, he was on the other side of Scrapiron, his hand reaching for the reins.

"What the hell are you doing up here, Shadoe?"

It was his voice that halted her. She ducked under Scrap-iron's neck for a better look and saw what her mind had not allowed her to register. Hank Emrich was staring at her with a blend of concern and anger.

Instead of a cutting reply, she could only drag air into her lungs.

He moved around the horse so fast she didn't realize what had happened until she felt his arms around her, offering support and an unexpected charge of heat. Dizzy already from the fall, she felt the reins slip from her fingers and she could not resist his forceful arms as he drew her against him and held her.

"Take it easy." One arm was wrapped around Shadoe's waist and he could feel the pounding of her heart, sense the slackness in her body as she almost fell. If he had not been holding her, she would have hit the ground.

He eased her away from the horse and over to a fallen tree where he sat her and gently pressed her head down between her knees.

"Just take long, slow breaths," he said. His fingers slid through her silken hair, and in the distance a hawk cried. The sense of the past was suddenly so strong for Hank that he felt dizzy himself. The soft feel of Shadoe's hair, the delicate scent of honeysuckle on her skin; he felt as if he were falling, falling deep into the past, and he wanted to make no effort to stop it.

As soon as the dizziness passed and she felt the sweet relief of oxygen in her lungs, Shadoe forced her head up. He moved his hand, allowing her to straighten. Even when he no longer touched her, she could feel where his hand had been. Her skin felt naked, vulnerable, and she recognized that feeling as longing. For what once had been, for that one touch that had always seemed to complete her. For a dream that was long gone. When their gazes met, she saw the young man she'd left behind nearly twenty years before.

And this time she wasn't afraid. His dark gaze was open, pain shimmering for an instant before he covered it.

"Are you okay?" His voice was roughened by his own emotions.

She nodded, unable to speak such a direct lie. It wasn't the pain across her chest or the bruises she'd received in the fall. She was hurting in a way she hadn't hurt in years. Deep beneath the bruises, her heart was cracking wide open. Tears stung her eyes and she focused on the dirt beside her boots where a line of ants marched determinedly toward a hole in the fallen tree.

"What happened?" Hank knew Shadoe hadn't fallen from the horse. He'd seen her ride in the competition. She wasn't the kind of rider who took a tumble without provocation. He glanced around the area, but there was nothing he saw that would have caused an accident.

Shadoe found it impossible to answer. Her throat was blocked with emotion that she couldn't afford to express. She rose, slowly at first, then with more confidence as she walked toward the wire. It took her a moment to find it, but when she did, she heard Hank's soft whistle.

"You could have been killed."

"Yes." She'd finally gotten a grip on her emotions and she turned to face him. "I was standing in the stirrups to look ahead. Otherwise it would have caught me right at my throat."

Hank's vision drifted from her eyes to her lips to her neck, and stopped at the level of her collar bones. "Let me take a look at that," he said.

Shadoe looked down and for the first time saw the blood on her shirt. The bleeding was minimal, but she knew the wire had left its mark.

"It's okay." She shook her head. As vulnerable as she was to Hank, she certainly didn't want him tending her wounds. It was too personal, too caring. She might just die from the treatment.

"Just to be sure it's not serious." He walked over to her and undid the first button of her shirt. His fingers fumbled the button, and he saw his hands were shaking. Shadoe looked steadily at a tree. When at last he'd managed to move the collar of her blue denim shirt aside, he saw the ugly mark of the wire. The skin had been torn and cut, but the external damage was not serious. Already the tender flesh was bruising, and he saw the first dark mottling in her beautiful bronzed skin. He wanted to touch her, to soothe her and wipe away the damage, but he could not. Beneath the injury was the swell of her breasts, and as much as he wanted to comfort her, he also wanted more.

"No serious damage, but I know it hurts. When we get home, we'll put some ice on it." He had to step away or he was going to take her into his arms and kiss her. That was the one thing he wasn't certain he could survive.

For Shadoe, the entire world had narrowed to the feel of his gaze on her chest, the knowledge that his fingers brushed the naked skin of her throat, and the urgent beating of her heart which had begun to awaken so many parts of her body. If her injury was painful, she didn't feel it. Pain sensors were shut down. What she felt was a sudden and nearly overwhelming desire. She had lain in Hank's arms along Silver Flash Creek. They had picnicked and camped and fished and dreamed of their future together, laughing and talking, and kissing. They were waiting only to finish high school. They had promised Jimmy they would wait. In the end, they had waited too long.

Hank carefully rebuttoned her blouse and stepped back from her.

"This hasn't been your week, has it?" he asked.

Something of the understatement of his words caused her to smile. "You could say that."

As natural as if they'd taken a hike together he put his hand under her elbow and led her back to the fallen tree. "Sit down for a few minutes."

Shadoe did as he asked, feeling as if her will had been suddenly suspended. Hank had stepped out of the woods and taken charge. It seemed as right and natural as drawing the pure mountain air into her lungs. His very touch was soothing. Later, alone in her bed at night, she'd pay a terrible price for this, but she had no intention of running away from him now. She had faced some truths on her ride to Silver Flash Creek, and she acknowledged another one. When she'd left Montana, she'd been running from Hank and her feelings for him as much as running away from the tragic loss of her father and brother.

Hank sat beside her and started to talk. He could not trust himself to let the silence continue. "Remember the June night we camped out up here with your dad and Joey?"

At first Shadoe balked at the memory, but then she had a clear image of the campfire, of her father's face across it, highlighted by the flickering flames. There was Joey, too, all blond excitement at being allowed to camp with them. And Hank, bringing up another load of firewood so they could sit up late into the night and listen to her father's stories.

"I remember." She was surprised that the memory made her smile. In the past such thoughts would have brought pain.

"Do you remember? That was the night your father told us about Crazy Horse's vision."

"I remember." Shadoe scuffed the dirt with the toe of her boot. "I was thinking about that only a little while ago."

"Do you remember what Jimmy said?"

Shadoe looked up at Hank. His eyes were animated, his expression tense. "What?"

"He said that Crazy Horse understood that if the settlers weren't stopped immediately, it would be the end of the Indians, the death of the wilderness."

The pleasant ease that had developed between them disappeared. Shadoe sensed that Hank was using the past, using the memory of her father, for his own purposes. "My father was talking about something in the past, Hank. The Indians did fight, and they lost their land anyway."

He saw her tense, but he had to go on. This was the moment he'd been waiting for. The chance to explain to her why he was so dedicated to releasing the wolves. If he could tell her exactly right, then she'd understand. Maybe, if they could settle this issue between them... "Jimmy was right, Shadoe. If we don't save something of the wilderness and simply allow it to be what it is, then we'll lose everything."

"The ranchers are a part of this state. We're not destroying the wilderness. We're not paving and building and cutting down trees. We *do* live here and protect the land. Just because we don't want our livestock killed by a pack of wolves doesn't mean we don't care about the wilderness." The more she talked the angrier she got.

"This is a special place, Shadoe."

His very sincerity infuriated her. "You think I don't know that? You think you have some rare spiritual connection to this country?"

Her anger ignited his. "I do have a special connection to this land. A bond you'd never understand. I'm not the one who threw everything away to go off to college, to drive around in a sports car and throw parties for celebrities. I was forced out of my home because you..." He stopped himself. The anger had been quick-hot, and it was gone as fast as it had come. Shadoe was staring at him, her chest rising and falling in short, rapid breaths that he knew would soon erupt into angry words.

"This is all personal with you, isn't it? You don't give a damn about the wilderness or the wolves or the ranchers. This is your way to heap revenge on me and everyone else who gets in the way. Tell me, Hank, when did you pick the site to release the wolves? Was it sometime this winter, *after* you'd learned I was back in Lakota County?" She stood up, her chest hurting, along with her ribs, her backside and mostly her heart. "Was it after you left your pocketknife in my barn?"

"Believe what you'd like." Hank stood also. He was furious with himself. Why had he even thought he could talk to her? Being up at Stag's Horn, every evening staring out into the glittering velvet of a Montana night, he'd lost his mind. He'd allowed himself to believe that somehow he could talk to Shadoe, make her see that it wasn't her pitted against the wilderness. He thought somehow he could reach out and touch her and discover that her heart was still that of the young girl he'd loved. But that was not true.

"It's true, isn't it?" Even Shadoe was surprised by the searing pain. "You did decide on this location after last October, didn't you?" She'd never really believed the wolf release was directly aimed at her. She could see in his face, though, that she was right. "And you were in Scrapiron's stall?"

"Only when I brought him home, Shadoe, but my knife is missing. As far as locating the wolves to hurt you, I find it fascinating that you think you're that important." He hurled the angry words at her. "If I were so determined to do something to hurt you, wouldn't it be much simpler to take a direct approach?"

"What are you doing on Double S land?" It suddenly occurred to Shadoe that Hank had appeared out of the woods. Was it possible that she'd been chasing him?

"I was doing my job." He tried to control his temper. The one thing he had to keep in mind was the wolves. No matter how angry Shadoe made him, he could not jeopardize the release.

"Would that job include stringing a wire across the path?" Shadoe was so mad she didn't care what she said.

At first he couldn't believe what she was accusing him of. When he looked into her face, he saw that she was dead serious. "Don't be a fool. Why would I try to hurt you?"

She didn't have an answer for that, but then she didn't understand anything about him any more. "I warned you once about trespassing on Double S land. I see you didn't believe me." She gathered up Scrapiron's reins in her hands. "The ranchers don't have a lot of weapons, Hank, but we intend to use what we have."

"Does that include arsenic?"

She swung up into the saddle before she looked at him. "No. I wouldn't poison an animal, not even a wolf. But I do intend to call the television station as soon as I get home. I think they'll find it interesting that the spokesperson for the rancher's coalition was attacked today on her own property while a federal agent was trespassing at the very same spot."

Hank started to reach out and grab her arm, to hold her until she admitted that she knew he'd never try to harm her. But did she really know that about him? He had his doubts about her.

"I don't know what you might do, Shadoe. At this moment, I wouldn't put anything past you."

She turned Scrapiron. "I won't use poison, but I will use public opinion, and I've had years of training in how to make it go my way."

"I didn't think you'd stoop to lying."

"Oh, but you thought I'd use arsenic. You have a very strange sense of degrees of evil." She could see she'd gotten to him, and it felt good. "I won't be lying anyway. Simply stating the facts. You're here. I was injured by a booby trap. I'm not going to accuse you—I'll let the public draw their own conclusions."

Hank felt as if he'd spun backward in time. Back to a place he didn't want to be. Shadoe had no way of knowing—did she?—that the scenario she had painted was the one that would get him fired, and likely brought up on charges. It had been five years before that a television reporter had leveled almost the exact same charge against him, and tried to pin him with charges of assault and attempted rape. The woman had been discredited, but Hank's career had suffered, and this time he would not escape with a reprimand and lack of promotion. But he'd be damned if he was going to try to explain this to Shadoe. First of all, she wouldn't give a hoot in hell, and secondly, she might get too much satisfaction from it.

Shadoe nudged Scrapiron along the trail until she came to the wire. Pulling a pair of wire cutters from the pouch that was tied to the side of her saddle, she clipped the thin strand and watched it snap back into the trees.

"If I were you, I'd be more concerned about who tried to high wire you than figuring out a public relations campaign." He was concerned about the wire, but she'd never believe that.

"Why don't you investigate?" The question stung with sarcasm.

"I think I will."

"Well, be sure you do a thorough job, because I'd better not catch you on Double S land again or I'll press charges. I mean it, Hank. Billy won't like it, but he upholds the law."

Hank leaned down and picked up his gun. He held it loosely in his right hand. He watched as Shadoe put her heels into Scrapiron's ribs, urging him home. He was left with a number of serious questions about the wire and the man he'd been pursuing once again on Shadoe's land—almost as if he were being deliberately led into encounters with Shadoe. Those were concerns he had to address, but the one question he couldn't seem to shake was, would there ever come a day when Shadoe Deerman failed to get under his skin?

Chapter Eight

Shadoe took the longer route home. The ranchers were holding a strategy meeting that evening, and she was expected at Hoss Kemper's house, but the encounter with Hank had stolen her fire. She wanted only to be alone. As soon as she was half a mile away from him she lost the anger that had kept her back erect and her eyes snapping. Now the pain would no longer be kept at bay. And the questions. What was he doing at Flashing Silver Creek, on Double S property? Was it Hank she'd seen in the woods? If so, was he watching her? And why? What motive could anyone have for watching her take a trail ride on her horse?

Beneath all of the questions was the sense of loss. For a few minutes, the years had fallen away and she had stepped into the past. His touch on her hair, on her chest, his arm around her waist had been so natural. So perfect.

So much a lie.

And his half-spoken accusation burned in her heart. He would still own Copperwood Ranch if she hadn't fled Montana like the demons of hell were pursuing her. He'd never said that to her. No one had. But it was true. Completely true.

Hank's parents had died when he was fifteen, but they had left him the ranch and enough money to survive. It was Shadoe's father who had convinced him to buy more cattle.

Hank and Jimmy were going to work together, father and son. Joey would become a partner, too, as soon as he was old enough to help. And Shadoe would be daughter and bride. But Jimmy's death had changed it all. Hank had lost his investment, and ultimately the ranch. Shadoe, who had fled Hank and Montana, had not known about the financial complications until Copperwood was already sold at auction.

Hank had sent her urgent messages—and she had torn them up without reading them because she thought he was asking her to return to Montana. Connie had never mentioned a word about the other, the money and the cattle.

And Hank would never believe otherwise.

Halfway home, Shadoe pulled Scrapiron to a walk. He'd had enough galloping for the day and there was no point letting him exhaust himself simply because she wanted to run away from Hank faster. At that thought she straightened her back. She'd come to Montana because she was tired of running. She was done with it, and not even Hank Emrich was going to make her turn tail again.

Fifteen minutes later she topped a hill in the horseshoe pasture and spotted the roof of the barn. As she drew closer, she saw that Jill's pickup truck was parked at the double doors. Concern made her urge Scrapiron into a trot.

As soon as they were in the barnyard she swung to the ground. Reins in hand, she hurried toward the stalls. She found her friend sitting on a tack trunk drinking a cold cola.

"What's wrong?"

Jill swallowed and sighed. "The horses are fine. I can see that's your first worry."

"Thank goodness." Shadoe took a deep breath of relief. But the worried look was still on her friend's face. "What is it then?"

Jill shook the cola and watched it foam in the tinted bottle. "In a word, Hank."

"I know." Shadoe busied herself untacking Scrapiron and rubbing him down.

"You don't know this. Or at least if you do, you must be psychic."

Peering over the horse's withers, Shadoe waited with brush in hand. "Well, are you going to tell me or are you going to tease me?"

"I wish this were a tease." Jill stood up. "I got a call about an hour ago, from a woman in Washington D.C. Does the name Kathy Lemon mean anything to you?"

Shadoe had moved the brush and was working on Scrapiron's hide. "Not a single thing." Even though she spoke pertly, she was beginning to have a very bad feeling.

"She was a television reporter in D.C."

"Not exactly my circle of friends."

"Not yours, but Hank's."

Shadoe continued to ply the brush, her face carefully composed to show no expression. "So? I suppose in the years that have passed, Hank has had plenty of female friends. I've led my life."

"It isn't that, Shadoe. In a way I wish it were." Jill shrugged. "I know you deny it, but I've always felt you still have feelings for Hank. What you and he felt for each other was a lot deeper than high school puppy love. Even we could see that. It was…magical."

"It *was* love, and it *is* the past." Shadoe couldn't even muster pretend anger at her friend. Her encounter with Hank had left her too raw to feign indignation. "Just tell me the point to all of this."

"This woman called and said she saw a news clip of you, about the wolves. Hank was also in that clip, and she recognized him. She recognized you, too, from some of the things he'd said about you." Jill hesitated.

"So far this doesn't sound like anything I'm going to need medical attention to recover from." She did feel slightly better. Jill was good at making a mountain out of a molehill.

"Shadoe, this woman said Hank made threats against you. She said he was always talking about getting even with you about the past. She said he was a very bitter man and capable of anything and that in the past his badge had protected him from prosecution. She called to warn you." Jill shook her head and then went to her friend. "She called Billy trying to find you and when you didn't answer your phone, Billy gave her my number."

Shadoe didn't believe a word of it, not for an instant. Hank wasn't the kind of man who would hurt a woman. Not even one who'd caused him to lose his ranch.

"I know you're thinking this isn't possible, but Ms. Lemon said he had done the same thing to her and that he had ruined her career and—"

"You listened to this?" Shadoe dropped the brush in the grooming kit and walked around to face her friend.

"I didn't have much choice. The woman kept rattling on and on, and I have to tell you, Shadoe, she struck me as sincere."

"Kooks can sound sincere."

"She had dates, times. She even said she'd filed charges against him with the wildlife service. His friends helped him get off, but she said we could check with Harry Code to verify her accusations."

"This woman was a television reporter?" Shadoe was trying to grasp what her friend had told her.

"For WDAT in D.C. She said Hank cost her her job."

"Maybe, if she was running around making wild accusations, she needed to lose her job." But the first inkling of doubt had crept into Shadoe's mind.

"She said he physically assaulted her. That he tried to...rape her." Jill sounded less certain, as if maybe she'd begun to try to match Hank with the described actions. She gave voice to her doubts. "Even I find that a little hard to swallow. Hank never was the type to physically attack another guy, much less a woman."

Against her will, Shadoe's mind returned to the night Scrapiron was let out of his stall. Hank had been right there. And again up at Silver Flash Creek, where a thin metal line could have killed her. Was it possible? In anger she'd considered the possibility. And rejected it. Now she found fear made her want to push the thought out of her mind. But she wasn't running away again. Not from anything.

"Did this Kathy Lemon leave a telephone number?"

"She did." Jill followed Shadoe as she took Scrapiron to the stall.

"Good." Shadoe threw the latch. "Because I have a few questions for her."

"What if it's true?" Jill asked, horror in her tone.

"Then at least we'll know the measure of the enemy."

"Oh, Shadoe." Jill took her friend's shoulders and held them. "I can't bear to hear you call Hank the enemy, as if he were a horrible person or something awful."

"If he's done the things this woman accuses him of doing, then he is awful, Jill. The best we can do is ask smart questions and see what's true and what's not."

"Will you believe her?"

"I don't know. But I will believe Hank's personnel record with the wildlife service, and that's something I think Billy can check on for us no matter what Ms. Lemon says."

Shadoe started toward the house and Jill followed, her shorter legs having to work twice as hard to keep up with Shadoe. "I only hope we're doing the right thing."

Jill had the number in her purse, and Shadoe dialed the phone while her friend made a pot of coffee. Neither of them wanted coffee, but Jill needed something to do. Shadoe heard her rummaging in the kitchen as the phone rang six times, seven, then eight. She was about to hang up when a woman answered. In two sentences, Shadoe had confirmed that she was talking with Kathy Lemon, former newscaster and current television publicity woman for a mail-order cosmetics line.

To Shadoe, Kathy sounded sane, stable and well-meaning. As Kathy ran down her professional achievements, Shadoe found that she was comparing herself to the woman on the other end of the line. The similarities were striking. Both had grown up in the west and gone south for an education. Where Shadoe had gone immediately into advertising, Kathy had followed her ambition to become a network anchor. And she had a good start, to hear her tell it, until she'd run amok of Hank Emrich and a story regarding the illegal importation of exotic birds.

"Hank promised me a scoop, but what he did was wreck my credibility," Kathy Lemon said.

"Why should I believe you?" Shadoe found she was gripping the phone.

"Believe or don't. It's just that he mentioned you so often. I mean all the time. At first I was a little jealous..." She paused. "I guess I should tell you I was attracted to Hank. Very much so. Until I discovered what kind of man he really is."

"What happened with the birds?"

"Hank and two other agents had set up a sting. They could have gotten the local dealers easy enough, but Hank wanted the suppliers, the folks down in the islands who trap the birds. He knew if he arrested the stateside dealers, then the suppliers would just find a new outlet for the birds. Hank wanted to shut them down."

Shadoe listened. So far, it sounded perfectly like Hank. He never did a job partway when he could go whole-hog.

"I got onto the story through a friend of mine in the Wildlife Service. I had everything. I knew as much about the bird scam as Hank, and he cut a deal with me. I would hold my story if he would tell me when the bust was coming down so I could get some action shots. It would be the story that made my career. It would have proved I was a good reporter and able to function under stress."

It wasn't difficult to see the importance of the story to Kathy Lemon, but Shadoe was having a hard time seeing any fault in Hank's behavior. "Go on," she said.

"I did everything Hank asked, and I had live cameras and everything ready to roll at the time and location Hank gave me. Except he had given me bad information. After convincing me to hold the story, he betrayed my trust by sending me out to the wrong place. I looked like an idiot. The news producer was so furious that all of the cameras had gone out on my story and there wasn't a single camera to cover the drug arrest of the mayor of the city that as soon as I walked in the door, he fired me. And then he blacklisted me with all the other stations. I couldn't get a job cleaning toilets in a news station. I was finished in the business."

Shadoe waited, but Kathy Lemon didn't continue. Finally Shadoe asked, "My friend said something about physical assault?"

"Rape is what I'd call it. Or attempted rape."

"That's a harsh accusation."

"Hey, in case you haven't run across Hank lately, let me warn you, he's a pretty harsh guy."

"Did he try to…attack you?" Shadoe couldn't bring herself to use the word *rape*. Not in connection with Hank. They had driven each other mad with desire, and he'd never, never pushed the issue when she'd said no. They'd both given their words to her father, and Hank was the kind of man who kept his promise. Or at least he used to be.

For what seemed an eternity, Kathy Lemon did not answer. "He hit me and tried to attack me. I got away."

Shadoe expelled a sigh. She had no words for Kathy's charge.

"He wasn't successful, but what he did was worse than rape." Kathy Lemon sounded angry. "He called me to meet him in a darkened warehouse. He said he had information for another story to give me, to make up for what he'd done before."

Panic was building in the other woman's voice. Shadoe's heart was beating faster as she listened.

"I got there and the place was completely black. It was a bad part of town. I knew that, and because I'd been fired, I didn't have a backup camera crew. I was going to do this myself with some equipment I borrowed, just to prove I was a good reporter. Anyway, there wasn't a story. There was only Hank, and that's when he told me what he could do to me if he wanted, and what he intended to do to you when he got the chance. He knocked me to the floor and fell on me like an animal. A watchman came in the building and I got away."

Before Shadoe could say a word, the woman burst into tears. "I've warned you. That's all I meant to do. Please just leave me alone now." She slammed the telephone down.

Shadoe was left holding a buzzing receiver. Her heart felt as if it had been stepped on.

"Well?" Jill held out a cup of coffee to her.

"Did Billy say what she'd said to him?" Shadoe took the coffee and sipped, the bitter brew too strong but exactly what she needed.

"She didn't really talk to him. Just to me. And she obviously told you a lot more than she told me." Curiosity was eating Jill alive.

"I need to talk to Billy."

Shadoe stood up and the light from the kitchen window slanted across her chest. For the first time Jill noticed the dark stains on the yoke of her friend's shirt. "What happened? That looks like blood."

"It is." Shadoe frowned. "I ran into Hank up by Silver Flash. We had an argument."

"Hank didn't hurt you." It was both a statement and a question.

"No." Shadoe shook her head. "I don't know."

"You're not making a lot of sense."

"I know." Shadoe held up her hands. "I can't believe Hank had anything to do with what happened."

"What *did* happen?"

"Someone had strung a wire. Scrapiron was galloping when I hit it. Lucky for me, I had stood to look at something we were chasing in the woods. The wire caught me across the chest instead of the neck." She fell silent at the horrified expression on her friend's face.

"You could have been killed. That wire could have broken your neck, or severed an artery, or—"

"I was lucky." Shadoe trembled as a chill touched her. Her father would have said that her spirit had been touched by someone who had crossed over to the clouds. A warning.

"You don't really think Hank did that, do you?"

"No." She looked at Jill and saw the fear. "In my heart, I don't believe it. In my mind, I intend to take nothing for granted."

"Let's drive into town and see Billy."

"What about the cattle?"

"Curly's over at the ranch. I'll give him a call and ask him to run over here." Jill was already pulling her keys from her pocket.

"I'd better feed first." Shadoe wanted desperately to talk over the events with Billy, but Curly had been more than generous to help her while she was at the competition. He was Jill's employee, and he was paid for his help, but it

was added time and added chores, and it wasn't right to
simply expect him to pick up the slack.

"I know what you're thinking." Jill had her purse in one
hand and the clutch of keys in the other. "Curly's wife just
had another baby. That's four. He's delighted for the extra
cash, and you always pay him fairly."

"Call him and ask."

Jill dialed the phone with her keys jangling while Shadoe
changed her blouse. In less than a minute they had Curly's
consent and were on the way to Athens.

THE BATTERED STETSON was tipped to the back of Billy's
head by the time Shadoe finished telling him about the
telephone call. She left out the charge of rape. If Hank had
been found guilty of rape, he'd be in jail. She couldn't say
such a thing without more proof. Jill was sitting on the edge
of her chair watching them like a hawk.

"What are you going to do?" she finally asked when
neither Billy nor Shadoe made a suggestion.

"Do my job." Billy sat up and straightened his hat.

"That's not very helpful," Jill complained. "You always
do your job. What are you going to do about Hank?"

"I never did get to see those wolves. I guess I'm going
to take a drive up to Stag's Horn and see for myself what
all this trouble is about."

He stood up and motioned to the door.

"You want us to leave?" Jill didn't believe it. "Just like
that, you're showing us the door."

"I always knew you were a smart girl."

"Billy!" Jill was exasperated. She turned on Shadoe.
"And you're just as bad. You act like now that you've told
him, that's all there is to it."

"Let's head on home." Shadoe couldn't meet Billy's
eyes as she stepped through the door and out into the street.
It was a beautiful day, and shoppers were moving up and

down Main Street in the small town. This was the place she'd grown up. She knew eighty percent of the people she saw, yet she felt as if she'd stepped into a stranger's shoes. On the drive to Athens, and as she'd watched Billy's expression as she told her story, she felt worse and worse. It was one thing to suspect Hank and quite another to vocalize those doubts to a man who had known and admired Hank all of his life. By telling Billy, she had hurt him, Hank and herself.

Without saying a word, she got in the truck with Jill and waited for her friend to start the engine.

"How about we go over to Hoss's and get a barbecue?" Jill was suddenly contrite. She could see the turn of events had upset Shadoe considerably.

"Sure." Shadoe hadn't eaten since breakfast. She wasn't hungry, but it was something to do and it would keep Jill from telling her how much she needed to eat.

Several folks on the street waved and smiled, and Shadoe automatically returned the gestures, but her heart and mind were elsewhere. Jill threw her long looks, but refrained from asking a single question. A fact that Shadoe knew was out of character with her friend.

Hoss's barbecue and burger joint was called The Pit. It was the place for teens to meet after school, where they climbed in and out of one another's vehicles and did their best to confuse the waitresses who came to the cars and trucks to take and deliver the short orders.

Both Shadoe and Jill had spent their high school years stopping by The Pit for an after-school snack, or ending up there late on Saturday night for a final milkshake or cola. While the young folks claimed it in the afternoons and on date nights, it belonged to the families and adults of Lakota County the rest of the time. Hoss Kemper made good barbecue.

"Sandwich and lemonade." Shadoe pulled some money from her pocket but Jill shook her head.

"This is my treat." She gave the order to a cute teer and sat back, staring into the weathered wood of The Pit In a moment the back door opened and a big man walked toward them.

He went to the passenger side and reached in to give Shadoe's shoulder a squeeze. "You were wonderful on television last night. You blasted that fed right out of the water. Are we still set to meet at six?"

Shadoe raised her eyebrows. "I'd completely forgotten."

Hoss grinned. "We can't have our spokesperson going senile on us. No telling what you might say when you get in front of the cameras."

"Maybe we should find a more reliable speaker." Shadoe didn't mind the teasing, but at the moment her heart wasn't in the fight.

Hoss leaned down and looked at her. He was twenty years older than her and not one of her father's closest friends, but well-known to the Deerman family. His spread of four hundred acres was to the west of the Double S, and between his cattle and his restaurant, he hadn't been a regular in community activities, but he always catered official town functions.

"Hey, Shadoe, we're counting on you. Is something wrong?"

Jill leaned over so she could talk. "Shadoe had an accident today. Someone rigged up a clothesline across a trail on her property and she hit it."

"You're lucky you weren't killed." His gaze studied her closely. "Are you sure you're okay? We can postpone the meeting until tomorrow."

"I'm not hurt." Not physically. She tried for a smile.

"Hey, I've got a thought. Why don't you check over at the hardware store and see who's been buying clothesline wire? I mean they could have gotten it anywhere, but it might be interesting to know who's been buying the stuff around here.''

Jill slapped the steering wheel. ''That's a great idea, Hoss. What about it, Shadoe?''

''Sure.'' She nodded because her voice held no enthusiasm. ''Sure, that's a good idea.''

''And by the way, I was planning on serving barbecue at the meeting tonight, so don't stuff yourself here. Wait 'til it's free.'' He patted Shadoe's arm. ''Better get back to the kitchen. No telling what those clowns will put in the sauce if I don't watch them. Everyone thinks they have the better recipe, even the busboys.'' He laughed as he turned back to the restaurant.

The waitress brought the food and Jill paid her. Before Shadoe could settle the sack on the truck seat, Jill had the motor running.

''We're headed to Kyle's Hardware.'' She didn't give Shadoe a chance to back out.

Main Street in Athens was only a mile long, and the hardware store was on a cross street at the other end of town. Within three minutes they were parked and on their way inside.

''Let me do the asking,'' Jill said. ''The way you're acting, folks will know it's serious and Kyle might clam up.''

Shadoe couldn't help but smile. Kyle Rolofson loved to talk and he had a memory like an elephant about who bought what and what they were building or repairing. But if he thought he was revealing any personal business of his customers, he clamped his mouth shut.

''Hey, Kyle,'' Jill called as she kept walking to the counter at the back of the store. ''You got any clothesline wire? I think with the good spring weather I'm going to put my sheets out on the line. Get the sun-kissed smell in them.'' She grinned at the young man.

Kyle Rolofson shook his dark head. "Funny you should ask about clothesline wire. Those federal agents bought every bit I had. About six hundred feet. I thought to myself they were going to be doing an awful lot of laundry up on that mountain for a bunch of men camping out in the woods."

Chapter Nine

"Hello, darlin'," John Carpenter moved to Shadoe's side with a smile as sexy as a kiss. It took him only a few seconds to figure out that something was wrong. "Are the horses okay? Did that mare foal?"

John's immediate concern eased the anxiety that had been building in Shadoe all day. "Cricket's fine, and the baby too. A very nice little stud colt. Another potential Luster."

"Then what's troubling you?" John brushed her hair back from her cheek and forced her to look at him. "I see worry in those dark eyes and I'd rather see dancing."

No matter how she tried, Shadoe couldn't resist John's good nature. She couldn't stay mad at him, or aggravated when he didn't follow through on things he'd promised. If she'd been in love with him, he would have kept her tied in knots. But she wasn't, and he was a terrific friend. One she cherished.

"I'm okay. I—"

"Someone rigged up a clothesline wire at Silver Flash Creek and she nearly killed herself." Jill interjected the pertinent facts before Shadoe could answer. When she saw her friend turn to her with a frown, Jill held up a hand. "You wouldn't have told, and the other ranchers need to know. With six hundred feet of wire, someone could have booby-trapped other areas. We need to be on guard.''

Jill was right, but her conclusion was an assumption, and one Shadoe didn't want vocalized until Billy had investigated. She looked around Hoss's spacious home and noted that the sheriff was nowhere around. ''I'm fine,'' she reassured John. ''I took a lucky fall. A few bruises and some wounded pride. Is Billy here?''

''Not yet. He called in and said he'd be late.'' John's brow was still furrowed. ''He sounded like he had a bee in his bonnet, too.'' He looked down at Shadoe. ''Is there something you're not telling me?''

Before Jill could spill the beans, Shadoe shook her head. ''Nothing I know for a fact, John. Believe me, when I do know the truth, I'll tell everyone here.''

''I'm not ready to let this go, but I got some information that the federal boys have hired a big-name environmentalist to give a news conference today. It should be on the six o'clock news.'' John signaled to Hoss, who turned on the set. The cluster of eight ranchers found seats and settled down to watch.

The lead story was the environmental expert, who made a case for restoring the natural balance of the ecosystem via the wolves. Instead of cattle and horses and sheep, James Bradley pointed out that wolves would thin the herds of deer and other wild creatures, which were their natural prey, rather than livestock.

At first Shadoe listened to the words, but then she found herself watching the clips of the wolves. Some of the footage had been taken in Canada when they were wild and free, and she reacted to the images with a pleasure that almost frightened her. They were magnificent animals, especially the large male that seemed to be the pack leader. His golden gaze stared directly into the camera and seemed to fix on Shadoe.

The talk around Shadoe disappeared. The voice-over of the television narrator faded. Shadoe stared into the eyes of the wolf. She felt her skin prickle, and a surge of fear made her stomach knot. This was the wolf from her dream. He was no ordinary wolf, but a creature with human cunning. His gaze held her, paralyzed, before he lifted his nose to the cold Canadian air and howled a challenge.

"Look, there's Hank." Jill nudged Shadoe in the ribs and broke the spell as the film footage changed to Hank, deep in the snow, as he and several other men ran to retrieve the wolf they'd darted with sedatives.

The clip ended abruptly and returned to the television news desk then shifted to a more current interview with Hank.

"There's enough wilderness for all of us, if we protect it." Hank spoke calmly. "The wolves are no serious danger to anyone. Not ranchers, campers or tourists. Precautions must be taken, but if we all use care and common sense, the wolves will roam the wilderness." Hank took a breath. "I have a great personal stake in this project. As a native of Montana, I feel this is the right thing to do. Those who oppose it do so for selfish reasons. We have to look to the future, to what is right, not what is convenient." He started to say something else, then reconsidered. "Thank you." He nodded to the reporter, who hadn't been able to get a single question in, and got up. He unhooked the mike and left.

"That was Hank Emrich, U.S. Wildlife Service agent in charge of the release." The anchorman recovered quickly and moved on to the next story.

"Well, well, old Hank should have been a preacher." Hoss smiled as he passed platters of barbecue sandwiches, but his face was too red, as if he'd been hovering over the hickory fire.

His remark was met with nervous laughter. Shadoe

looked at the faces around her and recognized the expression. They felt they had been betrayed. It was the same look she'd seen earlier that day on Hank's face. The idea of it, on top of the strange feelings she'd gotten from the wolf, made her stomach clench tight. There was no way she could force a mouthful of food down, no matter what anyone said.

"He as much as said we were willing to sacrifice the wilderness for our own greed and personal gain," Red Jeffreys said. His sense of betrayal had turned to anger. "I just can't believe Hank would do a thing like that. We went to high school together, and he knows the problems ranchers face."

The argument was picked up and batted around the room. Shadoe held her plate and tried to force the image of the wolf from her eyes. It seemed to have been etched against the backs of her eyelids, the golden gaze haunting her, holding her. Waiting to kill her.

A light tap came at the door, and it opened to reveal Billy Casper. He stood in the threshold, his hand on the knob.

"Well, come on in, Billy," Hoss urged.

"I've got some official business here." Billy looked angry, too. He finally stepped aside. Hank Emrich entered behind Billy and the gathering of ranchers fell instantly silent.

"You obviously didn't see the news, Billy. Hank's not welcome here." Hoss put down his sandwich and stood up.

"He has something to say." Billy's voice was calm, but meant to be obeyed. He nodded to Hank. "Go on, tell 'em."

"Late this evening someone took some bolt cutters and snapped the lock on the cage of the large male wolf. He was set free about five o'clock today."

For three beats of her heart, Shadoe heard absolutely

nothing but the ticking of the clock in the hallway. Then a babble of voices broke. There were questions and threats in equal measure.

"The wolf is alone. Without the others he doesn't stand much of a chance to survive. But he will get hungry, and I want to urge you to bring your stock in to closer pastures. We're setting traps for him now and I feel certain he'll be captured shortly."

"You feel certain! Can you guarantee me that he won't go after my sheep?" Gerald Pritchett was furious.

"I can't make any rash promises, Gerald. Except one." Hank looked around the room slowly. "Someone deliberately set that animal free. I do promise you that I will find the person responsible for this, and when I do, he or she will pay the most severe penalty the law will allow me to extract."

Before anyone could respond, Hank stepped back through the doorway and slammed the door behind him.

Billy surveyed the room, settling on Shadoe's shocked face. He waited until he had her attention, then nodded. "I'm going to make myself an old-fashioned shot of whiskey," Billy said loud enough for several people to hear. A moment later he left the crowded room and went to the bar near the patio.

Shadoe followed him, slipping through the ranchers as they argued the best course of action to take in this latest development of the wolves.

She found him alone, one boot propped up on the bronze bar rail. "What Kathy Lemon said, is it true?" She couldn't wait for formalities.

Billy turned to her. His face showed his concern. "He wouldn't deny it." He lifted the glass and swallowed half of the amber liquid.

"What about the pocketknife?"

Billy finished the whiskey before he answered. "He said

it had been stolen from his tent." He finished the drink. "He was like stone while he listened to me. Then he said, and I quote, 'Facts don't seem to matter here. If Shadoe believes it, then it must be true.' Then he walked away."

Shadoe recognized his words as those of hurt and anger. But he *hadn't* denied the serious charges Kathy Lemon had made against him. She saw that Billy had the same worry she did. Was it possible Hank was guilty?

"What about the wolf?"

"That was a shock to Hank. One of the other agents came to tell him right about the time I said I needed to hear him deny it. Instead of answering me, he went up to the cages to see what had happened."

"Someone cut the bolt?"

"Clean as a whistle. And they knew which one they were releasing. The biggest, the leader. The pack may not survive without him."

Shadoe stepped up to the bar and poured Billy another drink, taking a half measure for herself. "Billy, is it possible that one of the agents released that wolf?"

Billy sipped the whiskey this time. "I'd say it's more than possible. I'd say it's probable. That place is hard to get to. Someone could have come up through the woods, but the terrain is treacherous. I'd say whoever did it walked straight up the trail from the camp to the cages."

Shadoe concentrated on the bite of the whiskey as she took a tiny swallow. She wasn't much of a drinker, but the burn helped calm her. "Then it could have been Hank?"

"It could have been." Billy wasn't willing to give her that. "It could have been someone else up there, too. Someone who doesn't care about those wolves the way Hank does."

"What's going to happen to the wolf?" Shadoe knew that if he came on any of the ranchers' property, he'd be dead. But the federal agents were trying to trap him. Were they using live traps or the lethal leg holds that could cripple or kill him?

Billy gazed into the back of the bar and his voice took on a pensive note when he finally spoke. "Hank called the wolf Thor." He looked at Shadoe. "He let it slip before he thought. He knows how much danger the animal is in now. From us, and from the other agents. They can't afford to have him do something, like kill some cattle or sheep. If they have to, they'll kill him before the ranchers do."

For a split second Shadoe was caught again in the golden gaze as the wolf stared out of the television and directly into her.

"Shadoe!" Billy's hand caught her elbow and steadied her. "That fall you took must have done more damage than you thought." He eased her up on a bar stool.

"No," she shook her head, clearing away the last vestiges of the wolf. "I'm fine." She gave him a wry grin. "Thinking too hard. It made me dizzy."

"I'm going back to the office. There are some facts I want to check out."

"About Hank?"

He nodded. "About this Kathy Lemon. Don't you think the timing of her call was a little fortuitous?"

"She said she saw a news clip about me. And my mother did see one in West Palm Beach."

"It's possible. It's also likely this woman was notified by someone here in Lakota County. Someone who wants to cause trouble for Hank." He pushed back from the bar. "Or the ranchers."

"How?"

"If anything goes wrong and the ranchers are blamed, this won't end with a clean victory. You can count on that. If this goes badly because of an act of violence against those wolves, there'll be major repercussions. You have to understand, the federal boys are in a bad position on this."

Shadoe hadn't considered that scenario. "You're right."

"I'll give you a call when I have something definite." He straightened his hat and headed out.

Shadoe swirled the barely touched liquor in her glass. Her mother found solace in drinking. Easing the glass to the countertop, she walked back into the den where the ranchers were taking a vote.

"Shadoe!" Jill cried. "You've just been unanimously elected as the Coalition of Lakota County Ranchers spokesperson. I'm going to try to get the Billings station to give us some rebuttal time. But we're going to have to get lots of facts and figures about wolf kills and all of that." Jill was excited, and the rest of the ranchers looked at her with expectancy. "You will do it, won't you?"

"Sure." Shadoe couldn't back out now, even though she kept seeing little mental movie clips of the male wolf slipping through the trees, a flash of silver in the deep green gloom. "I've got to head home." She smiled at them all. "I took a fall and I'm not feeling as good as I thought I was."

John instantly appeared at her elbow. "Let me drive you."

She started to decline, but the idea of going home alone to her doubts and fears was daunting. John was good company, and he wouldn't consider her foolish if she asked him to check the barns with her. "Thanks."

Lost in her own swirl of thoughts, Shadoe realized they were halfway home before John spoke. She'd been ignoring him, and felt a twinge of guilt until she caught the tension in his voice.

"I don't mean to be pushy, Shadoe, but Jill told me about the rest of what happened today."

Shadoe had a fleeting moment of pure aggravation with her big-mouthed friend. "I don't want to talk about this until I have a chance to find out the facts."

"Worried about Hank's reputation?" John's tone was sarcastic.

"As a matter of fact, I am." Shadoe's temper ignited. "You don't know the whole story, and the last thing I want to do is damage Hank again, without cause. If he's guilty, that's one thing. If he isn't, to spread rumors or make accusations could do irreparable damage. I don't want to be a part of that."

"And if he's guilty and decides to take action against you again, you could be dead."

"How would Hank know I was going to ride up to that particular area of my ranch? I've been home longer than six months and haven't been near Silver Flash Creek. I didn't tell him, or anyone who might have told him."

"Who did you tell?"

Shadoe hesitated. "Jill. Maybe I mentioned it to Doc Adams. And I told you that I'd been wanting to explore that area." She looked over at him. "And I don't suspect any of the three of you."

His grin was visible in the lights of the dash. "That's a good thing. At least I'm that far ahead of Mr. Emrich."

Shadoe felt her anger ease. So it was a jealousy thing with John. Well, she'd been bitten by that devil and knew the pain. If John was worried that she had something going with Hank, she could at least put those demons to rest. "John, as far as I'm concerned, Hank is the past. I just don't want to hurt him again." She sighed. "He lost Copperwood because of me. Not something I did deliberately, but something I did without thinking, without considering anyone except myself. I don't want to add another injury."

"But he's the past?"

The hope in John's question made her hesitate before she answered. Was Hank really the past? What they had dreamed was gone, dust blown by a fierce wind, but her feelings for him were complicated, and now wasn't the time to try to explain that. "There's not a chance of anything between me and Hank." She reached across the seat and touched John's arm. "I don't think we can go back in time. Not any of us."

John stared into the Montana night. "I think that's a message directed at me."

"I wish things could be different."

"If Emrich hadn't shown up, they might be." There was anger in John's voice. "I saw the way you looked at him when he walked in at Hoss's. You looked like a starving woman at a buffet."

"That's not true." Shadoe felt the heat rise to her cheeks at even the thought.

"It's true." John's foot pressed harder on the gas.

"Slow down, John. Please." Shadoe saw that the speedometer was climbing past seventy, and the road was narrow and winding.

"I moved here and bought that ranch, thinking we could make a life together."

"I never implied that was something I wanted." Shadoe tried to walk a thin line between brutal truth and an effort to spare John's feelings. "I didn't even know you'd bought Copperwood."

"You talked about that ranch all the time. About the plans you'd made."

"And I left that life behind me, John."

"You're here. Back in Montana."

Shadoe threw up her hands. "What is that supposed to mean?"

"You wanted to settle down, to raise horses. That was part of what we shared. The two of us together, we can breed some fine quarter horses."

"Except you never wanted to settle down. That was one of the things I loved about you. You were so damn free. I wanted to be that way, but I couldn't."

"I've changed. I've been trying to tell you that." He pulled down the drive to her house.

Shadoe opened the door before the truck stopped. This was too much. After the day she'd had, she didn't have enough patience to deal with John without saying something she'd regret. "I asked you not to make me feel cornered. That's the only thing I wanted. Apparently it was asking too much." She slammed the truck door and started running toward the house.

John kept the engine idling and opened his door to step out. "The past isn't so easy for me to put behind, Shadoe," he called out. "I came here to be with you, and I've gotten in neck deep. Jill helped me get a good price, but I'm in debt up to my ears."

At the front porch, Shadoe stopped. Her heart was pounding in her ears and she felt sick. "I didn't ask you to do anything," she said, but it was only a whisper. As she watched, John got in his truck and drove away.

A dark figure materialized from behind a fir tree on the lawn. "Do you make it a habit of driving all of your men into debt and then abandoning them?" Hank stepped closer.

Shadoe managed to stop the scream. Hank had startled her, but she'd never give him the pleasure of letting him know it. "What are you doing here?"

"Who set the wolf free?" He stepped so close that his breath was warm on her face.

Shadoe's eyes had adjusted to the moonlight, and she stared up at him without wavering. "Maybe you should use your much-touted investigative skills to find that out. I thought you federal agents got some kind of high-level training. Or maybe you should just call Billy in. He is a real lawman, after all."

"Why go to all that trouble when you can simply tell

me?'' His voice was lazy but there was a current of danger in it.

"Go to hell.'' She turned to the door, key in hand.

Hank's hand on her shoulder was sudden, harsh. He clamped down hard enough to make her wince.

"That wolf is out there, alone and lost. He's my responsibility, Shadoe. I don't know if that means anything to you, but it means a helluva lot to me. I brought him here, and I'm going to protect him. And I want to know who cut the lock on his cage.'' He pulled her closer, so that she could feel his heart beating through the light jacket she wore.

The accusations made by Kathy Lemon came back to her. She had said Hank had tricked her into meeting him alone and then attacked. She had said he was a man made violent by his anger and desire to seek revenge—because of her. According to Kathy Lemon, Hank carried a longtime grudge against Shadoe and intended to get even.

Hank's fingers bit deeper into her shoulder, sending a jolt of fear through her. And a lightning bolt of anger.

"Or what, Hank? What will you do if I don't tell you?'' She knew it was worse than stupid to taunt him, but she'd never been one to back down.

"What did Kathy say I did to her?'' Hank knew he was doing the worst possible thing, but he couldn't help himself. He sensed Shadoe's fear—of him. Of someone she'd known better than she knew herself. "What exactly did Ms. Lemon accuse me of?''

It was his tight smile that frightened Shadoe more than his question. "You tell me.'' The racing of her pulse had become a constant, but she was also beginning to think instead of simply reacting. She was five miles from the nearest neighbor, and she was all alone with a man who was angry, and possibly capable of violence. He was also a man with a badge, which gave him a certain immunity from the law.

"Tell me!"

She kept her lips stubbornly closed.

"Did she say I hit her? That I pushed her? That I..."

Shadoe couldn't stand it any longer. The Hank Emrich she had known would never bully anyone, much less a woman. "She said you raped her." She hurled the information at him and he actually looked stunned.

"That's impossible." His voice had lost its edge.

"It's possible, and it's the truth." She shook her shoulder free of his hand. "Based on your behavior tonight, I wouldn't say it was out of the question." With as much dignity as she could muster, she turned back to the door, inserted her key and pushed it open. "You've been warned Hank. I'm calling Billy right now to press charges against you for trespassing. And assault. I waited about the incident up on the mountain. Billy wanted to let you have a chance to give your side. Now I see clearly what your side is." She slammed the door behind her as she went inside.

Chapter Ten

In the glow of the lantern, Harry Code's face was eager. He sat with his hands folded on top of a card table and stared at Hank, not offering a chair.

"I've been waiting for you for over an hour," Code finally said. There was anticipation in his tone. "I thought you'd gone looking for that wolf."

Hank knew that Code had something juicy going on—he was far too self-satisfied to have day-to-day business on his mind. The hour was late; the summons to Code's tent completely out of the ordinary.

"I was following some leads." Hank kept it as noncommittal as possible. After his encounter with Shadoe, he'd camped out the remainder of the night and the next. Code had obviously been eagerly awaiting his return.

"I didn't realize those leads would take you to hide in the front of Shadoe Deerman's lawn."

So Shadoe had called and reported him. He felt a sting of betrayal, and knew the emotion was completely out of line. He'd gone down there in the dark and all but accosted her. In fact, if she told about the grip he'd taken on her shoulder, it could be considered assault. Shadoe's complaint, along with Kathy Lemon's lies, could easily put his badge on the line.

"I wanted to ask Ms. Deerman some questions."

"Weren't you given a direct order to stay off the Double S Ranch?"

"My first goal is to find the wolf. The second is to figure out who turned that wolf loose." Hank tried to keep the anger out of his voice.

"And that gives you the right to ignore an order?"

"Listen, Code, I believe Shadoe knows more than she's letting on. I had a few simple questions to ask her. I wanted to save some time so I took the direct route. Some of those ranchers may have the wolf."

"Do you know what I think?" Harry sat perfectly still, his hands calmly flat on the tabletop. "I think you're personally involved in this case on several levels. None of them professional. I'm tempted to pull your badge right now, but because I understand the chain of command, I'm going to let the boys in Washington decide this one."

Hank wasn't aware how tense he was until he felt the relief at Code's statement. He'd expected Code to demand his badge on the spot. It would take weeks for the Washington office to process the complaint, and by then, Thor would be back in custody, or the wolf project would be scrapped. Hank realized Code was watching him closely.

"Don't count your chickens, Emrich. I'm sending you to Washington. Pronto. We have enough trouble with the locals without you violating express orders not to trespass on private property. You can cool your heels up on the Hill. I don't need a troublemaker on this job, and I won't have one." Code's voice was level, without any inflection of anger.

Hank listened to him with his temper growing. Code had thought it all out, had figured the best way to get at Hank. Sending him away while Thor was on the loose was the worst thing he could do. And he had decided to do it. There were a million things he wanted to say to Code, but he kept his lips firmly pressed together. He'd been known to dig his own grave with his big mouth. He was in deep enough already.

"Have your things packed at dawn. I'll have Cal take you in to the local airport. I want you out of here. Yesterday." Harry stood up. "You're dismissed."

There had not been a single opportunity for Hank to defend himself, and even if there had been, it wouldn't have done any good. Harry Code hated him. Had for years. It had amazed Hank that Code had agreed to let him oversee the release. And now Hank had put himself in a position where Harry could act against him.

Stepping from the tent into the night air, Hank knew there was no one to blame for his situation other than himself. Shadoe had twice warned him off her property. He'd gone back for the third time. Because he had to ask her about the wolf. And... He forced himself to confront the truth. And because he wanted to see her. When she'd pulled up with that cowboy, he'd been angry. Mad at her for riding home with another man. He'd let his personal life get twisted up with the wolves, and the result was the mess he now found himself in.

Hank's tent was solo, modest and set back from the others, and he went inside and quickly began to stow his gear in a backpack. When he had his few clothes packed, he discovered that his .38 was missing. Thinking he was mistaken, he searched the entire tent. To his fury, the gun was gone, as was the pump action rifle he used when he was on guard duty. It was obvious that Code had ordered one of the other agents to confiscate his guns, even though the pistol was a personal weapon and was not service issue. Harry Code didn't have the backbone to pull Hank's badge, but he would sneak into his tent and steal his weapons. Or order one of his minions to do it.

Hank felt the scabbard on his belt where he kept his hunting knife, wondering again who had taken his pocketknife and how they'd gotten it. It had disappeared the night Cal's brakes had been tampered with. And reappeared at Shadoe's. More than strange. Almost too coincidental to be anything other than deliberate. As if he were being set up. And Shadoe was somehow involved. He felt the loss of his guns more keenly.

He'd become more and more reliant on the guns in his work, but there had been a time when he'd been able to protect himself with the knife. Jimmy Deerman had taught him how to use the blade like a warrior. Hank pulled the bone-handled knife from the scabbard. The blade caught the light of the candle in the tent, and for a split second, Hank felt all of the anger and frustration of the past few days disappear. He could hear Jimmy's voice talking about the ways of the warrior. "A man does not act in haste or emotion. Even vengeance is done with honor and deliberation. The knife is an honorable death, for animal or man. It is a death met hand-to-hand, face-to-face."

Hank put the knife back in the scabbard and hefted his backpack. He wasn't going back to Washington. Not on a bet. He had captured the wolves and brought them out of their native land to a place where all the odds were against them. This was his project, not Code's. Harry didn't care two figs for the wolves or what happened to them as long as it didn't turn out to be a public relations problem. In fact, Hank wouldn't be surprised if his boss turned them all over to the ranchers for execution if it was the more expedient thing to do.

Peering out through the tent opening, he made sure that the agent on guard duty was nowhere in sight. He stepped into the night, moving away from the trail toward the deep woods. He was going after Thor. And if he couldn't capture him, then he would kill him. Face-to-face. An honorable death, not trapped or poisoned. In the spirit world, Jimmy Deerman would hold Hank responsible for such a thing.

There was also the possibility that Thor would kill him. Hank was not fool enough to discount that outcome, and he accepted it fully as he sought the shelter of the forest.

SHADOE STARED into the plate of over-easy eggs and bacon and knew she couldn't eat a bite.

"You had to do it," Jill said as she ate. "And you have to eat. There's no point sitting at the table, moping around because you made Hank stop harassing you. I mean just because he has a badge doesn't mean he has a right to jump out of the bushes and terrorize you." Jill's voice became more agitated. "If John had seen him up there, manhandling you, he would have beat the smithereens out of him, and it might be just what Hank needs. He's changed, Shadoe. There's something dark about him now, like all of this rage is bottled up inside and ready to explode."

"He didn't manhandle me." Shadoe shook her head. "He made me mad, and I shouldn't have insisted that Billy report him."

"You're worried about his career?" Jill was incredulous. "He trespasses and virtually threatens you, not to mention the fact that he was the guy who targeted this neck of the woods for those damn wolves, and you're concerned that when he stepped out of line he might be punished for it? You are too much. You're still carrying a torch for the guy." Jill stood up and went to the counter for the coffeepot.

"That's not it." Shadoe felt the pressure of tears at her eyes and didn't understand why she was suddenly so weepy. "Hank lost Copperwood because of me and my family, Jill. I didn't know that when I left to go to college. Mother didn't tell me a thing, and naturally Hank was too proud to explain the situation. Now, because of me, his job is threatened. There's a pattern here, and I don't like my involvement in it."

"Hey, news flash, Shadoe. No one held a gun to his head and made him buy those cattle. That's the way the ranching business goes. I could lose my shirt any season, and with those wolves around I well may lose the Bar Three. As far as last night, Hank acted on his own. He ambushed you in your own yard. He's responsible for his own actions. You can't take on that burden of guilt. If he'd been doing what he was supposed to be doing, he wouldn't be in trouble now—if he even got reprimanded. We don't know for certain that he was even called on the carpet. Knowing those guys, they probably gave him a promotion."

Shadoe pushed her plate away. "Well, that's one thing I can check. I'm going up there, and I'm going to talk to Hank. We need to settle some things between us that are twenty years too long in the making."

Jill's brows drew together in a frown. "Don't give them a reason to arrest you. You're the most potent weapon the ranchers have, Shadoe. You're a great spokesperson, and if they could trump up some charges against you, it would damage our case."

"I only want to talk to Hank."

Jill saw the determination on her friend's face. "Want me to go with you?"

The offer was tempting, but Shadoe shook her head. "No, this is something I really need to do alone." Together they walked out to climb into Jill's truck.

Jill dropped her at her truck, which she'd left at Hoss's house the night before. She tried not to think as she headed north, toward the range of mountains, which had once seemed like paradise.

The passing scenery was so familiar, and Shadoe felt overwhelmed by memories. This was the land of her father, and the pain that it evoked was one reason she had fled Montana. Jimmy Deerman's laugh was present in the call of a hawk that swooped out of the sky and dove into the forest. His gentle touch was on the breeze that came in through the open truck window and filled the cab with the promise of summer.

Shadoe considered the possibility that she'd been mistaken in coming back to the range. She had thought she was tougher, better able to handle the losses. Maybe she was wrong. Or maybe it was the fact that she was driving to see Hank Emrich that made her doubt herself and all of her decisions. He and her father were irrevocably twined in her mind. When her father had died, she'd run away from Hank. She'd fled from everything that reminded her of Jimmy and how much it hurt to let him go. She had done what she had to do to survive, but it hadn't been a courageous path.

Her father would have been disappointed in her, as she was disillusioned with herself.

She accepted that judgment and focused her eyes on the winding road. That was what she had to tell Hank. Maybe once she settled this between them, they could both go on with their business. They were on opposite sides, but they did not have to be bitter enemies.

With that determination, Shadoe felt as if a large boulder had been lifted from her shoulders. For the first time since Hank had arrived, Shadoe felt a real anticipation to see him. She urged the truck faster and took in the beauty of Stag's Horn as she drew closer and closer to it.

She left the truck beside the road, just where she and Jill had parked once before. Starting up the steep, narrow trail, she expected Hank to hail her, to stop her once again before she got too close to the wolves.

But the trail was empty of all humans. A few chipmunks scampered among the trees, and birds rustled in the leaves and tiny branches. Shadoe climbed the steep trail with brisk efficiency. The climb made her warm and she removed her light jacket, tying the arms around her waist.

The chatter of the birds and chipmunks suddenly ceased, and she felt her scalp prickle with a strange foreboding of danger. She halted, then slowly began to turn.

The wolf was only twenty feet behind her. He was bigger than she'd ever expected, and he'd apparently been following her for a little ways. His golden eyes held her gaze, his pink tongue hung between white teeth that marked him as young and capable of a quick kill.

Shadoe thought her heart had stopped. For what seemed like an eternity she couldn't breathe, couldn't feel the beat of her own heart. There was only a ringing in her ears that filled the woods with complete silence. That and the wolf.

She saw him in exact detail. His silver-gray pelt was beautiful, thick and full. He was lean, but not starving, and he seemed in perfect health. He watched her without a shred of fear, as if he knew he were the lord and she merely a human.

For a single instant, Shadoe recognized his power and his beauty, and then the blood rushed into her heart and she felt her muscles spasm with fear.

Slowly the wolf turned and disappeared into the forest. In three seconds he was gone, absorbed by the deep shadows and thick trees.

She stood perfectly still, waiting for her heart to calm. If she tried to take a step she'd fall flat on her face. Looking at the trail where the wolf had stood, Shadoe thought perhaps she'd hallucinated the wolf. He had been so...conscious of her. As if he'd sought her out to pay her a visit.

Her father had taught her that there was a balance between animal and man, and that as long as man did not ruin the balance with overpopulation, there was a bond with nature. He also believed that some rare animals could transcend their nature and make contact with another species. It was almost as if the wolf...

"No..." Shadoe spoke aloud and felt her knees weaken. She sat down on the path and put her head in her hands. "No, that isn't possible." She was acting like a crazy woman, buying into a bunch of superstitions and foolishness her father had entertained her with beside the campfire late at night.

Jimmy had taught her respect for the old ways, for the traditions of his people. He had shown her, and then allowed her to pick her own path.

She stood up abruptly and went to the place where the wolf had stood. It was possible that she had imagined the whole thing. The business with Hank had brought her father too close to her mind, and her heart, and the result had been a vivid moment of imagination. She bent to the rocky ground, satisfied that she would find no evidence of the wolf. As she hunted, her certainty grew. She had tricked herself, a matter of her emotions taking control of her mind.

She was about to give up when she found the print. It was almost as big as her hand. Four large toe pads and a central, triangular footpad. The marks of the nails were deep, strong, a clear indication of the weight of the animal.

Shadoe touched the print and felt for a moment the lingering presence of the animal. There was no doubt the wolf had been there.

She stood up, disorientated and suddenly afraid. Above her a hungry crow cawed and fussed. She looked up at the bird and watched it wheel in the blue sky, giving her another little jolt of vertigo. Stumbling over to a tree, she had just placed her hand on the bark when the shot ripped through the silence of the woods and the tree beside her head exploded.

Shadoe dropped to the ground and rolled instinctively. She took refuge behind a large rock.

"There he goes!" A man's voice cried and there was the sound of another shot.

"Damn! You missed." A second male voice spoke.

There was the sound of shells being reloaded. "Don't worry, we'll get him. We have to before he makes trouble."

Shadoe felt a moment's relief that the men had not actually been shooting at her, but that comfort disappeared when she realized they were after the wolf. They intended to shoot him down.

"Hey!" she called out loudly. "Hey!" She stood up, looking north, toward the direction the shots had come from.

"What the hell?" One of the men pointed at her and they both took off running in the opposite direction.

Without a second thought, Shadoe gave pursuit. Why were the federal agents running away from her? As the answer came to her, her feet slowed. The men weren't federal agents. They were locals who'd come out to hunt the wolf and kill it. She saw a flash of one as he jumped behind a tree. She stopped and let them go.

The silence of the forest settled around her, along with a sense of hopelessness. Her encounter with the wolf had done something, changed her somehow. To the point that she had stepped forward to try to protect him. She smiled grimly to herself as she set her feet back on the path to the camp. Wouldn't Hank Emrich get a big charge out of that little scene? After moaning and groaning about the wolves, she'd actually tried to defend one. Well, she had no intention of reporting the two hunters. The wolf had escaped them, and if they were foolish enough to return so close to the camp of the federal agents, then they'd surely be caught swiftly enough. In fact, she was surprised the area wasn't already swarming with agents at the sound of the gun.

It was close to noon when she walked into the camp, so she didn't find it unusual that there was no sign of life around the tents. The platform that had been erected for the press conference was still there, the flowers dead from lack of water. She glanced around, looking for what might be a mess tent.

"I don't know where he is."

The voice came to her, clearly irritated.

There was a mumble of other talk, and then the same voice. "Hank's a big boy. He knows the rules. I have full confidence in him."

Shadoe walked toward the largest tent where the voices came from and hesitated just at the open flap. There was nothing to knock on, so she stepped inside.

She was greeted by the surprised faces of at least fifteen men. She searched them each carefully, one by one. "I'm looking for Hank Emrich," she said to the man she recognized as Hank's boss, the man she'd faced off against at the press conference.

"Well, well, isn't that amusing. So are we." Harry Code's voice dripped with sarcasm. "I doubt it's for the same reason, though. Hank appears to be missing."

Shadoe knew instantly that Harry Code hated Hank. Instinctively she bristled. "First you lose one of the wolves, now you've lost one of your agents. This is a real bang-up operation, isn't it?"

Her fiery retort took Harry aback. He gave her a longer look, assessing the intelligence he saw in her face. "Ms. Deerman, the spokesperson for the ranchers, isn't it?"

"I'm Shadoe Deerman. I'm looking for Hank."

"Unfortunately, Hank is no longer with us." Harry waved the men out of the tent. He ignored Shadoe for a moment as he gave them their orders. "He's on foot. He couldn't possibly have gotten far, but remember, he knows this area like the back of his hand."

"I'm sure Hank has gone on to Washington." A clean-cut agent held his ground, refusing to be put out of the tent. "Hank would not disobey a direct order. He knows the consequences. You're making a big deal out of this, Harry, and there's no need to send out a search party for him.''

Shadoe watched the scene unfold with amazement. ''What's happened to Hank?'' She shifted the question from Harry Code to the other man, who seemed more concerned about Hank's well-being.

''He's left the camp—''

''He took off last night because he knew I'd reported him and he was going back to Washington for discipline. He ran.'' Harry plowed over Cal Oberton's statement.

Shadoe looked at the angry Harry Code. What had Hank ever done to earn this man's total dislike? She'd sensed the conflict between them at the press conference, but this was outright hatred. She addressed her next question to the other man. ''Hank isn't here?''

''No.'' Cal took her arm. ''I think it would be better, Ms. Deerman, if you left the premises.'' Before she could resist, he propelled her out of the tent. ''Come on,'' he whispered in her ear, directing her back toward the path she'd come up.

When they were a safe distance from the camp, he pointed to a rock for her to take a seat. Shadoe had a million questions, but she kept them all to herself and watched the man who stood beside her. He was about Hank's age, of slighter build. His blue eyes were worried, and his face was pulled into a frown as he swung his gaze to her.

''How did you know my name?'' she asked.

''Hank's talked about you a great deal.'' Cal's expression grew rueful. ''I was beginning to think you were something he'd dreamed up. I mean, he never even mentioned another woman's name.''

Shadoe looked down at the ground. ''Where is he?'' She had a bad feeling. Very bad.

''The truth?''

She looked up. ''You're a friend of his?''

"Cal Oberton. We went through training together and for some unknown reason, we're normally assigned to the same project. Now you asked where Hank is. I was hoping maybe he was with you."

Shadoe shook her head. "The Double S would be the last place he'd go."

"I see." Cal's voice sounded as if he did. "I didn't believe it when Harry said you registered a complaint. Hank must have been his usual tactful self and made you mad as hell."

Cal's good-natured understanding made Shadoe smile. "That's one way of putting it, but Hank probably feels the good-natured part of it comes from my end."

"Well, he was a little torqued out about that wolf. Hank and I have worked a lot of cases together, and he's always concerned about the wildlife, but these wolves are something else. There's some link between him and these animals." Cal hesitated. "Hank likes to push the envelope. I'm afraid this time he may have gone over the edge." He looked directly at Shadoe. "After the complaint you filed, Code ordered him back to Washington for disciplinary action. Sometime last night Hank packed his equipment and took off. We've been hunting him all day."

"Took off? Without a trace?" She recalled Harry Code's words—that Hank had run away. "Hank isn't the type of person to run away from his problems." No, that was the type of person she had been, once.

"As I said, Hank was personally involved with these wolves. I don't think he's run." Cal looked into the thick forest. "I think he's out there, looking for Thor."

Shadoe didn't respond. Deep in her heart, she knew Cal Oberton was correct. Hank wouldn't abandon the wolves. But he had gone out alone. Without the support of his fellow agents or the ranchers. She stood up. "I need to see

Mr. Code and explain that the complaint I registered was done in a moment of anger.''

Cal shook his head. ''That won't make a bit of difference to Code. He's been looking for something to nail Hank with and you just gave him the hammer. Taking it back now won't help Hank.''

''But at least if I wrote a letter, or explained—''

Cal's head shook again. ''My best advice to you is let it go. Harry can't do a thing until we find Hank. Maybe then it would help. But if you go to him now, he'll have plenty of time to figure out a way around you retracting the complaint. And he's been wanting to put it to Hank for a long, long time.''

Shadoe hesitated. She hated to leave the camp without straightening out the mess she'd made, but maybe Cal knew best. ''Okay,'' she agreed. She'd talk it over with Billy and see what he thought.

''You don't have any idea where Hank might be, do you? If we could find him, we might be able to straighten this out before it goes any farther.''

Shadoe was struck with a sudden thought. ''There's a cabin. It's on state property, just north of my ranch. We used to go there and camp a lot when we were younger. Hank knows about it, and he knows that my father and the local ranchers always kept it stocked with food and wood for a fire.'' She felt dead certain Hank would head for the cabin if he intended to stay in the mountains on a hunting expedition.

''Great!'' Cal put his arm around her and squeezed her tight. ''Listen, we have to get to Hank and convince him to come back to the camp. If he doesn't, Code's going to pull out all the stops.''

''Hank isn't easy to convince about something he doesn't want to do.'' She knew that from long experience.

''You can do it, Shadoe, if anyone can. The man has

been in love with you for years.'' Cal started down the path. ''If we don't bring him in, Harry's going to label him a rogue agent. And Hank could lose a lot more than his badge.'' He looked back at Shadoe. ''He could lose his life.''

Chapter Eleven

Shadoe replaced the telephone and sat for a moment with Totem in her lap. The cat purred as Shadoe's fingers stroked her fur. "Where is old Billy?" she asked, but Totem had no answers.

She stared at the telephone, mentally urging Billy to call her back. She'd left messages for him at the sheriff's office, at the barber shop and at Hoss's barbecue where he liked to hang out for lunch and at other times when the coffee or company were good. It was odd that no one had seen him.

The incident with the gunshot in the woods nagged at Shadoe. She hadn't reported it to the feds, but it was something Billy should know. The ranchers needed to be kept in line. If they killed the wolf, it would be a disaster, as Billy had pointed out. Based on their hunting skills, they were as likely to kill each other—or an innocent by-stander—as they were the wolf. Any way she cut it, the would-be hunters spelled trouble. Billy needed to know. Dang his hide, where had he gone?

Holding Totem in her arms, she went to the front balcony and stepped out into the afternoon sunlight. She had about five hours of daylight left. Just enough.

"I might as well do it," she said as she put Totem down.

"I'm driving myself crazy just hanging around here worrying."

Picking up a rifle, she went to the barn. In fifteen minutes she had Chester and Ray, two reliable geldings, saddled and ready to go. Riding Chester, she set off toward the north leading Ray. It was a crazy notion, but she intended to bring Hank back down with her, whether he wanted to come or not. She was positive he was holed up in the cabin.

She pressed the horses into a ground-covering trot and tried to put her mind in neutral, but she kept coming up with plans on how to handle the rapidly approaching encounter. Hank would be furious. She knew his temper well, though over the years he'd honed an edge on it that hadn't been there as a young man. He would resist all efforts to talk sense into him. But he was in this mess partly because of her—no matter what Jill said—and she was going to make the effort to put things to right. There was no undoing what had been done in the past, but she could assume the responsibility for her actions. It wouldn't change anything, except her feelings about herself. She was sick of turning tail, worn out with running.

Once she'd gotten things straight with Hank, she was going to come back to her ranch and start working with the new foals and honing Luster's skills for the next competition. Since the competition in Billings, she'd had eight calls about breeding to Scrapiron, and the mares would be coming in the latter part of the month. With stud fees and mare care, this was a good first step in her horse-breeding business. There would be testing, teasing and breeding, and she wouldn't have a spare minute to worry about Hank, or for that matter about John. She was thoroughly disgusted with both of them, and men in general.

As she headed north, the pastureland gave way to rockier terrain. The open meadows were replaced with steep trails sheltered on both sides by firs and a few hardwoods just brave enough to show the first tips of greenery. The wild-flowers were beginning to dare the spring, and Shadoe pulled Chester to a halt as she crested a steep rise and looked down into a valley showing the russets, pale greens, yellows and blues of a Montana spring.

The land caught at her heart with a sudden fierceness that pushed everything else from her mind. There was no place like it, no sensation equal to that of topping a crest and seeing the untouched wilderness fall away beneath her feet in a rolling vista of colorful wildflowers surrounded by boulders and trees. This land spoke to her blood, to her need to be free and alive.

How had she denied this love for so long?

Sighing, she nudged Chester forward and Ray obediently trotted along beside her. She was more tired than she'd thought. Watching for the wolf had worn her down, but she couldn't forget that the big, powerful killer was out there somewhere.

It was three o'clock before she neared the cabin. She'd have about fifteen minutes to fight with Hank before they had to leave to return—or face the dangers of traveling back along the mountains in the dark. As willing and game as Chester and Ray were, they didn't have the surefooted-ness of mules or pack burros. She trusted them, but she also knew that they had been bred and trained for some-thing other than mountain climbing in the dark. And cer-tainly not with a wolf on the loose.

Hank could argue on horseback—and she was sure he would fight until the mountains gave back his grumbling. To her surprise, she found she was smiling at that thought. In times past, she and Hank had sat up entire nights de-bating a point or an idea.

Two hundred yards from the cabin she dismounted and tied the horses to a scrub tree. She was ninety-nine percent positive Hank would be at the cabin, but there was that single possibility that someone else was there, some camper or one of the other ranchers. Or maybe even the person who'd been in her barn. It always paid to be cautious.

On the long ride, Shadoe developed her own theories about what had been happening in Lakota County, and they involved a third party. She didn't believe Hank would turn Thor loose knowing that every rancher in the area would be out to shoot him on sight. Without the pack, Thor would be more likely to move down to ranches rather than hunt with his comrades in the wilderness.

Hank absolutely hadn't turned Scrapiron loose. She'd seen him and the intruder at the same time. That left a third party.

But if Shadoe could resolve some of the problems she faced in Montana by adding an unknown third party, she could not do the same for Kathy Lemon's accusations against Hank. She'd slapped Hank with the charge and then gone into the house. She'd given him no time to respond, if he had an inclination to do so. Not really. This time she wanted a yes or no—while she looked into his eyes. One simple answer.

When she came within sight of the cabin, she stopped. The place looked deserted. If she hadn't known Hank as well as she did, she would have simply said the cabin was empty. But he had been trained by a master—her own father. Jimmy Deerman had known how to walk without leaving prints, to wander through the wilderness without upsetting the animals around him. And he'd also known how to stand so completely still that he didn't register on a person's vision. Hank knew those things, too.

Shadoe walked directly to the front door. One thing she didn't want to do was startle Hank, especially if he was asleep. And he might well be if he'd spent the better part of the night and morning walking down from Stag's Horn.

"Hank." She tapped on the door lightly. "Hank!"

She heard his footsteps and composed her face into a blank. She might be able to hide her expressions, but she couldn't deny the sudden rapid beating of her heart, or the feeling of breathlessness that made her inhale deeply before the door opened.

"Shadoe." He spoke her name and looked at her for a moment as if he had stepped into a long-awaited dream. Then his features hardened.

His face was stubbled with a light growth of blond beard, and his eyes looked tired. It was a look Shadoe recognized from a time long past, and she felt a twist of pain. She had been the source of that look.

"Get your gear." She spoke softly, knowing he would resent an order of any kind. "We need to head home before it gets any later." She had not meant to say home. For all of her rehearsing on the way up the trail, she'd bungled it at the very last. To cover her embarrassment, she went on. "I brought a horse for you. You'll like Ray. He's a lot like you. Stubborn."

Hank ignored her attempt to lighten the moment. "How'd you know I was here?"

"Lucky guess. I went up to talk with your boss. He said you'd cut out." She used the term deliberately. Her emotions were in turmoil, and she'd always been able to draw a rise out of Hank with minimal effort.

Hank gave her a black look and walked back into the cabin.

He hadn't invited her in, but Shadoe followed him anyway. She took in his pack against the rough-hewn wall, the chair pulled up to the window where he'd been gazing down into a small clearing. Watching. For what?

He went back to the window. Shadoe felt terribly awkward. Hank stood with his back to her, gazing out as if she weren't there. She'd already told him why she was there— to take him home. Apparently, he wasn't going to mount

Ray unless she could convince him with a little more than logic. Now she had to tell him *why* she was there.

It was damn hard to do with him giving her his backside. She cleared her throat, but he continued to ignore her.

"Don't make this any harder, please." She swallowed and waited for him to turn around. Her gaze lingered on the sunlight in his blond hair, the softness of the blue flannel shirt he wore. It would be the same color as his eyes. It would be soft and smell of him. She'd always loved to fall asleep with her head resting on Hank's shoulder as he drove her home from a dance or a movie. He had been her source of comfort, of total security. If he would only turn around and look at her. But he didn't.

"Hank, I owe you an apology." She took a hesitant step forward. "For making Billy call your boss...and for when I left Montana. I shouldn't have done it the way I did. I just couldn't do it any other way at the time." She swallowed. "I was weak. After Dad was killed, I didn't want to care about anyone or anything. I just shut myself down and ran."

He turned slowly then, stopping when he fully faced her. His blue gaze moved over her face, as if he meant to read the truth in her features rather than her words. "For a long time, I thought it was something I'd done."

She nodded and felt a lump in her throat. "I know that now. At the time, I didn't think about how it would feel to you. I *couldn't* think about anything except getting as far away as I could. Or drown in the horror of it all." She swallowed twice. "So I ran. And I ran some more. And it got so that it was easier to run than to stand still and think." She shrugged, knowing that she was on the verge of tears. If she ever allowed herself to start crying, it would take a long time to stop. Tears were weakness, and Hank had seen enough of her weakness.

"I would have helped you."

Shadoe forced herself to look at him. She owed him that much. He would have helped her. By running, she had denied him that way of assuaging his own grief. "No one could help me, Hank. When Dad died...I didn't allow myself to feel anything for a long, long time. I couldn't let you help me because I would have had to feel something for you. You always made me feel, sometimes more than I thought I could bear."

More than anything in the world, Hank wanted to step over to her, to brush the tears away from her cheeks and hold her against him. He knew the feel of her, the way her chin would touch just at his breastbone, the way her fingers would curl on his chest. The need to touch her was a terrible pain, but he resisted it. It seemed that Shadoe Deerman was a continuation of bitter lessons for him. He had to learn that this was the past. Whatever they had shared was over. He forced down his desire to reach out to her and found the residue of his anger.

"And what about me? You simply left. No telephone call. No address. Your mother wouldn't tell me where you'd gone. There was talk you'd been put in a hospital." He laughed, but it was bitter. "I called every hospital, even the mental institutions, in the state of Montana. And then someone told me that you could be there under an assumed name. But I didn't give up. I started going to each one, looking for you."

"Oh, Hank." She couldn't help the tears now. She could see him, a kid of eighteen, spending his Sundays looking for a girl who had simply vanished. The fact that she had been more dead than alive didn't relieve her of the pain she had given him.

"Finally, about nine months later, Jill told me she'd gotten a letter from you. She said you were in college, and that you were dating a senior. She said I should forget you."

Shadoe brushed her tears away with the back of her hand. She was overwhelmed by emotion, and she wanted to walk out the door and ride—to escape to anywhere except where she was standing. But her days of running were over. "Mother insisted that I put Montana behind me. She said it would only make it worse to stay in touch with my old friends. I finally wrote Jill, because I was so homesick and so alone. But I made it sound like everything was fine. I made up the part about dating someone so I didn't sound so pathetic." Shadoe smiled and shook her head. "Always the pride. Always."

"By the time Jill got your letter, I was neck-deep in debt at Copperwood. A smart man would have let it go then, but I hung on and on, until when it did go, there was nothing but bad debt for me."

"And so you went east and went into the wildlife service."

"I got a scholarship."

"And you came back to Montana."

"Just long enough to establish the wolves. There's nothing here for me any longer." He felt the first flash of satisfaction at the expression on her face. But that moment was short-lived. He had hurt her, and he found that it did not truly relieve his own suffering. The damnable truth was that it only heightened it.

The pain his words generated surprised Shadoe. At last she looked away. "And I came back to try to find the part of me I left here. My courage." She turned so that her profile was to him. "I didn't know exactly why I came back here until this very minute. But it's the truth. I can't go forward with my life until I find the rest of myself."

"Like the old warrior Two Crows." Hank's voice had softened a tiny bit. He knew her well enough to know what this admission cost her. Whatever she had done in the past, he had to admire her for this moment. "He lost his courage in a fight with a bear."

"And he couldn't go to the land of the clouds without it." Shadoe remembered. Vividly. It was one of her favorite stories that her father had told.

"He was too old to walk the mountains, so he went on a dream quest." Hank took up the story.

"And in the dream, he saw that his courage had been found and taken by an eagle. He knew that she would not willingly return it to him. He would have to trick her." She felt like the old warrior, except she had no dream to show her where she'd left her courage. She was stumbling along in the dark, without even the guidance of a dream. "The warrior was lucky. He found that part of himself he had lost. I'm not so certain I'll be able to do the same."

Hank watched her carefully. The sunlight seemed to be pulled deep into her hair and sent back in bright sparks among the dark strands. She held herself straight, her shoulders back. She was still proud. To his surprise, he found that his anger toward her was greatly diminished. She had admitted her weakness to him. Both Shadoe and her father had been too proud.

"Well," she said as she turned back to him, her cheeks red. "That's what I wanted to tell you. It doesn't do much good now, but you had a right to know what happened." She had to find a way out of the past, and that was to look to the future—just a few steps down the road would do it. The immediate road led back to the Double S. "We have to head back to the ranch. We've wasted too much time here already. As it is, we'll have to take the last few miles in the dark, but once we get to the range, I think Chester and Ray can make it blindfolded." As she spoke she could hear her voice grow stronger, more assured.

"I'm not going anywhere."

He spoke so calmly that Shadoe thought she might have

misunderstood. He'd sounded reasonable, not hardheaded and ornery. "Hank, your boss is organizing a search party to look for you."

"Code is an idiot."

"That may be, but he's out to get you. He's acting like you're some kind of criminal. You've got to go back up there and straighten this out." Surely Hank was smart enough to see he was playing into Harry Code's hands.

"Sure." Hank pushed the chair aside with angry force. "Just go explain to Harry. He's such a good listener. And he's particularly sympathetic to me."

"If those agents waste their time hunting you, who's going to find the wolf?" Shadoe knew this was her best ploy. Hank would do whatever he had to if it meant safeguarding the wolf.

He knew Shadoe was manipulating him, but it didn't detract from the truthfulness of her statement. If Code put the entire team out searching for him, no one would even attempt to find Thor. Nor would they properly guard the rest of the wolves. With Harry Code in charge, there was no telling what would happen to the animals.

"Okay." He went to get his pack. "But I want a promise from you first." He lifted the pack and stopped in front of her.

"What?"

"Promise me that you'll keep the ranchers out of the wilderness until we can find the wolf."

Shadoe's gaze dropped from his. "I can't promise that."

He sensed immediately that she was hiding something from him. "What is it?"

"When I went up to talk with your boss, I saw the wolf." A chill brushed across her skin at the memory. For an instant, it was as if she saw the animal again. His presence was so intense, so unforgettable. "And I saw two hunters. They took a shot at him and almost got me."

"Did you know them?" Hank's voice was urgent.

She shook her head. "I honestly didn't get a look at them. I swear to you, the members of the coalition haven't made any plans to harm the wolves. None at all. But that's the small group I know. Some of the members are strangers. I don't know them well enough to say they wouldn't take it on themselves to hunt the wolf down. Some of the ranchers, particularly the small ones, are upset by all of this."

Hank shouldered the pack. "Let's get home." He had no intention of turning himself over to Harry Code and possible transfer to Washington D.C., but Shadoe didn't have to know about his plans. As usual, he found that he was better off working alone.

The sun had taken on the more golden tones of late afternoon, and Shadoe led the way to the horses. The silence between them was not awkward, but it was noticeable. The cabin had been charged with emotion. Now, in the open air, she simply couldn't think of a thing to say. Except to ask Hank about Kathy Lemon, and now wasn't the time for that.

"The horses are just over there. I tied them to a shrub in the shade." She pointed behind several big boulders.

She was in the lead and when she climbed over the rocks, she stopped. The area around her was empty. Her first thought was that she'd brought Hank to the wrong place, but he immediately walked over and examined the hoofprints.

"Looks like they got pretty excited before they took off."

Shadoe walked over and bent down. The hard ground was battered and scarred where the horses had twisted and turned, shifting and moving. She went to the tree where she'd tied them. Strangely enough, the bark was undisturbed. "They must have pulled free."

Hank didn't say anything.

"They're probably halfway home by now." Shadoe turned and looked south, as if she might be able to pick up their trail.

Hank examined the tree where they'd been tied, then moved out to search the ground. He walked in a circular pattern, occasionally stopping to examine something.

After finding a shady spot, Shadoe sat down on a rock. The prospects for the night worried her. First of all, the horses at the Double S needed attention. And more acutely, she and Hank were trapped together. She checked the position of the sun. It was way too late to start hiking back to the ranch. The only alternative was staying the night in the cabin—with Hank. She felt a surge of dread. This was something she hadn't bargained for. Not at all.

She looked up to find his jaw set and his gaze on the ground. He was an intense man. He'd been an intense boy, never giving up on anything that he really wanted. Except her. And she'd left him no choice. Her own thoughts made her anxious.

"Chester and Ray are well trained. I can't imagine them taking off like that. Just pulling free." She spoke to chase away her own thoughts.

Hank's expression was grim. He stood up and came to sit beside her on the rock. "I'm not so certain they pulled free."

"Hank?" Shadoe saw more than his usual tenseness.

"I can't say for certain because the ground is so hard there isn't a good track, but it appears to me someone untied them and led them off."

"Who?" The word was almost a yell.

"There's no way to tell." Hank shrugged. "The ground is just too hard, but it looks as if they took off side by side. Their hooves have chipped the rocks in places. It was a walk, steady and in tandem. That just doesn't sound like two horses that got so spooked they tore free and headed home.''

Shadoe closed her eyes. "No, it doesn't." She pushed her hair back from her face, a gesture she used when she was upset. She didn't have to tell Hank that the chances of getting Chester and Ray back alive were slim to none. "Rustlers, maybe?" They were awfully isolated to be hit by horse thieves, but it was possible. Cattle and horse rustlers hit a herd, stealing five or six head here and there until they had enough for butcher. It was a business where buyer and seller didn't ask a lot of questions about brands or origins of stock.

Hank heard her sorrow in her voice. "I don't think it was a rustler. Not up here."

She looked up, startled. "Then who?"

"I think it was the same man who turned Scrapiron out, and the same person I was following when I was down at the Double S. The same man who stole my knife and left it in your barn to incriminate me." He got up and walked to the ground where the horses had been. He looked at the area for a moment, then came back to Shadoe.

She sensed something in his stance, in the way he stared at her. "What is it?"

"I have to ask myself if maybe this mystery man isn't working with you."

Shadoe stood up slowly. She was afraid with all of her blood pounding in her ears that if she moved too fast she would faint. "What exactly are you saying?"

Hank glared at her. "I'm saying that maybe I've been set up. From the very beginning."

Chapter Twelve

Hank struck the match and put fire to paper. In a moment the small sticks of kindling were burning cheerfully. The sound of the crackling fire only heightened the silence between him and Shadoe.

From the pantry she had found canned chicken, mushrooms, rice and assorted spices. A casserole was baking in the gas oven, filling the small cabin with savory smells and a sense of homeyness that made her twitch with an anxious emotion she couldn't pin down. On one hand, it seemed the most natural thing in the world for her to be in the cabin with Hank, the fire leaping, bright yellow flames in the hearth, and supper bubbling in the oven. They had shared so many nights like this one, with and without her father.

But twenty years had passed. She had only to look at Hank, one boot hooked on the hearth, his gaze captured by the flames. He was a man, not a boy. He was also not any happier about being stranded on the mountain than she was.

As she mixed the ingredients for biscuits, she found a nugget of possibility in the idea that the man who had turned the wolf free might have been the one who stole Chester and Ray. If that was the case, she might be able to find her horses, unharmed. She started to break the silence by telling her thought to Hank, but she stopped.

The very idea that he thought she had somehow entrapped him was beyond belief. How could he think such a thing? Her anger returned on a wave of hot fury, and she mixed the biscuits with herculean force.

The sound of angry cooking came clearly to Hank, but he didn't look up. He had a lot on his mind, and looking at Shadoe, dark hair hanging about her shoulders, wasn't conducive to clear thinking. He had not asked her to cook, just as she had not asked him to build a fire. They had fallen naturally into the pattern of the old days.

Hank had the sudden, disturbing feeling that if he looked up, he would see the sixteen-year-old girl he'd loved with all his heart. Maybe, just maybe if he went to her and held her tight, he could prevent everything that had happened. Hank had known broken bones, animal bites, bitter cold, baking heat, but nothing compared to the jolt of pure pain in his chest that came with that thought. He almost moaned aloud but caught himself.

He was a fool, opening old scars and letting them bleed again. He was worse than a fool for tormenting himself with possibilities that existed only in his mind.

If he turned and looked at Shadoe Deerman, he would see a thirty-six-year-old woman who was furious with him. Because she couldn't hit him, she was beating a bowl of biscuits to death in the kitchen.

He heard the oven door open. There was the scrape of the casserole coming out and the biscuits going in. Suddenly, the idea of sitting across the table from Shadoe and sharing a meal with her was more than he could take. He turned, catching her as she bent over the oven. He had to face the truth that as a grown woman, she was even more beautiful than she'd been as a girl. Gone were the sharp angles, the hesitation of youth. She was rounded, strong and very confident. She closed the oven door and stood up, turning to face him. Her face carried the flush of heat from the oven.

"I'm going to scout around," he said.

Shadoe opened her mouth to tell him that the food would be ready in fifteen minutes, but she never said the words. She had no appetite. Her mind and body and emotions were in such turmoil that the idea of eating saddened her. The thought of calling Hank to supper, as if they were on a date...or sharing the evening voluntarily...was too hard. She said nothing as she watched him go out the door.

The Montana night had grown cold. Even though the Double S was only fifteen miles away, the elevation of the cabin made it much colder here after the sun had set. Shadoe put plates, flatware and napkins on the table, adding the hot chicken and biscuits. For herself, she poured a cup of fresh coffee and took it to the fire. Common sense told her to eat, to get it over before Hank returned and avoid the awkward event of supper. Her stomach simply rebelled at the idea.

Pulling an old rocker up to the fire, she sipped the coffee, stared into the flames and tried not to think about the past, the present or the future. She fastened her attention on old movies she'd seen and tried to recall titles, actors and plots. Anything except her immediate surroundings.

After half an hour, Shadoe got up and went to the window. Hank's continued absence worried her a little. She knew he was probably as uncomfortable as she was and that he was staying outside deliberately. Still, what if something had happened to him? He didn't have a gun, only a knife. That much she'd observed. They were far enough into the mountains that he could have run across a bear, even a mountain lion. Or that big silver wolf.

A knife was no weapon against such animals.

What if he was lying outside, wounded and bleeding?

She put down her cup, got her jacket and went out into the night.

The black sky was pure velvet, and a three-quarter moon gave good illumination. She'd gone only half a dozen steps from the porch when she saw Hank. He was sitting on a boulder staring into the night sky. His back was slumped, and he seemed to be in deep concentration.

Moving silently, Shadoe went back inside the cabin. It was clear he preferred the cold of the night to her company. There was no need to force herself on him. The best thing to do was go to sleep and be ready for a long walk home at first light. There was so much to do at the ranch. Scrapiron had an automatic waterer and plenty of hay, so he wouldn't suffer from the lack of a couple of meals. The other horses had been left in pasture where they could graze and drink from the clear mountain streams that cut through the spring grass. Nothing would seriously suffer from her one-night absence, but she had to get back by dark the next day. And that meant a long, steady walk. Sleep was the ticket.

Once inside the cabin, though, she was confronted with a new dilemma. Where to sleep? There was one bed. A double. And not even a sofa. She could take the bed and leave Hank the rocker. Chances were he wouldn't even return inside so it would be foolish for her to sleep in a chair. Except.

She went to the bed and removed the top quilt. In front of the fire she arranged the rocking chair with a small table so that she could sit and put her feet up. As her last act, she fed the fire, hoping Hank would decide to come inside before it went out completely. If the fire died, she'd awaken stiff and frozen. Well, too bad. She kicked off her boots, got in the chair and arranged the quilt as snugly as she could. Sleep wasn't going to come easily, but it would come. She was bone weary.

Outside the cabin, Hank continued to stare, motionless, into the night. He'd heard the cabin door open and sensed Shadoe's approach. He'd almost felt her, like a touch, as she'd drawn nearer to him. Using rigid discipline, he'd also made himself not react to her presence. He'd seen something along the edge of the woods. Or perhaps it would be more accurate to say that he'd sensed something. Something alive, and big, and watching the cabin.

The possibilities of what that might be kept him motionless.

There was no reason for anyone to spy on him or Shadoe. No legitimate reason. It was possible that some of the federal agents had tracked him to the cabin. It was also possible that the watcher had something to do with Shadoe. Only time would tell. So he'd held his slump-shouldered pose, acting as if he were deep in thought and unaware of his surroundings while he was as alert as he could be. Whatever it was, man or beast, it would have to make a move sometime. Hank had to know more about it before he could formulate a plan. By remaining still, he'd hoped to draw out the watcher—and to send Shadoe back to the safety of the cabin.

The second possibility—that whatever was in the woods was a wild creature—would also be affected by his stance as a sentinel. A wild animal, under normal circumstances, would see him and depart. Few animals, even bears or wildcats, were naturally aggressive with man. Given the chance, they would depart without a confrontation. He was counting on that since he had only a knife for protection.

The minutes stretched longer and longer as the still night seemed to freeze time. There was no movement, and Hank began to wonder if he'd imagined it. He was about to give up, to stand, stretch and face the difficulties of entering the cabin when he saw it again. Just the flicker of something.

More of a sixth sense than something his eye could register. He froze.

Just at the edge of the woods, what seemed to be molten moonlight shifted among the trees.

Hank held his breath. It wasn't possible. Was it? He looked.

Thor stepped out of the trees, moving fully onto exposed ground. He walked directly toward Hank, his gait sure and steady. He was not hurried, nor was he afraid.

Hank thought for a moment he was dreaming. This was the waking dream of a warrior that Jimmy had filled his head with so many times as a boy. The wild creature came with a message to the dreamer, bringing a prophecy, or a gift.

Hank wanted to shut his eyes, then reopen them—to check reality. But he simply could not take his gaze off the magnificent animal that walked gracefully toward him. Not even for a second. One part of Hank didn't want the wolf to be a dream.

"Thor?" he spoke softly into the night.

Fifty feet away, the wolf stopped, his golden gaze catching and holding Hank's. His teeth were bone white in the moonlight, his tongue pink and moist as he panted and stared at Hank. A low growl came from deep within his throat and he shifted his gaze to the cabin.

SHADOE STEPPED OFF *the wooden porch of the cabin and onto the ground in her bare feet. Behind her the light from the lamp spilled onto the rough boards of the porch. Slowly, very slowly, the door closed, blocking off the rectangle of light. She was alone in the darkness.*

The stars overhead were scattered like billions of tiny diamond chips. The night was incredibly warm, and she had a sudden desire to feel the gentle breeze on her bare skin. Very slowly she stepped out of her clothes. There was no one to see or disturb her. In a burst of joy, she began to dance in the light of the moon.

Spinning and weaving in the magical moonlight, she danced to the tune she hummed softly under her breath. She was completely happy. Totally safe. She danced across the clearing in front of the cabin to the edge of the woods. The night was balmy, a perfect summer night, and she had not been so happy in years. Montana. She had come home.

Deep in the woods there was the hoot of an owl. The sound came again, and with it a shiver of apprehension crossed her skin. The warm summer breeze shifted, coming from the north and bringing the cold of the snow-capped mountains to her. She looked back to the cabin and saw that it was much farther away than she'd thought. A long, long way and the ground looked frozen and cold.

Suddenly there was the sound of something in the woods, the brittle snap of a stick, and once again, the mournful hoot of the owl. Shadoe froze. The old ones believed that the owl came through the woods in search of a spirit to claim. The owl was the harbinger of death.

There was the flutter of large wings, and through the darkness the owl's voice echoed, "Shad-doe! Shad-da-doe!"

She stepped backward, away from the woods where the owl called to her. She'd fancied herself free and safe, and she was neither of those things. She was merely foolish. She had to get back to the cabin, to safety.

As she turned to run, she heard the sound of fast movement in the woods. Something big was running, running in the trees. She turned to look but saw nothing in the silver glow of the moon.

In the distance there was the cry of a young horse. For a horrible moment, Shadoe was torn between her desire to run to the cabin or to go to the horses. She started forward, knowing instinctively that she had to save the young ani-

mal. The dread in the foal's cry sent a surge of fear into her heart.

Unarmed, completely vulnerable, she stepped into the darkness of the woods. Beneath the trees, the air was freezing, and the cold moved from the ground up to her knees, up her bare legs to her torso, to her head. She was swallowed by the darkness of the woods. Not even the moon could penetrate the shadows cast by the huge trees.

Through the darkness came the sound of something following her. A shaft of moonlight fell in a circle. Not twenty feet away, the wolf stood, watching. Gold eyes stared into her dark ones and held. To Shadoe, it seemed the coat of the wolf had drunk the light. He glowed with silver power, moon touched.

She ran. Her feet tripped on brambles and sticks that were suddenly in the path. With each step she took, the wolf advanced one pace. He did not surge forward, but he kept even with her, step by step. He was unhurried, waiting.

She remembered then. Look, listen, think, then act. She could hear her father's voice guiding her. A thin line of trees marked the end of the woods, and she moved toward the biggest of them. Her hand brushed against the big trunk, the bark sharp and abrasive. She hugged close to it, trying to elude the wolf. Sidestepping, she prepared to make a run across the clearing. The wolf appeared, still twenty feet away, watching as if it were eager for the chase. With a cry of desperation, Shadoe started across the frozen, empty ground.

She ran, her feet barely feeling the sharp and jagged rocks. Moving with the grace of a deer, she bounded toward the cabin. She was determined to live, and that made her strong. The ground churned beneath her feet, and suddenly she was on the hard boards of the porch. She flung open the door and hurdled through it, closing it behind her *and throwing the lock. She had made it! She had made it inside!*

To her horror, she heard the sound of scratching at the door. Insistent scratching. She went to the window and slowly pushed the curtain aside. Her heart squeezed with fear as she looked into the wolf's golden gaze. He stood with his paws on the windowsill, staring at her through the glass. Saliva dripped from his pink tongue and he seemed to know her. Golden eyes stared into hers, speaking in a language she did not understand. But it was clear the animal knew her, and had come to her for a reason.

The wolf's mouth opened, white fangs exposed, and she screamed.

AT THE SOUND of Shadoe's anguished screams, Hank broke eye contact with the wolf. They had stood each other off for a full five minutes. Looking away from the wolf, Hank started toward the house. He'd covered only twenty feet when the body of the animal sprang past him and leaped up on the porch. Turning to face Hank, the wolf growled low and deep, then jumped from the porch and ran for the woods.

For just an instant, he watched the wolf disappear, then he hit the door with the weight of his body, slammed it open and rushed inside.

The fire was a bed of glowing embers with only the occasional flicker of flames. Framed against the fire, Shadoe sat in the chair. The quilt had fallen about her waist, and her eyes were closed. In her sleep she struggled, fighting some presence that threatened her.

"Shadoe!" Hank went to her and without thinking, he scooped her into his arms. Moving gently, he carried her to the bed and put her down.

She was still struggling, still in the throes of her night-nare. Her arms came up and she fought, pounding against his chest, crying and thrashing.

"Shadoe." He spoke softly, touching her cheek with his fingers. When that didn't awaken her, he shook her shoulder. "Wake up, Shadoe. It's a dream. Wake up." He shook her harder, watching as her eyes slowly opened and she looked up into his gaze.

"Hank!" She was breathless as she reached up and grabbed him, burrowing her face against his chest. "Oh, God, Hank, it was the wolf."

At her words he felt a chill brush down his neck like the touch of an icy finger. "The wolf?"

She was still caught by the last tentacles of the dream. Outside the cabin was the wolf and danger. Inside was Hank. He was so good, so solid and so real after the terror of the animal. She ran her hands inside his jacket, feeling the softness of his shirt and the beating of his heart against her palm. Nothing in her life had ever been so wonderful.

"What wolf?" Hank asked. "Did you see a wolf?"

"The one in my dream. He keeps coming after me. In the snow, in the woods. He's a big silver wolf, and this time he came up on the porch, and..." She felt him stiffen. "What?"

Hank eased her back onto the bed so that he could look deep into her eyes. "You've dreamed about this wolf before?"

"All spring." She tried to find a smile, but the dream was still too much with her. "He's beautiful," she admitted reluctantly, "but he's stalking me. He waits in the woods for me." The expression in Hank's eyes frightened her. "What is it?"

He gently brushed her silky hair from her cheek. The feel of her skin was so delicious. He saw her lips part as he took a deep breath, and suddenly there was no holding back any longer. He bent toward her, moving slowly so that she had plenty of time to halt him with a touch or word.

His lips touched hers, at first a feathery touch that chilled him while it promised delicious warmth. Her lips were softer than anything he could remember. At the gentle probing of his tongue, she opened her mouth and gave him access.

For Hank, that willingness was like oxygen to fire. His desire flamed, growing with each touch, each delicate feel of her beneath him. She coiled one hand in his hair while the other slipped around his back, pressing him down to her.

Hank heard a moan, and wasn't certain whether it was his or hers. It was burned away in his need for her. They kissed with a fierceness that took them both by surprise. Shadoe opened her lips for his exploration, she lifted her chin, exposing the sensitive areas of her neck. One hand beneath his jacket, slid over his chest, fingers exploring with need and a white-hot desire that made her burn with longing for him.

Hank shrugged out of his jacket and his arms went around her, pulling her against him as he settled on the bed beside her. Her hair spilled over his arm as she clung to him, and he ran his fingers through it and thought of silk and water. His fingers tightened, bringing her head back so that he could look into her eyes. For what, he couldn't have said. But he saw it there, at last, a need for him as great as that he felt for her.

Shadoe stared into his eyes and felt a twist of desire that was almost painful. Never in her life had she wanted anything more than to feel Hank's hands on her, to know him completely and totally as a man. The terror of the dream, the hurt and anguish of the past, she pushed all of it aside. His fingers were at the buttons of her blouse while she worked his own shirt free. They tugged at each other's clothes with a need that was more than desperate. For twenty years they had denied themselves this moment, and neither could wait any longer.

As Shadoe peeled his shirt down his arms, Hank managed to stand and kick off his boots. He returned to the bed and pressed her back with his weight. He felt every inch of her beneath him, all softer, rounder than he remembered, but so achingly familiar. "Shadoe," he whispered in her ear, his voice thick with emotion. He lifted himself so that he could look down at her.

Shadoe felt the burn of hot tears behind her eyes, but she smiled up into Hank's face. She could not say that what they were doing was right. She could not say that one or both of them would not regret it. But neither could stop it. They were long past the moment when common sense or logic could save them from each other—or from themselves.

She reached up and brushed the backs of her fingers against his blond stubble. Her thumb touched his lips, and she felt the kiss he placed upon it, but her eyes were held by his gaze. So dark, so intense. She traced the line of his jaw with her hand, feeling as if she were blind. Each touch, each new sensation made her want to cry out with pleasure.

He supported his weight with one elbow, while his other hand moved along the contour of her hip, touching, caressing, exploring her leg, moving down the outside to her knee and starting on the slow, tantalizing journey up the inside of her thigh.

Her breath caught in her throat at the intimacy of his touch, but his hand moved across her abdomen to her belt. His eyes asked her to stop him if she could as his fingers unbuckled her belt, then the snap of her jeans. When she made no protest, he shifted to his knees and grabbed her jeans by the cuffs, pulling them off with one smooth motion.

Shadoe had to smile at him. Though they had never slept together, they had come close more than once. She had always teased him that he could remove her pants faster than she could herself. "You still have the touch," she said.

He stood beside the bed, unbuckled his own jeans and dropped them to the floor. Stepping out of them he stood beside her.

The fire had burned lower, but the glowing embers cast enough light in the room for Shadoe to see him. Muscles had replaced the lean body of the boy, but when she gazed into his eyes, she saw again the Hank she remembered. She lifted her arms to him, and he sank down on the bed beside her.

He kissed her slowly, rolling on top of her, tantalizing her with tiny touches, a kiss that started at her neck and moved slowly to her chest. He worked the clasp of her bra, sliding it from her shoulders with hands that hugged and caressed each inch of her.

With one finger he drew a line from the hollow of her throat to her navel.

"Do you know how many nights I've dreamed of this?" he asked.

She shook her head, unable to trust her voice to answer.

He kissed her again, this time with more restraint, but Shadoe could wait no longer. She found her fingers pressing into his back, demanding the feel of him on top of her. Her need for him spanned twenty years, and for the moment, she was willing to sacrifice whatever was required for that precious moment of complete unity.

For Hank, the consequences of the night were like soft whispers at a closed door. He heard them, but he did not listen. He had been in love with Shadoe Deerman from the first day he saw her, walking along the sidewalk and into the grammar school in Athens. She had worn long braids and kneesocks, and she had looked up at him with a solemnness that the other girls had mocked. From that moment, he had lost his heart. The years of separation had only intensified the pleasure of this evening.

Whatever happened in the dawn, he could not stop himself. He didn't want to.

Chapter Thirteen

Shadoe pulled the quilt more snugly under her chin, lifting it also over Hank's back. She was curled into his chest, his long, solid arms and legs wrapped around her for warmth. Even as she sighed into the pink light of dawn, she could see her breath frost in front of her. It was cold in the cabin. It was going to be a long, cold walk down to the Double S. Even worse would be getting out of bed, leaving behind the haven of pleasure, and peace, they had found at last.

She cast her thoughts forward and discovered a mental picture of herself cresting the last swell of land, topping it bathed in golden sunlight to see the ranch below her. Hank stood at her side. The image was neither past nor future, but a fantasy. Still, Shadoe couldn't suppress a smile as she pressed her forehead against Hank's chest and listened to the soft rhythm of his heart. Maybe… She pushed the thought away before it could fully form. Fantasies were for young girls.

They were both tired. They had gone to sleep only an hour or so before dawn. Twenty years of longing and desire had been packed into one night. They had remained awake, touching, until exhaustion had finally demanded that they sleep. Now, the day, with all of the unknowns, stretched before them. But the night that was past had proven beyond a doubt that they were equally matched with passion and desire. Shadoe felt the blush creep up her cheeks as she remembered. It was not often that two living creatures were so perfectly attuned to touch and response. She had never doubted that with Hank, making love would be wonderful. She had not expected it to give her such a feeling of peace and total satisfaction.

He stirred beside her, and she lifted her face so that she looked into his eyes as he opened them.

"I was afraid last night was a dream," he said. He touched her cheek, letting his hand slide down her neck, then along her shoulder and arm, moving finally to her waist and hip. "Nope, you're flesh and blood."

Shadoe had thought she would be shy with him, but there was no awkwardness. Nothing had ever felt more right. "Dawn is breaking."

"If I could have a single wish, I'd get us another day, two if I were greedy. Shadoe, we have to work things out between us."

She nodded. Could they? Would it actually be possible to find some compromise? "I'd like that, Hank." She eased slightly away from the warmth of him. They had reached a plateau with their personal feelings. Before they could progress any further, they had to deal with the issues that had brought them back together. "You have to find that wolf before he kills."

"Or before someone kills him," Hank countered. Shadoe's words reminded him about the wolf and her strange dream. It was a subject he didn't want to broach, but it had been too powerful to ignore. She had a right to know. "Last night, when you were asleep in the chair. What were you dreaming about?"

She didn't have to try to remember. The dream was vivid. All of the wolf dreams were so intense they were unforgettable to her.

"I was outside dancing and saw movement in the woods.

An owl hooted, but instead of a hoot, it called my name. Then one of the young horses began to scream in panic. I knew the wolf was hunting one of the foals, so I went into the woods to find my horse. That was when the wolf appeared. He was there, waiting for me. Stalking me." Her voice trembled. "And I ran back to the cabin, and he jumped up on the porch."

Hank's hands grasped her shoulders and pulled her close. She could hear his heart, pounding now instead of the gentle rhythm of sleep. "What is it?" she asked, almost afraid to hear his answer.

"Last night, when I was outside, there was something in the woods."

Shadoe knew the truth, almost as if it were inevitable. "He was here, wasn't he?" This wasn't possible. They were talking like people who had lost their minds, seeing wolves, reading dreams. Hank started to speak again, and she forced herself to listen.

"He ran right past me up to the porch. He never made an attempt to harm me at all." Hank's voice was hesitant. "Up on the porch, he growled when I tried to approach. Then he left. He's been watching me, Shadoe. I know that sounds foolish, but it's true. Almost from the moment I captured him. He's been keenly aware of me. Not like an ordinary wolf." He laughed, but it was halfhearted. "Maybe all along he was following me to get to you."

Shadoe felt as if a rock had lodged in her throat. Hank's words angered her because they frightened her. "Why would a wolf seek me out?" She looked into his eyes, caught by the sincerity she hadn't expected to see there. The look tempered her anger considerably. "You know what's wrong with us? We're both victims of Jimmy Deerman." A rueful smile touched her lips. "We grew up on his campfire stories of animals and magic, warriors and the wilderness. We're both too susceptible to the idea of that wolf.''

Hank kissed the top of her head. ''That wolf wasn't an idea. It was flesh and bone, and it behaved in a most peculiar fashion, for a wolf. I have no idea what's going on, Shadoe, but if we work together on this, maybe we can find out.''

She nodded. ''And we'd better get started. It's going to be a long, hot walk.''

The pure light of dawn brought action, but it did not bring the sense of safety and return to normalcy that she had anticipated. They ate the cold casserole and hot coffee for breakfast, taking care to tidy and secure the cabin before they left. Shadoe had no pack, so she went to look for the rifle that was always kept in the cabin. To her surprise it was gone, as were all the shells.

''I looked when I first came in.'' Hank shrugged. ''No telling who's been by here.'' He tried to hide his uneasiness. A rifle had been left in the cabin since he was old enough to remember. None of the ranchers who used the place would have taken it, without leaving another to replace it. The gun was left for emergencies, and sometimes, in the mountains, circumstances required a weapon for survival.

''Let's head home.'' Shadoe closed the door and they stepped off the porch together, stopping to examine the print of a large wolf beside the path.

''It wasn't a dream,'' Shadoe said softly.

''No.'' Hank took her arm. It hadn't been a dream at all, and that was what worried him.

They walked steadily, pausing for water from the canteen or some of the dried fruit Shadoe had raided from the pantry. Then they walked on. They spoke of the past, of small incidents that were neither too joyful nor too painful. The secret pleasure of the night was between them, filling the soft silences that occasionally fell as they struggled up a steep incline or sat, exhausted, to rest.

They walked south. The sun rose steadily at their right shoulder until it centered overhead, high and hot. Shadoe calculated they were a little over halfway home. There had been no sign of the horses—or the wolf. She felt her anxiety grow the closer she got to home. Were Scrapiron, Luster and the others okay? Had Jill thought to check on them when Shadoe didn't answer the phone? Jill called almost every evening. Surely she'd think something was wrong. Shadoe tried to calm herself with those assurances. And she tried not to glance forward at Hank too often.

She found she could not look at him without thinking what his touch could do to her. To let even the memory of his kiss whisper through her mind was torment. With all of her desire to hurry home, she also wanted to settle down beside a small stream that whispered through the newly greening grass and gaze into his eyes.

Hank set a steady pace, but he was painfully aware of Shadoe. He made sure she kept up without straining herself, and he fought down the urge to pull her into his arms and press her down to the earth. He could see her worry, and he understood. When he looked at her, he felt such a mix of emotions, he wasn't certain what they meant.

Did he regret what had happened between them? He wasn't a man much given to regret. This time, though, he knew that he had set himself up for harsh consequences. He'd felt the loss of Shadoe once before. If possible, this time it would be worse if he lost her. Still, he could not honestly say he would undo the night just past. He cast a look over his shoulder and her half-parted lips sent a rush of desire through him that was a physical pain. He turned his attention to the trail and walked.

The path led down a sharp incline to a small gorge where Hank heard the murmur of another small stream. With the snows melting in the spring sun, the energetic streams would pop up in beds that had been dry through the winter—and would dry again in the July heat. The sound was merry, reminding Hank of the fun he and Shadoe had once shared so casually, splashing together in the cold mountain water. They had been children. Such innocents.

She drew abreast of him. The expression on his face made her smile. "I'd ask you what you were thinking, but it's as clear on your face as if it were written in indigo ink."

"I'm thinking that no matter how much we need to get home, we should take a rest beside that stream and cool our feet." He grinned at her. "I think I feel a fever coming on. A dangerous fever."

The urge to get home was strong, but the desire for Hank was stronger. Shadoe nodded, her heart beating faster at just the thought.

Their first warning was the click of metal. Hank tensed instantly, putting Shadoe to his off side as he looked up the sides of the gorge. He should have known better than to linger in a place where they could be so easily ambushed, especially when they were virtually unarmed. He'd known there was danger about. His hand went to the dagger, and he felt her drop into a crouch.

"Shadoe, are you okay?"

The voice came from above them, and they both whirled and looked into the barrel of the gun held by John Carpenter.

"*John!*" Shadoe gasped the word. "What are you doing?"

"Looking for you." He held the gun steady at Hank's chest, but he eased his finger slightly away from the trigger. "Has he hurt you?"

"No!" She finally grasped the situation—as John might

possibly read it. "No, he hasn't hurt me," she reassured the cowboy. "It's okay. I went up to find Hank."

Reluctantly John lowered the gun. He pushed his hat back slightly and stared down at the two of them. "I've been trailing you for about fifteen minutes. I rode up here to this gorge, hoping I could set up an ambush, if it was necessary."

Hank said nothing, but Shadoe could feel his anger. He was furious at the thought that someone would think he'd hurt her. Well, John's assumption was partly her fault—and a lot Hank's. Hank had stalked back into town with an attitude a mile high. He hadn't bothered to speak to any of his old friends, to try to show who he was or who he had become. His actions had done nothing but antagonize the ranchers. Now with John, she was in the picture. It was something they needed to clear up. The two men had enough reasons to dislike each other without John thinking Hank had abducted her.

"It's okay, John. Someone stole our horses and we got stranded. We're headed back to the Double S."

John eased along the gorge until he was on level ground beside them. "I've got Chester and Ray."

"You do?" Shadoe couldn't contain her delight.

"I caught them early this morning trying to make it home." He gave Hank a dark look.

"Are they okay?"

John looked back at Shadoe. "Thirsty. Tired. Maybe a little ragged around the edges but they aren't hurt. How'd they get away from you?"

"Someone untied them." Hank's sentence was an accusation.

"Well, partner, if you can't tie a horse, I'd think about learning some good knots." John lifted one eyebrow in a challenge.

"Stop it." Shadoe stepped between them. "*I* tied the

horses and they were secure. Someone turned them loose, but thank goodness they aren't hurt.'' She looked behind John. ''Where are they?''

''Hobbled in the stream. They needed a drink, and I needed them to be quiet.'' He motioned the way for them to follow.

After Shadoe had found the horses and looked them over carefully, she finally joined the two men above the clear, amber stream. They were glaring at each other with deep distrust.

''Ray and Chester are fine.'' Her words dropped into the silence like a stone in a well. She went to the pack, got the canteen and refilled it at the stream. As she worked, Hank spoke. The tone of his voice was easy, almost casual. She felt a whisper of anxiety in his words.

''Where'd you find the horses, John?'' he asked.

''They were up above the Buffalo Pasture,'' he answered warily, as if he sensed the danger in Hank and his questions.

''They made it all the way back.'' Hank's tone was conversational.

''Yes, they were eager to get home. They couldn't find a way around the fence.''

''I suppose you were just out walking around the Buffalo Pasture, maybe looking for some old buffalo bones for an archeological expedition you're planning to host. Or maybe you were just out for a little exercise.''

''Listen, Emrich. I don't have to take your cute tone and not so subtle innuendoes. If you want to know, Jill called me early this morning. She'd been calling Shadoe and hadn't gotten an answer. She asked me to stop by the Double S and check on things, just to be sure.''

Shadoe found herself holding the canteen and listening. She'd been curious, too, how John had found the horses. It made perfect sense that Jill would call him.

"Must have been some kind of instinct that took you straight up to the most northern of Shadoe's pastures."

"You can skip the sarcasm. I was looking to see if any of her horses were gone. I checked the barn, the west pasture, the Butterfly Field, the Cottonwood Pasture, and finally I was headed up to the Buffalo when I heard the horses calling each other. Once I saw them, it was easy to figure they'd come from the north." John cocked his head slightly. "But just to be on the safe side, I called Jill and she told me about some old cabin. That was where I was headed, still wondering why she was riding one horse and leading another when she disappeared. It wasn't too hard to pick up the trail she left behind."

Shadoe stood up and brushed her wet hands on her jeans. "Well, thank goodness you found the horses, and they're here. Let's mount up and ride the rest of the way back. I'm more than sick of walking."

The men stood with her, but they refused to pick up her lighthearted tone.

"Were Scrapiron and the others okay?" she asked John.

"Fine. I gave him some hay and checked the water." He smiled at her. "Everything's fine, Shadoe, now that I know you're safe." He started to put his hand on her shoulder, but she bent to pick up a rock.

She held it up to the light, admiring the stone veined with pink, then turned to Hank. "An arrowhead." She handed it to him without thought. He had once collected them, and she'd always given her finds to him to keep.

Hank examined it critically, watching out of the corner of his eye as anger clouded John's face. "It's a good one," he declared, feeling the sharpened edge of the rock with his thumb. "Beautiful. Probably a ceremonial tip. Saved for a sacred hunt or a vision quest."

With those simple words, Hank created a moment of

intimacy with Shadoe. She looked at him, helpless to hide her feelings.

"Shadoe, we need to talk." John reclaimed her attention. "I owe you an apology for the other night."

Shadoe shook her head, as much to clear away the magic Hank created as to ease John's conscience. "Forget it, John. I have."

"You forgive very easily these days."

She looked past him. "Maybe I'm learning a little about growing up. It's about time." She walked past both men, picked up Chester's reins and mounted. "I'm tired, dirty and I want a cup of hot coffee and a long bath."

"An agenda even I could appreciate," Hank said, picking up Ray's reins and mounting. "Though I like my original plan much better."

Shadoe turned her horse so that neither man could see the pink that touched her cheeks.

"What are you going to do after your soak?" John asked Hank. "Half the county's out looking for you. If I'm not mistaken, there's some type of warrant."

Shadoe felt the words like a blow, but one look at Hank's face showed he wasn't concerned at all.

"What warrant?" she asked John.

The look he gave her was both angry and satisfied. "Trespassing. Harassment. You should know, Shadoe, you're the one who filed the complaint. Then there's the little matter that the federal agents are looking for him for some of their own charges."

Shadoe looked at Hank. "We'll straighten this out when we get back home." She nudged her horse in the ribs and started down the trail toward home.

When they arrived at the ranch two hours later, Billy was waiting for them on the porch of the Double S, his forehead furrowed with anger and concern. He walked down to the barn to greet them, pausing in the doorway as they untacked the horses.

"You two are in enough hot water to start a natural spring." He nodded to John. "Glad you rounded them up. At least Hank will have a chance to voluntarily clear this up. And Shadoe may get the spanking her father always threatened but never gave." He glared at her.

"I'd better get home." John led the big chestnut he'd ridden to a stall in the barn. "I'll give you a call later, Shadoe."

"Thanks, John." She walked out of the barn, away from Billy and Hank. She put her hand on his arm and looked up at him. "Thanks for finding the horses. I was worried sick. And thanks for coming to my rescue, though I wasn't in any danger." She wanted to make that clear.

"Are you sure you're okay?"

"Fine. It's been a…long day."

"We need to talk."

The one thing Shadoe wasn't up to was another conversation with John. "Let me rest. I'm really dead on my feet."

"You're worried about him, aren't you?"

"Yes." Hedging the truth wouldn't make it any easier on John in the long run. "Part of his troubles are my fault. This goes back a long, long way. It isn't just recent events."

John nodded. "I see." He picked up the reins and led his horse to the trailer. Halfway there, he turned around. "I wasn't All-Around Cowboy in 1992 because I quit. I haven't given up, Shadoe. Not at all."

She waved goodbye to him, his declaration making her sad.

"He's got it bad for you."

Hank's unexpected words startled her. She turned to find him right behind her. "Leave it, Hank," she warned him.

John wasn't something she wanted to talk about, especially not with Hank.

Billy walked out of the barn, his face as angry as when he went in. "Hank, here, refuses to go up to Stag's Horn and straighten this mess out."

Shadoe looked at him, startled. "I'll explain that my call was a mistake."

Hank shook his head. "Harry Code wants nothing more than to send me back to Washington. If I go back up to camp, he'll do just that."

"Be reasonable, Hank, they're going to issue a federal warrant for you." Billy spoke with force. "They'll pull your badge."

"That wolf is my responsibility." He looked at Shadoe. "I brought him here."

"Don't be a fool, Hank." Billy was growing redder in the face. "This is your career."

"No," Hank said, "this is my life. The job is just a small part of it. I realize that now."

"What are you going to do?" Shadoe knew he'd grown quiet on the ride home, but she hadn't a clue what he'd been thinking. She didn't like the way he was looking.

"I'm going to find Thor, protect the other wolves as best I can." He looked at Shadoe, then Billy. "Riding home, I realized that I'm in the perfect position to guard them. No one knows where I'll turn up. I'm a free agent."

"You're a wanted agent," Billy snapped. "They'll have a warrant out for your arrest."

"Maybe." Hank shrugged. "Code is capable of anything."

"No maybes about it, Hank. Code is letting it be known that he suspects you're the one who cut the lock on that wolf's cage. He's telling the local media you had a personal agenda here in Montana, that you've used the wolves for revenge. I hate to say it, Hank, but he's got the whole countryside fired up against you."

Hank nodded. "Harry Code always was an excellent showman, and I suppose the television cameras are eating it up."

There was an edge of bitterness in his voice that caught Shadoe hard.

"Half the newscast this morning was devoted to you and those wolves. He works hard at looking good for the cameras." The last was spoken with contempt by Billy.

"Let's go up to the house, since the horses are settled," Shadoe said. She wanted a chance to talk with Billy. Maybe they could devise a quick strategy to make Hank see the light.

"We'll throw some hay and check the water," Billy said, nudging Shadoe toward the house. "Go on up. We'll be there in three shakes of a lamb's tail."

"Thanks." Shadoe felt as if her bones were worn out. She started up to the house, already smelling the pot of coffee she was going to put on to brew. She'd made it to the front door when she decided to go back down to the barn and ask Billy to stay for a steak. With any luck at all, Hank would fire up the grill, and she could throw together a salad. It would be good to have Billy there—for several reasons, one of them being he might be able to talk more sense into Hank than she could alone.

She turned back to the barn, retracing her steps. The two men had ducked inside. She wasn't particularly listening, but she couldn't help hearing their voices, raised in argument. She stopped just at the door, wondering whether she should go on back to the house and start the coffee or interrupt.

"If you think Code's bad news, you're in for a bigger surprise. I just heard today that the television station in Billings has hired a new reporter."

"I don't care who the television station hires." Hank couldn't hide his irritation. "All those people care about is air time and ambition. They distort the facts to highlight the drama. I've known more than enough of them to realize they're all image, no substance."

"You should care."

"Give it a rest, Billy. I'm not going back up the mountain and hand myself over to Code because some snot-nosed reporter has decided to make me a villain. Code has been trying for the past three years to bust my chops."

"Hank, WSTU has hired Kathy Lemon."

Inside the barn there was silence. Outside, Shadoe could hear the painful beating of her heart.

"She's been out of the business for a couple of years now. She was selling cosmetics in one of those infomercials." Hank was surprised. It showed in his voice.

"It seemed a little coincidental to me, too." Billy sounded worried. "Hank, she made some serious charges against you. To Shadoe. And to me. We've never really discussed this."

"That woman just won't go away."

"Are they true? Did you use that woman the way she said?"

There was a long silence, and Shadoe felt as if she needed to sit down. She waited, afraid to breathe. Scared to make a noise or she might miss Hank's answer.

"Yes," he finally said. "I knew her, and I used her. Or misused her, depending on how you look at the situation. But she begged for it, Billy. She wanted it so bad that she set herself up."

"Dammit, Hank." Billy's voice was sharp. "Dammit all to hell."

Shadoe felt as if she'd been slapped, hard. Her ears rang, her stomach knotted. Her balance was precarious as the blood rushed to her head. Before she could make her legs work, could force herself to go in the barn and confront Hank, she heard a car coming along the drive. Dusk was falling, and the vehicle that approached had its headlights on bright, and it was traveling at a fast speed. Shadoe watched, disoriented. It came straight to the barn at a very fast pace, sliding on the gravel as the driver slammed on the brakes. He was half-out of the car before it stopped.

"Is Hank Emrich here?" the driver asked.

He was blond, fit, wearing a flannel shirt and jeans. Shadoe thought she recognized him, but she wasn't certain.

Hank came out of the barn, followed by Billy. "Cal! What are you doing here?" He stepped toward the car.

"Dammit, Hank, I've been hunting you everywhere. Do you have any idea how much trouble you're in?"

"I've been trying to tell him," Billy said.

Shadoe stood slightly out of the conversation, her dark eyes on Hank. Still reeling from Hank's confession, she wasn't able to take in Cal's urgent presence. She was still arguing with herself, remembering Hank's tenderness, his lovemaking that seemed designed to give her all the pleasure possible. He wasn't the kind of man who took women, who used them, who felt they deserved such treatment. Surely she hadn't heard him right. He'd confessed to using Kathy Lemon as if it were nothing.

"Hank, you've got to turn yourself in," Cal said urgently. "Code is getting ready to blame everything that's gone wrong on you. He's having a field day."

"Let him." Hank's voice was almost a growl.

"You have to come back and explain things." Cal was almost begging. "The entire project is in jeopardy."

Hank shook his head. "If I go back, he'll just send me to Washington where I'll be 'detained,' as in chained to a desk in some Washington office. That amounts to being arrested without the benefit of a formal charge, as you well know. At least by staying here, I can guard the wolves."

"Guard the wolves!" Cal was incredulous. "If you go within half a mile of that camp they'll have you in leg irons. You're about to be a renegade agent, Hank. Do you understand what that means?"

Hank looked at Cal. "Exactly. It means that I get to use whatever force is necessary to protect those wolves." He nodded slowly. "In fact, you can take that message to Code for me. You tell him that I'm prepared to do whatever is necessary to safeguard this project. Tell him I've done it before, and I'll do it this time. He'll understand what I mean."

"Hank!" Billy's voice held censure. "That's a threat."

Hank looked at his old friend. "You're right, Billy. That's exactly what it is. And this time I mean it."

Chapter Fourteen

Shadoe, Billy and Hank watched as Cal's taillights disappeared down the drive. Cal had argued with Hank for another ten minutes, then accepted defeat. Hank would not listen to reason from him, or Billy. Shadoe had no advice to offer. She watched Hank's chiseled jaw in the falling dusk. She could remember the planes of his chest, the swell of muscle in his back and legs. Tears had collected in her eyes, but she would not allow them release. She would not cry for Hank, or for her own foolish heart. At last she'd gotten exactly what she deserved from Hank.

"Shadoe, would you loan Hank a horse?" Billy's voice sounded as if he'd asked the question once before.

"I've got to go after the wolf." Hank was speaking to her in a tone that was filled with intimacy, with caring.

She ignored the stab of pain in her heart that his voice caused. "I'm not fond of the idea of one of my horses being used as wolf bait."

There was stunned silence. Billy spoke first. "Shadoe?"

"It's okay." Hank moved toward her, as if he intended to touch her.

Shadoe backed away from him.

"What is it?" He looked at her, then at Billy. "What happened that I don't know about?"

Billy was looking at Shadoe as if she might be a caged cat.

"What's going on, Shadoe? I swear, you're generating enough electricity that if you held a lightbulb, it would glow."

"Take Winston. The buckskin next to Chester in the barn. Don't let anything happen to him, Hank. It's in my best interest if that wolf is caught. Once you've got him, bring Winston back. Then I never want to see you again." She turned then and ran, unable to hold back the tears any longer. She listened, but there wasn't the sound of footsteps coming after her.

BLIND ANGER pushed Hank up the mountainside to a campsite five miles from the Double S. He was still a long way from where he wanted to be, but he simply was too weary to go on. Winston was a good horse. Not the brightest animal he'd ever ridden, but calm and steady, perfect for the job he had before him. Shadoe had chosen well, if not graciously. Even at the thought of her he felt another flare of fury.

He'd thought, at last, that they'd reached some understanding. Tentative, yes. More physical than intellectual, for the moment, but there had been so much emotion there. With time, and talk, he'd felt certain they could find their way back to each other.

Except Shadoe didn't want that at all. As soon as the cowboy had appeared, she'd grown distant. And finally cold and hard. She had no desire to commit—at least not to him. Not on any level. He'd been a damn fool to ride along with his hopes high and his heart singing. This time she hadn't run away to hurt him. No, she was through running all right. But that didn't mean she'd changed. At least not where he was concerned.

He kicked another small branch into the fire and poured

a cup of bitter camp coffee. Billy had seen to some supplies while he was saddling Winston. He had come out of the house as grim-faced and angry as Hank felt himself. All he'd said was that Shadoe had refused to talk with him at all, as if he, too, had been tarred with the same brush as Hank.

A high wind pushed a cloud over the moon, and for a moment the cloud's edges were lined in silver. Jimmy Deerman had said that a moon-shot cloud was a sign of troubled gods, a coming wind of change. Hank couldn't agree more. He didn't need an omen from the sky to tell him things were bad and probably going to get worse. Along with his troubles with Shadoe, he'd failed to protect the wolves.

He sat forward, pricked by his own inability to take care of creatures he felt responsible to protect. Cal had assured him that the remaining wolves were in good physical shape. The delay in the release was having a negative impact, though. The time in the pens was beginning to wear on them, turning them into pacing, neurotic animals. They needed to be set free.

Without Thor, though, did the pack stand a chance of survival? What was best for the wolves? Hank looked beyond the campfire into the night.

Two golden eyes stared back at him.

At first he didn't believe it. Very slowly he reached for the rifle that Shadoe had provided, albeit grudgingly. The wolf stepped closer to the fire, staring at him without blinking. Thor was totally unafraid of the flames—just as he was unafraid of Hank.

Hank lifted the rifle, sighting down the barrel directly into the wolf's hypnotic gaze. At this distance, he could get a clean head shot. It was the right thing to do. To leave Thor out to fend for himself, without the pack, was a cruelty worse than a bullet. He could already see that the muscled body was leaner, almost drawn-looking. If he didn't kill him now, the wolf would go after someone's stock. Thor needed the other wolves to successfully hunt the wild game that would be his natural prey. Alone, though, he would have to take the easier livestock. The ranchers might not be kind enough to hand out a clean kill, and Thor was already too far down from the safety of the woodlands, too close to the civilization that hated and feared him on sight.

Hank pressed his finger to the trigger, sighting carefully. Sometimes a person just had to do the hard thing to make it right.

"I'm sorry, Thor," he whispered as he took a breath.

The wolf never flinched. He stared into the gun as if he could defy it, or as if he did not accept the power that it had to destroy him.

Hank took another breath, then slowly lowered the gun. He could not kill the wolf. Not with a hunting rifle. Not with Thor staring at him. There was dishonor in such an action. The odds were too much in his favor.

For a moment longer, the wolf watched him. Then he turned away from the fire and trotted into the darkness of the night.

Hank laid back against the saddle he was using for a pillow. He felt as if he'd been brushed by magic, some special message that had been given him, if he were acute enough to decipher it. First the cloud, then the wolf. It occurred to him that the wolf was following him, again.

"Yes!" He sat forward at a sudden thought. If Thor was willing to follow, he could lead the wolf back to the rest of the pack. With Thor there to take charge of them, he could release the others. Once free, they would be on their own, to survive or not. But at least it would be a fighting chance. The opportunity that he'd meant to give them long ago when the project was initiated.

It was the only way the release would work at all. Once

Harry Code and the ranchers were confronted with a fait accompli, there would be no stopping it. Whatever Harry's secondary motives toward the wolves might be, his plan would be foiled. Once the wolves were gone, there would be nothing to do but wait and see if they survived on their own.

Hank felt a surge of energy. At last he knew what he should do. Once the wolves had a fighting chance, then he'd turn himself in to Harry and see what he could salvage out of his career. Maybe there would be nothing left. And maybe he didn't care. The idea of a sailboat and a long, solitary cruise seemed suddenly very appealing. Perhaps there was an island out there, sand and blue ocean, where he could forget about mountains and wolves and Shadoe.

He put his head against the saddle that smelled of soap and horse, and closed his eyes. Sleep came instantly.

He awoke with the first light of dawn, stiff, sore and still angry at Shadoe. She was the first thing he thought of, and images from the night they'd shared made him scowl over his morning coffee. In one night she'd managed to get under his skin, and it wasn't going to be easy to get rid of her. He remembered, with bitterness, her father's story of a powerful warrior who fell in love with a spirit woman. Though the other members of the tribe warned him against her, he'd been unable to resist. He had gone down from the high mountains to meet her in the grassy plains where the buffalo grazed. They had held each other in the moonlight, unable to let go until dawn approached and she fled before the warm sun could turn her into mist. The warrior was left alone, with only memories of her. She was under his skin like salt, burning and itching, until he could endure her absence no longer and threw himself off a cliff.

Hank stood up and kicked dirt on the small campfire, making sure it was dead. Well, he'd given enough of his skin, and his life, to Shadoe Deerman. He was moving forward, and never again would she have a chance to wreak havoc in his life.

He saddled the buckskin and headed north, taking it slow and easy on the rough terrain. When the ground was level, he let the gelding canter, and in two hours he was in the dense woods of the national forest.

There was no way to be certain, but Hank thought he'd caught a glimpse of silver trailing him through the trees. He didn't trust his vision, but he did trust his instincts. Thor was with him, following. The plan was going to work. For the first time in hours, he felt as if his life had direction.

He camped another night, this time in the higher elevation of the mountains and without benefit of a campfire. If what Cal had said was true, there would be search parties out looking for him. A fire was too dangerous, and he was too close to his goal to risk detection. The wolf was still with him, he felt sure, though Thor had not paid him another visit. There were other creatures in the woods, though. Hank could hear them, and they drew closer than they would have if he'd had a fire. Too alert to sleep, he rested against the saddle and listened to the night sounds.

Nearby, Winston moved lazily through the clump of rough grass where Hank had hobbled him. At times the horse would lift his head and listen, as good a watchdog as Hank could ever find. If anything really dangerous came up, Winston would let him know. He closed his eyes and was tormented on the edge of sleep by a dream of Shadoe. In the dream she was coming toward him, all grace and sinew and hunger. Only fifteen steps away, she turned into a wolf. A small silver-and-black female. She came to him, eyes dark and blazing, mouth open. He watched in awe as she licked his hand.

Still aroused by the dream, he was startled awake by the sound of Winston shifting uneasily. In the distance there was the cry of a coyote, answered by another a good two miles away. In the cold, clear night, sound traveled easily, amplified by the rock walls of the mountains.

"Easy, fella," he said to the horse. The coyotes wouldn't normally approach a man. Just to be on the safe side he pulled his rifle from his pack and laid it beside him before he fell back into a troubled sleep.

SHADOE FLIPPED ON the television and watched the scenic views of Montana sweep across the screen, followed by sirens and a fast-paced clip of music. WSTU News At Ten flashed across the screen, and the camera focused in on Rob Richards, the middle-aged anchor who had been covering the news for the past twenty years.

When the camera pulled back, Shadoe got her first look at Kathy Lemon. She was coanchoring the news.

"Well, she's pretty," Jill said with a roll of her eyes as she put her glass of cola on the coffee table and picked up a handful of chips. "Really pretty."

Shadoe frowned. It was true, but Jill didn't have to keep pointing it out. The newscaster was blond, slender with blue eyes that seemed to sparkle. Her voice was pleasantly modulated with a trained, homogenized accent—and familiar. She was the woman who'd called Shadoe about Hank.

"At least Hank has good taste in women. She's..."

At Shadoe's injured look, Jill hushed. "I'm sorry." She shrugged. "Who would have thought you'd carry a torch for the guy for twenty years, especially since you walked out and left him like you did."

Shadoe got up from the sofa and started out of the room.

"Hey, I'm sorry," Jill called after her. "I didn't mean that the way it sounded. It's just that Hank is bad news for us ranchers, and I hate to see how he can get to you. I thought when you came back to Athens that you'd finally put the past behind you."

Shadoe sat back down on the sofa. She stared at the

television where Kathy Lemon was talking about storm damage in the central part of the state. "*I* thought I'd put the past behind me when I *left* Athens. I guess there's no escape from it." She sounded tired, and she was. She'd spent a sleepless night thinking of Hank. She'd tossed and turned in bed to the point that Totem, fed up with her restlessness, had actually bitten her.

And she'd gotten up the next morning and spent the entire day doing chores and thinking about Hank. How could she have been so wrong about him? Was it because she wanted to believe—wanted to find something of the past she still missed with a fierce ache and had hoped that he would be the way to find it?

"I know you said you spent the night in the cabin with Hank. Did anything happen?" Jill's gaze was sharp. There was a suspicious look in her eye. "He didn't hurt you, did he?"

"Not in the way you're thinking." Shadoe sighed.

"What did he do?" Jill leaned forward and put her hand on her friend's knee. "Shadoe, he can be brought to justice if he did anything to you. I think it's fortuitous that Kathy Lemon is in this state."

"Fortuitous? I think it's beyond coincidental." Shadoe waved her hands. "How *did* she end up in Montana shortly after calling me out of the blue about Hank?" What had begun as a small doubt began to grow into serious suspicion. "This is a little more than coincidental. She told me she was out of the news business. How did she land a job as a coanchor, and at WSTU, no less?"

As she talked she grew more excited. This wasn't right. Things didn't happen this way—except in movies. Bad movies, where coincidence was the glue of the plot. She looked at Jill and her thoughts stopped dead. Her friend was staring at her hands, twiddling her fingers together in one direction and then the next. "Jill?" she asked.

"It would be a terrible coincidence, if I weren't to blame for it."

Jill hadn't looked up, and Shadoe leaned back against the sofa. "I think you're going to have to explain that one.

"I told her about the opening at WSTU. When she called, she said she was a broadcaster but hadn't worked in the field due to Hank. We talked a minute or two. She said Hank had gotten her fired and blacklisted, and I'd heard that Arny Evans was looking for a newscaster. A female. So, I just...told her about the job opening." She glanced up at Shadoe and at the expression of disbelief and anger, she looked back down. "I regret doing it. How was I to know they'd hire her? She just sounded so miserable in her job, and it was because of Hank...." She picked up her cola from the table. "I'm sorry, Shadoe. I had no idea the woman would actually get the job, and I had no way of knowing how it would upset you."

Shadoe swallowed back her anger, and her bitter disappointment that the flare of hope that had risen was now defeated. Jill was the type of person who went out of her way to help others, even strangers. It was like her, impulsive, helpful, to mention a job to Kathy Lemon. It was also out of her hands who WSTU hired.

"Forget it, Jill." She managed to make it sound sincere. "The station wouldn't have hired her if she wasn't qualified."

Jill finally looked up. "I am sorry. I should learn not to meddle. If I could undo it, I would."

Shadoe gave a rueful smile and shook her head. "She's in Billings. Not here. If it bothers me, I can watch another station."

Jill's smile returned. "That's the spirit. So tell me, what went on up at that cabin? I'm not leaving here until I know the nitty-gritty."

Shadoe tried to blink back the sudden rush of tears, but

it was too late. She stared into her cocoa until Jill removed the cup from her hands and put it on the coffee table.

"Spill it," she said, trying for a lighthearted note. "It couldn't be all that bad."

Shadoe nodded. "It's worse," she managed to say. She looked at her friend. "I did the stupidest thing."

"Don't tell me you slept with him?" Jill was braced for bad news.

"Worse than that." Shadoe tried to laugh. "I fell in love with him." She swallowed. "Or I should say I fell back in love with him. I suppose I never really stopped. And he's…he admitted to doing the things Kathy Lemon said he did."

Jill's face went from surprised to shocked. "He did?"

"He told Billy. I overheard them in the barn." Shadoe fought for control.

"So, he admitted it." Jill got up and got a box of tissue from the bathroom. She handed them to Shadoe, who pulled two and dried her eyes.

"He admitted it. Without even sounding as if he were sorry." Shadoe felt the tears building again. "He said she deserved it."

Jill nodded, and her mouth was set in a grim line. "This is going to sound very cold, Shadoe, but hear me out. I know this is causing you personal pain, but you had to find out about Hank. Trust me, it's better now than later. And this could have a beneficial effect on the coalition."

Shadoe wiped her tears with a tissue. "What are you talking about?"

"It won't hurt to have WSTU on our side in the fight. The television can sway a lot of public opinion, and I believe Harry Code isn't immune to media attention. I've spoken with Mr. Code, and he can be reasonable." Jill got up and started pacing. "I don't want you to think I don't care that you've been hurt. I do. If there was something I could do to Hank, I'd do it. But maybe this is even better." She swung around to face Shadoe. "Let's call that woman."

Shadoe looked beyond Jill to the television. Another reporter was doing a clip of a traffic accident. The scene shifted to the newsroom, and Kathy Lemon was on the air.

"We have an update from Lakota County."

At her words, Jill swung around also.

"Earlier today, Harry Code with the U.S. Fish and Wildlife Service, issued a press release. Federal arrest warrants have been issued for agent Hank Emrich. Emrich is charged with destruction of federal property and sabotage. He is believed to be in the national wilderness in or near Lakota County. He is considered armed and dangerous." A picture of Hank flashed up on the inset screen beside Kathy's head. "Citizens are urged to use extreme caution. If Emrich is sighted, a report should be made to the Lakota County sheriff's office. Do not try to apprehend this man. He is armed and dangerous."

The camera focused back in on Kathy. "Now we'll turn to the weather. What about it, Rob? More perfect spring?"

"No, Kathy, there's a storm brewing...."

Shadoe tuned out the weather. She stared blankly at the screen before she looked up at Jill. As she watched, her friend went to the telephone book and began to look up the number for the station.

"As soon as she gets off the air, let's call her. You two have a lot in common, and it couldn't hurt the ranchers' cause."

"I don't know, Jill." Shadoe had absolutely no heart to talk with Kathy Lemon, particularly about Hank.

"Well, I do know. Strike while the iron is hot, as my mother used to say. This is some of the best ammunition we've had. We could call an emergency meeting of the coalition, but I'm sure everyone will agree with me." She wrote the number on a pad.

"I don't think this is such a good idea."

Jill rounded on her. "You've got to quit protecting Hank. He isn't the man you thought he was. He's come back here out of some crazy sense of revenge, and unless we stop him, we're going to have those wolves slaughtering our livestock."

Shadoe was still unconvinced.

"You're the only one who can do this, Shadoe. If you don't do it for your horses, do it for the rest of us. We can't afford to lose this fight. You can find a job in the city again, but most of us can't. We're ranchers, and we have as much right to survive as the wolves."

Shadoe picked up the cocoa, which was only lukewarm. She didn't drink it but she held the cup in her chilled hands. Maybe it was for the best. Jill was right, she was being totally selfish. Once again, she was putting what she wanted before the needs of others. "Okay."

"Listen, Shadoe, with a little extra push, we might be able to get those wolves loaded up and back in Canada where they belong. This is the best thing for us, and for the wolves. Do you want to see them caught one by one in leg traps, or poisoned and shot?"

The very idea made Shadoe queasy. Somewhere along the way, they'd become less of an enemy, less the terrifying killers that she'd once viewed them as. Something of Hank's attitude toward them had rubbed off on her—his and her father's. It was the dreams. And the big silver wolf that seemed to linger just on the edge of her consciousness. What had Hank named him? Thor? That was it. It was the way Hank spoke of him, as if he were more than a wolf.

"Okay, the news is over." Jill extended the phone to her. "Call."

HANK DREW close to the Stag's Horn encampment at dusk. Using the failing light, he settled into a camp and waited for the darkness. The wind had picked up considerably, and he knew it was going to be a bitter night. The normal reds and golds of the sunset had been swallowed by a building mass of gray clouds on the western horizon. After finding the best shelter he could for the horse, Hank ate dried beef and watched the storm roll toward him. If it rained, he might leave traceable prints behind. That was the drawback. The asset was that a storm would cover the noise of him setting the wolves free. The animals were bound to be upset by his actions. He could only hope they were eager enough for freedom to run long and hard away from the campsite. And that Thor would be there to lead the way.

But he had no control over Thor or the weather, and he was determined to set the wolves free. It was now or never.

By seven o'clock, the cloud was totally black. There was no trace of moon or stars. The wind sang through the fir trees, whispering, moaning, promising a wild night. Hank made sure Winston was tethered and set out on foot.

He carried his knife and the rifle he'd borrowed from Shadoe. He had to be fast and ready for anything. The area was familiar to him—there wasn't much of it he hadn't tramped over during his youth. This knowledge stood him in good stead as he drew ever closer to the wolves. He'd decided on a northern approach, coming in on top of the pens. The camp was south of the wolves, and the terrain on the western side was treacherous. He could negotiate the rocks, but it would take so much longer. Time was his enemy now.

Would there be guards? He had originally posted them, but none of the agents had felt they were really necessary. They had groused and complained about the extra duty. Perhaps with Harry in charge, the wolves' guards had been discontinued. He could only hope that was true.

He caught the first glimpse of the metal cages and the supply tent about thirty yards from them. That was the tent where Doc Adams had nursed the poisoned wolf back to health. It seemed like a lifetime ago.

Hiding some twenty yards from the wolves, Hank settled down for a long, long wait. He watched the wolves, aware that they were on to his presence. They lifted their ears and whined, pacing in their pens and cages as they looked, one then another, in his direction. This was the way it had to be. He wanted them to become used to him before he made a move. Still, he found that he was holding his breath.

At half past eleven, the guard walked past the pens, a perfunctory check before he went back in the tent to light and laughter, the sound of other men inside. With the wind rising, Hank couldn't tell who they were by their voices. A small part of him didn't want to know, for surely these men would be in trouble in the morning when the wolves were discovered gone.

He went first to the pen of the pregnant female. She was due any day. She needed to find a den and have the litter. As he watched her move about the pen, Hank smiled. Doc Adams had worked wonders with her. She was fit—and eager to be free. He could read it in every line of her body. Her mate was beside her, watching Hank while the female looked beyond him, to the mountains.

"You're first." Hank used the keys he had to the locks. Harry Code had taken his guns, but he hadn't bothered to steal the keys. There was no reason not to do it the easy way since he knew the release would be blamed on him. The keys would cinch the circumstantial evidence, but so be it.

He'd inserted the key in the lock when the tent flap opened.

"I'll just check on her boys, then I'm going home."

Hank dove to the ground and then scrabbled to the safety of the rocks. If he hadn't recognized the guards, he had no trouble figuring out that the short rotund figure that approached was Doc Adams, on his way to check on the pregnant female wolf.

Hank cursed his luck. Now he'd have to wait until the next guard check. He didn't want the release in any way blamed on Doc.

Chapter Fifteen

An hour had passed, and the storm had settled in. The wind whipped the trees back and forth with such force that Hank felt that those anchored in the harsh face of the rock might be uprooted. Now the weather had developed into a serious threat. There was no rain yet, but the wind smelled of it, cold and wintery. He pulled his hat lower and crouched behind a rock. The weather worked both for and against him.

Even the sporadic attempts to guard the wolves had been abandoned with the coming of the storm. Two agents had come out after Doc left and made sure the pens were securely covered and that the wolves were not exposed to the elements. Then they had zipped the flaps of the tents and hunkered down for the duration of the storm. Their attitude seemed to be that no one in his right mind would approach Stag's Horn in such heavy winds. They were probably right.

No one in the tents would hear Hank at the pens, but the loud noise of the storm also worked against him. He couldn't hear the approach of anyone else. He could be caught red-handed, in the act, if his luck was running against him. He could only hope the earlier sight of the moon-cloud and the appearance of Thor were indications that his luck was changing for the better.

The wind was damp with the promise of rain. It was only fifteen minutes away, at most, he calculated. It was now or never. He eased to his feet and gave the circulation a chance to return to his aching legs. The keys to the pens were in his pockets, and he brought them out along with a tiny flashlight. He was as ready as he'd ever be.

Easing from rock to rock, he moved toward the cage of the pregnant wolf. He'd made a circuit of the pens, checking all of the wolves to be sure they were fit to go before he released the first one. There would be no second chance to set them free if any weren't ready to go tonight. During the long wait, he'd established a list—the pregnant female and her mate; the six females, then the seven males. He could only pray they would decide to run for the wilderness instead of coming after him. The release wasn't exactly supposed to be done by a single person, a cage at a time. If the wolves decided to attack, he'd be dead before the guards could even get out of the tent to check on the noise. If they heard anything at all above the howl of the storm.

Hank was twenty feet from the pregnant female's cage when she saw him. Her nose went up in the air, and some signal passed among the wolves. They turned in the direction where Hank hid. Normally too shy to meet a human's gaze, they stared at him with a predatory hunger.

Hank watched their behavior and felt a surge of hope. They had not been humanized by the capture. Man was still the deadliest of predators to them. They sniffed the wind and grew restless, alert.

"Easy, easy," Hank said more to himself than to the wolves as he shifted from behind the rock toward the cage. There was no cover here. He was in the wide open if anyone happened by.

Just as he made it to the cage the tent flap opened and a shaft of warm yellow light fell into the night. For the second time that night, he dove to the ground and rolled, holding himself perfectly still in the thick shadows. Not ten feet away, the wolves growled a warning. The storm and Hank's unexpected behavior were making them anxious.

In the open flap, a slender man stood, talking. "Hank went to a lot of trouble for those wolves. The least we can do is check them." Jim Larson stepped out of the tent flap. He was so bundled up that Hank almost didn't recognize him. Someone in the tent called something out, and Jim turned and answered. "I think Code's a jackass, and I'll tell him to his face. Putting out a warrant for Hank. That's absurd. He was a loner but he wasn't a criminal."

There was an answer from the tent, but Hank couldn't make it out. He felt a warm regard for Jim. He'd never expected the biologist to take his side, but it was gratifying to know that someone hadn't branded him a criminal.

Jim started toward the pens with a flashlight. He stopped and cast the light in on the wolves. Sensing their anxiety, he watched them closer. "It's only a storm," he told them. He moved the light so he could see all the cages. The illumination lingered a moment on Thor's empty cage as if Jim were speculating on what might have happened to the large male.

Moving slowly, he started toward Hank.

Hank was torn between lying perfectly still or making a dash for the rocks. If Jim turned the light on him, he'd be completely exposed. If he moved he might draw Jim's attention. No matter how Jim sympathized with him, he couldn't ask the biologist to risk his career by keeping quiet.

Hank was about to make a break for the rocks when there was the sharp report of a rifle. Uncertain where the shot had come from, he ducked instinctively. There was a second report and rock chips from the ground stung his face.

"Hey!" Jim Larson's cry was one of alarm, disbelief. There was a third shot, and to Hank's horror, Jim clutched his chest. He staggered forward three steps, then dropped to his knees with a low cry.

Not twenty feet from where Hank lay, Jim fell to the ground as the flap of the tent opened and one of the other agents called out into the night.

"Jim? Are you okay?"

Only the wind answered.

"Jim, where are you?"

Hank held his breath. He crawled to Jim Lawson and pressed his fingers into the carotid artery. He was dead. Hank couldn't see clearly, but the stickiness on Jim's chest indicated he had been hit in the heart. Knowing the killer was still out in the night—probably with a nightscope—Hank backed away from Jim and the cages, back to the relative safety of some rocks.

There was a commotion inside the tent, and Hank knew that his opportunity with the wolves was over for the night. In a moment federal agents would be all over the area. One of the team had been murdered. Why? By whom?

Was it possible the bullet had been intended for Hank?

The mystery man Hank had been pursuing all over the wilderness was still at large. Had he turned the tables and followed Hank? It was possible.

Hank cursed his own lack of awareness. He'd been so caught up with Shadoe that he'd let his mind slip off the facts. And now Jim Larson, a good man dedicated to preserving the wilderness, was dead.

Hiding behind the rocks, he watched as two men dashed out of the tent, guns at the ready. He didn't recognize either of them in their burly jackets, but he thought they were Fred Barnes and Sam Lindell. They eased away from the tent, backs together as they protected each other from possible attack, unaware that Jim was dead not thirty yards away from them.

Hank's first impulse was to shout a warning. Instead, he

inched backward, further into the wilderness and the night. A light rain had begun to fall. He couldn't afford to be caught now. There was nothing he could do for Jim. Not even to catch his killer. The gunshot had come out of the storm, and he hadn't seen a thing. The real danger was that the sniper was still out there, possibly drawing a bead on the other two men.

Hank picked up a rock and threw it in the direction of Jim's body. The men whirled, guns pointed, and the beam of their flashlights searched the ground in front of them. Hank tossed another rock.

The lights followed the sound of the rock, skimming the ground until they stopped on Jim's body. Hank heard the men exclaim and hurry forward, and he knew he'd done all he could to protect them. He had to get away before a search party was organized.

He glanced at the wolves. He'd have to make another attempt—and soon.

"Ms. LEMON, this is Jill Amberly, from Athens." Jill lifted one eyebrow at Shadoe as she held the phone to her ear. "That's right, you spoke with me when you were looking for Shadoe Deerman." She nodded. "Well, I'm glad it worked out for you." She shrugged helplessly at Shadoe. "Well, she's right here, and she'd like to speak with you."

Before Shadoe could escape, Jill thrust the phone in her hand.

"Ms. Deerman, I didn't expect to talk with you," Kathy Lemon said in her cool, effortless voice.

"It's something of a surprise to me, too. I didn't expect to see you anchoring the news in Montana."

"Thanks to your friend." Kathy laughed. "It turned out to be the opportunity of a lifetime. I can't believe anything good ever came out of Hank Emrich, but it seems that in trying to warn you about him I found myself the perfect job."

"Karma, perhaps," Shadoe said, hoping she didn't sound as fake as she felt.

"Whatever you want to call it, I'm grateful. I might even be willing to give Hank a thank you."

Shadoe felt something twist in the vicinity of her heart. "Oh, really. I would have thought you wouldn't care to be close enough to him to speak with him."

"I meant when he was arrested and in custody. Did you hear our story tonight? We had an exclusive. Straight from Harry Code's desk to our audience."

"I heard." Shadoe took no joy in Hank's predicament. Whatever he was, he cared about those animals. She was beginning to be very sorry she'd ever let Jill put the telephone in her hand.

"It's going to do my heart good." Kathy Lemon's voice turned brisk. "Well, what can I do for you, Ms. Deerman?"

"We're having a meeting of the Lakota County Ranchers Coalition tomorrow evening. I was wondering if you, or someone from WSTU, might care to cover it. We're going to have a guest environmentalist who believes the wolves cannot survive in the United States without preying on live-stock herds. We'd like to get our facts before the people."

"Excellent. Just a minute and let me get some directions."

Shadoe held a thumbs-up to Jill, who clapped silently with excitement.

"I've been meaning to take a look at that area out there," Kathy said. "I hear with this wolf scare there's some real bargains in real estate."

Shadoe swallowed. "A couple of the ranchers have talked about putting their places up for sale, but there's nothing definite yet. They're afraid if the wolves come, they won't be able to get anything for the land."

"That may make another interesting angle," Kathy said.

"I'm not sure about that. A story could start a land panic." Shadoe turned worried eyes on Jill.

"But it is news, Ms. Deerman. We don't select only the news that serves our purpose. At WSTU we report everything."

Something in the woman's tone got to Shadoe. "Don't you think it would be more ethical to report land prices dropping due to the wolves after the animals are released? If the Coalition has any power, the wolves will be taken back to Canada and a lot of good people will keep the homes and ranches some of them have worked for generations. This isn't a news story, Ms. Lemon, this is a possible tragedy." Shadoe felt Jill's hand on her shoulder and realized she sounded extremely angry.

"As I said," Kathy intoned dryly, "we don't make the news, we simply report it. Now, if you'll give me those directions."

Shadoe handed the phone to Jill. "If you really want her here, you give her directions. I should have listened to my instincts on this." She walked out of the room and into the kitchen. Why had she listened to Jill? Why had she let her life get so completely out of her control!

The kitchen door burst open and Jill stood there. "What in the world, Shadoe?"

"She wants to do a story on the ranchers selling out. I'm afraid it will drive the land prices down even more, panic more ranchers into selling." Shadoe sighed. "The irony is that the folks who'll buy the ranches will subdivide them. Pretty soon they'll be laying curbs and drainage for subdivisions and the wolves will be driven back to Canada the hard way." She sat down at the kitchen table and put her head in her hands. "If my head didn't ache so bad I think I'd cry. Here we are, torn between wolves and subdivisions."

Jill pulled out a chair and sat opposite her. "That's why we have to fight this harder. We can't let those wolves go free here, Shadoe. I know being with Hank made it harder for you, but you're the leader. Our spokesperson. We need you behind us a hundred percent."

Shadoe lowered her hands. "I don't know if I can, Jill."

"You have to."

"I've been thinking that coming back was the biggest in a long line of mistakes. I could go back to Texas and raise cutting horses. There's plenty of market there, and the winters aren't nearly so severe."

"Texas isn't Montana." Jill gave a lopsided grin. "This is your home, Shadoe. Your place. You've got to fight for it. For all of us."

Shadoe groaned. "What else could go wrong?"

There was a loud knock at the front door that startled both women. They jumped and screamed together, finally forcing Shadoe to laugh. "Look at us. We've turned into a couple of total ninnies. Someone knocks at the front door and we jump out of our skins." She got up and went to the door with Jill trailing at her heels.

The pounding came again, this time louder and harder. "Just a minute," Shadoe called as she pulled open the heavy ponderosa pine door. To her surprise, a wet Sheriff Billy stood on her steps with Doc Adams behind him.

"Come in," Shadoe motioned them in. "Jill, put on some coffee, and pour a couple of brandies."

"Thanks," Billy said, shrugging out of his wet coat. Doc did the same, giving Shadoe a hug as he stepped into the house. "Ah, those ribs are fine. You would have squawked like a chicken if they hadn't healed properly."

"Thanks for the hug, and the diagnosis," Shadoe said, kissing the vet on the cheek. Something about the expression on the two men's faces troubled her. It was Hank, she knew it. Her heart beat faster. He'd been in her thoughts since he'd ridden off on Winston. No matter how she'd fought against it, she couldn't stop thinking about him, wondering what he was doing. Had he managed to capture the big wolf yet?

Jill brought the brandy and handed it to the soaked men while Shadoe stoked up the fire in the fireplace and waited.

"Sorry to barge in, Shadoe." Billy cleared his throat. He looked at his watch. "It's going on midnight."

"I don't think you came out in a storm to give me the time." Shadoe tried to sound lighthearted. Even as she spoke she felt her heart thudding against her ribs. It was really bad for Billy to beat around the bush in such a fashion.

"It's Hank, isn't it?" Shadoe asked the question gently.

Billy nodded.

"It's bad, Little Missy," Doc said. "Really bad. That boy's in some deep trouble now."

"What is it?" Jill asked.

Billy shook his head. "One of the biologists up at Stag's Horn was shot tonight."

"That's terrible," Shadoe said, feeling the dread creep over her. She didn't have time to analyze why, she only knew the worst was yet to come.

"They found Hank's rifle beside him." Billy took over the story. "They think Hank was up there tampering with the wolves when Larson went out to check. They think Hank killed him, Shadoe."

For one stunned moment, no one in the room moved. "That's insane," Jill finally said, sitting down on the sofa as if her legs wouldn't support her any longer. "Hank may be a rat where women are concerned, but he isn't a cold-blooded killer."

"Where is he?" Shadoe asked. "Is he in jail?"

Billy went to her and put his arm around her, leading her to a chair. "He's up on the mountain somewhere, Shadoe.

No one saw him. But it was his rifle. And they found something else.''

"What?" Shadoe looked up at Billy.

"An arrowhead."

"An arrowhead." Shadoe repeated the words stupidly. "That's the evidence against him?"

"It's circumstantial, but several of the team members remarked on Hank's obsession with arrowheads. It seems he kept a collection from when he was a young boy out here."

"But the arrowhead could have been there all along. They're all over these parts."

Billy put his hands on her shoulders. "You make a good defense counsel, but you're preaching to the choir. I don't think Hank did this. The problem with the arrowhead is that a lot of the men there made the comment that Hank's last two vacations were back over here to Montana to 'hunt arrowheads.' That's what he told his friends. That's why they teased him about his obsession." At Shadoe's angry expression, Billy squeezed her shoulders harder. "It is circumstantial evidence, Shadoe. We'll try to prove him innocent."

Shadoe stood up. "Prove him innocent! I *thought* a man was innocent until proven *guilty*."

Billy sighed wearily. "I only wish it worked that way. Especially this time."

SHADOE CLOSED the door on Jill and leaned against it. It was past midnight, and every nerve in her body was tingling. She was tired but too keyed up to consider sleep. Hank, accused of murder. She still didn't believe it.

It was true that she'd had her doubts about him. But not murder. Never.

She gathered up the cups and glasses and took them back to the kitchen. Running hot water in the sink she tried to make the pieces fit together. The one incident that came back to her was the night someone had entered her barn and turned Scrapiron loose. That positively wasn't Hank. He said he'd been tailing someone. Someone who had been up at Stag's Horn around the wolves.

There was also the incident of the poisoned wolf. And Thor had been set free to meet a possibly gruesome end.

None of those things were Hank Emrich.

Which brought up Kathy Lemon. There was something about the last conversation she'd had with her that provoked distrust. It wasn't her ambition or lust for news. Shadoe was a competitor. She knew the cost of being the best. Competition wasn't for the faint-hearted—in any business. But there was something.

As she washed the dishes slowly, she tried to pinpoint it. It had to do with the newscaster's comments about property for sale. None of the ranches had been put on the market yet. There had been talk among the ranchers, but that was worry and fear talking. No one, as far as Shadoe knew, had listed with a Realtor. No one had gone that far. So, how had Kathy learned about it?

With the dishes half washed, Shadoe dried her hands. She paced the kitchen, knowing she had finally come upon the thing that troubled her. Newscasters had their sources. It wasn't inconceivable that someone had spoken with Kathy and aired their concerns and fears. Maybe she was jumping to conclusions.

Maybe she'd jumped to the wrong conclusion about Hank.

That thought burned like a hot brand, and Shadoe went up to her bedroom. She went through her closet for warm shirts, socks and jeans. Without thinking through what she was doing, she found a waterproof pack and stowed her gear. Back down in the kitchen she loaded up food supplies, flashlight and batteries, and her pistol. From the gun cabinet she took out a hunting rifle of her father's and the shotgun she kept handy. When she'd accumulated ammunition and put it in her pack, she got her coat, rain slicker and boots.

Even as she picked up the telephone, she tried not to think about what she was doing. Jill hadn't had time to get home yet, which was perfect. Shadoe dialed her number and left a brief message. "I'm going after Hank. Watch the horses for me. And don't worry. I'll be fine."

Before her mind kicked into gear and she thought about the consequences of her actions, she went down to the barn and saddled Scrapiron. He was the strongest of all her horses, the one most likely to make the trip in such terrible weather. He was not the best trained or the best suited, but he stood the greatest chance of getting her up the mountain and back. He was also the animal she could stand to lose least of all.

"Let's go, boy," she said as she led him out of his stall and mounted. The rain was falling at a slant, pushed by the wind. It was going to be a long, arduous ride, but Shadoe knew she had no choice. Hank had to be warned. She knew he hadn't killed anyone, and she didn't want him walking into an ambush, labeled a murderer. He was liable to be killed. She had to go.

Hat brim pulled low, she set out into the rain. Within two minutes, Scrapiron was soaked and cold and she let him trot. She had dismounted and was closing the gate at the Buffalo Pasture when she felt the hair on her neck rise. Beside her, Scrapiron shied and whinnied, a loud cry of fear.

Whirling, Shadoe could see nothing in the driving rain. The wind had picked up and the sky poured water. She was already regretting her decision, but turning back was out of the question. If she didn't find Hank first, chances were she'd find him dead. The more she thought about it, the more she realized he'd been set up.

She wasn't certain where he had gone. Certainly not back to the cabin. If his memories of the night they'd shared were anything like hers, he'd never set foot in that place again. He was camping. It seemed an impossible task to find him in the vast wilderness, but Shadoe knew the territory, and she knew Hank. There were two places she felt certain he would be. At least it was a starting place. By dawn, she would be close to the first.

"Easy, easy, fella," she soothed the horse as she moved to a rock to mount. Her saddle was wet and slick, her pants soaking. Just as she got in the saddle, Scrapiron lunged forward and to the left. His unexpected action almost unseated her, but she hung on. She followed his panicked gaze and felt her heart crash against her ribs.

The huge silver wolf stood just within visual range.

Her hand went to the scabbard and closed around the rifle. Moving slowly, she shifted over to the shotgun. He was close enough that the shotgun would be a more effective—and more deadly—tool. Very carefully she drew it out. She'd never fired from Scrapiron's back, and she knew she'd have only one chance. Once she made the shot the stallion would undoubtedly rear, bolt and head for home. If she missed, the wolf could be on her in a flash.

Just like in her dream, she felt him watching her. Stalking her. Her throat closed in fear. Still, even as she drew the gun up, he stared at her. He made no effort to approach, nor was he afraid of her. He simply stood.

Shadoe was transfixed by him. Though she held the weapon that could easily kill him, she didn't take aim. She found it was impossible to lift the weapon to her shoulder when he was staring at her with such...certainty. Was she dreaming again? Very slowly she lowered the gun and used her legs to keep her horse from bolting. As unsettled as she was by the wolf, Scrapiron liked him less.

The wolf turned slowly, trotting several yards into the

rain, almost out of sight. He turned back to look at her again.

Very carefully, Shadoe nudged Scrapiron forward. The wolf turned and trotted away again, then spun around to look. She followed again. This time he turned and kept going. It took all of Shadoe's persuasive riding skills to nudge Scrapiron on, but she followed the path selected by the wolf and prayed that she hadn't lost her mind completely. An animal that she loathed and feared, the same kind that had destroyed her family, was leading her deeper and deeper into the heart of the wilderness.

Thunder rumbled loud and threatening as Shadoe, the horse and the wolf traversed the northern trail angling toward Stag's Horn. The night was so dark that she was forced to trust Scrapiron to pick the path as she kept her head down and her gaze fastened on the bobbing silver tail of the wolf. Not once did he look back.

She wasn't certain how long she'd ridden, or how far they'd gone. All landmarks were obscured by the storm. At last the rain began to slack off and she found that she was high in the mountains. They'd covered far more ground than she'd realized, moving at a steady clip, walking only when the terrain demanded.

The sky had lightened enough so that she could tell she was on a cliff and she reined Scrapiron to a halt. The valley lay to the south of her, and ahead was the blacker-than-night outline of the highest mountains. On the eastern horizon, the dull gray sky was beginning to lighten with the promise of dawn. Deep in her thoughts about Hank, Shadoe had ridden the entire night.

She looked ahead and discovered that the wolf was gone.

For a moment she felt completely abandoned. She looked in all directions, noting that as the sky lightened, she could make out more and more landmarks that were familiar to her. She was exactly where she wanted to be.

Scrapiron was tired, but she urged him forward at a walk. If her calculations were correct, Hank wasn't far away.

They climbed another steep cliff and the narrow trail opened onto a small plateau. The area was flat and protected by rocks and trees. Shadoe had camped there herself, years before. She felt Scrapiron tense and her hand went automatically to her rifle. He whinnied so hard she could feel him tremble beneath her, and then Winston's answering whicker came through the dawn.

"So much for sneaking into camp," she said, patting the horse's shoulder. He'd done an excellent job of carrying her through the worst possible terrain. "I'm going to have to add sure-footed as a goat to your breeding résumé," she said, relief making her giddy. She walked on toward the place where she figured Hank had put his campsite. There was no point in trying for stealth. He would have to be deaf not to know she was there.

He was standing beside a wet bedroll and looked as bedraggled as she felt when she rode into camp. He looked at her, then bent to lift his gear.

"Jim Larson was killed up at the wolf site." She spoke first and fast. The silence between them was too hard to endure.

"I know."

His words startled her. He had no way of knowing. Unless he was there.

She felt him watching her, and this time she didn't make the mistake of jumping to any conclusion. "How did you know?"

"I was there. I saw it happen."

Shadoe slid from the stallion. When her feet hit the ground they were numb, and for a moment she thought they wouldn't hold her. But they did. "You saw it?"

"I went up to free the wolves." He was lifting his saddle as he spoke, headed for the buckskin who stood patiently now that Scrapiron was within sniffing distance. "I was about to open the cages when Jim came out for a check. Someone fired three shots, long-range rifle. One nearly hit me; one went wild; one hit Jim in the chest."

Shadoe bit her lip. "Did you know they've accused you of murder?"

She was surprised by the shock on his face. "Me?"

So her trip hadn't been in vain. "They found your rifle there." She hesitated. "And an arrowhead."

Hank settled the saddle on the gelding's back and turned to her. "When Harry said he was sending me back to Washington, someone took my rifle and my service pistol. I thought it was peculiar, but..." He reached under the horse and eased the girth tight.

"I came up here to warn you, Hank. They'll be out looking for you. It's going to be open season if you don't turn yourself in." They would hunt him down the same way they'd go after the wolves. With powerful scopes and night vision rifles. Hank wouldn't really stand a chance if they went after him. If they thought he was a cold-blooded murderer on the run. "I know it seems like I spend a lot of time getting you to come back, but here I am again." She tried for a lighthearted shrug, but there was fear in her voice.

"I'm not going back until the wolves are freed."

Dropping her reins to the ground, Shadoe stepped to him. "Hank, please. They'll kill you."

He looked at her. "You've wasted your time coming up here if you thought I'd go back and turn myself in to face a murder charge. I'm innocent."

"Hank..." She put her hand on his arm. "Please. Don't do this."

"I don't have a choice, Shadoe. This is something I have to do." Her fingers ignited a flame on his skin. Compassion, concern, simple kindness, he didn't care. Her touch was magic for him. He felt his heart rate increase and he knew if he didn't turn away from her he'd drag her into his arms.

Shadoe felt her body warm at his close look. Hank was not a killer. Whatever else he had done, he deserved a chance to defend himself. If he went after the wolves alone, he wouldn't get that chance. Shadoe lifted her chin. "Then let me help you."

Hank leaned closer. "What?"

"Let me help you. You can't do it alone."

"You want to help free the wolves?"

She shook her head slowly. "No, I don't want those animals freed any more now than I did last week. But I want you to live, and if it takes setting the wolves free, then I'll help you."

At first Hank couldn't believe what she was saying. One look at her, though, chin held high and eyes flashing, and he knew. If she had doubted him in the past, she was now risking everything for him.

"Are you sure?" he asked softly. His hand went up to trace a corner of her mouth.

"I'm sure." She lifted her own hand and placed her palm against his cheek. "I may be a fool, but I'm a certain fool."

He kissed her palm, drawing her into his arms. "Oh, Shadoe." He bent his head to kiss her. The tree behind his head exploded into splinters and the delayed whine of a bullet echoed on the morning air.

Chapter Sixteen

Shadoe felt like a rag doll as Hank threw her to the ground and then fell on top of her, covering every inch of her with his own hard body.

"Stay down," he ordered, as if she had any other choice.

She could hear the nervous stomping of the horses as they fought their natural urge to flee. Her own heart drummed in her ears, making the silence that followed the gunshot strangely loud.

After a moment, Hank eased his weight off her, but his hand held her pinned to the ground.

"I'm not going anywhere," she whispered.

Hank released his grip on her with a muttered, "Sorry."

Pressed close together they inhaled the smell of dirt, of turpentine oozing from the big pine that had been hit by the bullet, the scent of horses excited and afraid.

To Shadoe, the silence was terrifying. She expected another shot at any moment. The first had missed only because Hank had ducked his head to kiss her. Another second—he would've been dead.

"Come on." His grip on her elbow and his terse command got her up and moving before she could think—or refuse. Crouched down and moving fast, they darted behind several large boulders.

"Stay here. I'm going to Winston. The rifle's in the saddle." His voice was a tight whisper.

"I brought one," she whispered back. Before he could move, she gave a low whistle. There was the sound of iron shoes on rock and Scrapiron trotted toward them, head tossing and nostrils blowing his disapproval of the entire situation. She started to stand, but Hank pushed her down.

With two quick movements he pulled both the rifle and shotgun from her saddle and slapped the stallion on the rump to send him out of the way. Ducking back down by Shadoe, he said, "I didn't chase that devil all over the mountains for him to take a bullet meant for you."

"For me?" She was caught completely by surprise. The shot had missed Hank's head. Not her's. She scanned the direction she thought the bullet had come from. The forest gave up no secrets.

"Think about it, Shadoe. Someone was in your barn, setting your horse free. You were the one clotheslined in the forest. You show up here and bullets start flying." Hank ticked off the incidents. "I'd say you were the likely target, and someone has been following you. Think back."

She went over her trip. It had been wet and dark. She'd been so intent on following the wolf that she'd paid scant attention to what was behind her. Treacherous footing for her horse and the need to press forward had completely filled her thoughts. Someone could have followed her. But still... "What about you?" Shadoe wasn't willing to see herself as the target.

"Well, maybe me," Hank conceded. "But more likely you."

"I'm not the one accused of murdering a federal agent," she snapped. "That could be one of your buddies trying to settle the score."

"Maybe my boss, but not the agents or biologists. There are procedures..."

"Sure, like all law officers who've crossed over the line follow procedure. I guess they'd say something like, 'Come on out, Hank, so we can finish setting you up for murder. Maybe we'll kill the woman, then you, and make it look like we had to nail you because you killed her.' Just a little courtesy to a fellow officer so that he knows how it's all going to come down."

Hank was silent. He didn't like to admit it, but Shadoe had painted a pretty good crime scenario. If someone truly wanted to frame him for the murder of Jim Larson, the scene she had depicted would do it perfectly. He hefted the rifle and handed the shotgun to her.

Shadoe had gotten his attention, but she wasn't happy with the results. There was now a hunted look in his face that hadn't been there a moment before. All he needed was one more betrayal.

Hank shifted so that he could see around the outcropping of rock, which served as their primary protection. "Why'd you come up here?" Even as he asked the question, he was scouting the area, looking for any sign of life or movement. The wilderness was totally quiet. The smaller creatures had taken cover to hide from an enemy.

"To warn you." She let that sink in. "And to ask a question."

"I'm surprised that cowboy let you out of his sight." Hank tried to make it sound lighthearted, but the attempt failed miserably.

"John doesn't have a lot of say over what I do or don't do." Shadoe shifted. The rock she was leaning against was hard. Her legs were weary with the strain. "Don't you want to hear my question?"

Hank let the silence grow. He eased his position some, leaning back against the rock. He'd kept a keen eye on the horizon as they'd talked. "I think whoever was out there is gone."

Shadoe nodded. In the distance was the sound of a fussy jay. The birds were moving again, a fair indicator that whoever had been shifting through the trees with a rifle had pulled back, or gotten very still. It was a matter of waiting now.

"Why would they take one shot and leave?" She looked around, wondering if their assailant was that adept at blending into the woods. "We're sitting ducks here. They could easily wait us out."

"Maybe they don't have time. Maybe they need an alibi for where they are right at this moment and their available time has run out." He shifted, then reached down and picked up her hand. His thumb made a light circular pattern across the top. "Okay, ask your question. But I reserve the right not to answer it."

Shadoe had composed the question a thousand times in her mind. She had to ask it straight forward. "What happened between you and Kathy Lemon?"

"I told Billy."

Shadoe swallowed and found a lump in her throat. "I know. I heard last night."

Hank stroked her hand, turning it over so he could inspect the palm. "Is that what got you so upset?"

Shadoe felt a shiver of something crawl over her hand as he held it. He was asking her that question as if she didn't have a reason to be upset by his confession.

"Yes," she said. "That's what upset me so. It's difficult to hear that someone you care about casually confesses to slapping a woman around and then raping her, all for revenge."

Hank's grip on her hand grew completely limp, then tightened. She watched his throat work and his jaw clench, and for a moment she thought he was going to explode into a rage. Strangely enough, though, his hold on her hand calmed her. His touch was firm, but not harsh, not brutal. Not threatening.

"Tell me exactly what you know about Kathy Lemon." The only sign of his fury was in the tenseness of his body. "How did she know to call you?"

"She said you spoke about me. That you hurt her because you were angry with me."

"I should have asked you what she said. Exactly. Billy said something about the fact that she'd called his office." His jaw relaxed slightly. "Now I'm beginning to see a very ugly picture."

"Hank, you never answered my question." Shadoe bit her bottom lip. She felt like crying—and she wanted to run. As fast and as hard as she could. But she wasn't going to. "That's the problem here. You never told me yes or no. One simple word."

"It isn't that simple, Shadoe. I suppose it never is. I had an affair with Kathy." Hank's voice was deliberate, factual. "We met while I was working on a case involving the importation of exotic birds. Those poor animals were being smuggled into this country in sock tubes, at least half of them dying of suffocation. All so some jerk with five hundred dollars could pump up his low self-esteem by having an exotic creature in a cage."

Shadoe was surprised to hear more anger in his voice directed toward the bird importers than toward Kathy. She felt her own tense body relax slightly.

"I had those bastards nailed dead to rights. I wanted to expand the sting, catch the U.S. distributors and the guys catching the birds. Somehow, Kathy got onto the details of our plan. She insisted that she be there for the sting." He looked at Shadoe. "She was a very ambitious woman. It was one of the things I liked about her. She loved her work."

Shadoe nodded. This hurt more than she'd expected. Hank had actually cared for this woman.

"I knew how dangerous it would be for her to be there. Some people don't just hold up their hands and surrender." He expelled a breath. "So I lied to her and gave her a false location." His voice became hard again. "But I wasn't the only one telling lies."

In the silence, Shadoe heard the horses snuffling for a bit of grass. The forest around them had settled into a peacefulness that she envied. "What did she lie about?" she prompted softly.

"Because I knew there wasn't going to be an arrest, or a story, I insisted that she come alone. No camera crews, no lights. Then I was going to tell her the truth. But things got very complicated."

Shadoe's heart beat faster. "Tell me," she said simply. Now she knew why she'd never insisted on the truth. Not asking was a form of running. If she didn't wait for an answer, she could turn her back and get away without feeling too much pain. Listening to this was hurting her. She hurt for Hank, and she hurt for herself.

"The original sting was supposed to take place right after I'd taken care of Kathy. But the plan fell apart. The guys we were after didn't make the meeting. We had to set up another. In the meantime, Kathy showed up at the location I told her with several crews, remotes, ready to do a live of the capture of the bird dealers." Anger had returned to his voice. "She knew if she broadcast such a story it would blow our plan apart, but she couldn't resist. The story could have catapulted her to a major network."

Shadoe saw the link. "And when there was no bust, she was furious." So that much of her story had been true.

"Furious doesn't begin to describe her. She was enraged, beyond rational thought. She attacked me in front of the camera crews. It was quite a scene."

Shadoe could picture it. Hank trying his best to duck the blows of a woman who wanted to take his head off. "Did you hit her?"

Hank hesitated. "I put up my hand to hold her off, and she ran into it. She wasn't hurt, but she played it to the hilt."

"And the rape?"

"A complete fabrication. Her own camera crew will testify to that. In fact, if there had been the tiniest chance that I'd deliberately struck her, don't you think she would have pressed charges?"

Shadoe ignored that question. She needed more time to think about it before she answered. "And the birds?"

"Someone tipped the distributors. After eight months of work the entire case fell apart. I'm sure they're still doing their dirty business as we speak."

Shadoe felt the pressure of his fingers increase slightly on her hand that he still held, but she couldn't look at him. Not yet. She had to have a few moments to think through everything he'd told her. There were questions she had to ask, she just wasn't sure what they were.

"Shadoe?" His voice held his own question.

"Why did you tell Billy that what she said was true?"

Hank saw the hurt and confusion on her face, but the anger was not there. Neither was the fear that he'd seen earlier. "Because what Billy asked me was basically true. He said that she'd accused me of making her lose her job. That I'd lied to her about a story. That was true, as far as it went."

Shadoe's head came up and her dark eyes fastened their gaze onto his. "Billy didn't ask you about the rape or the assault?"

Hank shook his head, brushing back a strand of her dark silky hair that teased the corner of her mouth. His finger lightly caressed her skin. "Billy never said anything about that at all. Kathy pressed charges on the assault, but it never even went to trial.'' Hank's voice hardened. "But it did go in my record. The complaint. Even though I was innocent.''

Shadoe felt the pressure of her teeth on her bottom lip as she tried to concentrate. Hank's revelations left a lot of rough edges, and she wasn't sure what that meant.

"How did that woman know about me, Hank? How did she know to call me and tell me a passel of lies?"

Hank's face softened into a grin. "I had a picture of you in my bedroom. She asked who you were. Something in the tone of my voice set her off. She was very angry. It took me a while to figure out she was jealous, and by then she'd pumped me for quite a bit of information about you." Hank shrugged. "I didn't see any real harm, at the time."

"Did you…did you care for her a lot?"

"I thought I did." Hank moved her hand so that he held it between both of his own. "I liked her at first. She was energetic, determined, hard driving. She knew where she was going, and I did like that. But I didn't really know her, Shadoe. She had so many qualities that reminded me of you, I guess I deluded myself into thinking she was everything like you. But she wasn't.''

"What are we going to do?" That was the most important question. They were camped on a small plateau in the middle of a national wilderness. Everyone in the area was hunting for Hank, thinking he was a cold-blooded killer. There was a wolf loose, and someone had tried to kill them. But Shadoe felt a rising tide of joy in her heart.

"We are going to get out of here. Then *you* are going home, and I'm going to finish what I came up here to do.''

"Not without me." Her jaw was locked as stubbornly as Hank's ever dared to be.

"Now you stay put while I scout around."

"I'm as good a scout as you are." Shadoe started to rise, but Hank's hand held her in place.

His face was set, but there was laughter in his eyes. "We're going to have the rest of our lives to argue, but this one time, please, just do as I say."

"Hank..."

"Trust me," he said, kneeling down so they were eye to eye.

Shadoe leaned back against the rock. This was a challenge, a test not of her obedience, but of her heart. She nodded slowly. "I trust you, Hank."

He leaned toward her and kissed her lips softly, surprised once again by the full softness of them, by the heat of her mouth and her hands as they moved instinctively to caress his face and hair.

He eased away from her. "I want to check out the area just to be sure we're alone."

"And then..."

"We'll talk about a plan." He looked at her, heat in his eyes, but also determination. "Shadoe, why didn't Billy ask me about that rape? That's the one thing that troubles me."

"I don't know," she answered. It bothered her, too. "When he went up to talk to you and you wouldn't answer his question, he was upset, but not overly upset. No wonder."

"Are you sure you told Billy about it? Or did Kathy say she did?"

Shadoe thought back. "Actually, Jill told him. Maybe she didn't put that part in, knowing how close you and Billy used to be."

Hank stood up, nodding. "Maybe. Now stay put. I'll be back in fifteen minutes."

He was gone almost before she could blink, slipping through the woods soundlessly. Shadoe picked up the rifle he'd left her and started to take a position. But he had asked her to trust him. Reluctantly she slid back to a seated position, braced against the rock, and counted the seconds until he returned.

Hank reappeared as silently as he'd left. "Whoever it was is gone," he said, his face touched with a new kind of worry.

"What did you find?" Shadoe knew he'd found something, something that distressed him.

"Hoofprints."

"That isn't unexpected." She didn't follow. "It makes sense they were on horseback."

"That big gelding you brought for me. Ray?"

Shadoe nodded.

"I noticed he had a chip in his shoe. The prints back there had the same mark." He looked at her. "Whoever was shooting at us was riding your horse."

Shadoe started to protest, but Hank had learned to track from her father. He wouldn't jump to a conclusion. She had to believe him.

"Who could take one of your horses without stirring suspicions?" Hank asked.

"Curly. He comes over from Jill's to feed. Or Billy." She thought harder. "Hoss, if he had a reason. Just about any of the ranchers."

"That includes John Carpenter. He's done it before."

Shadoe looked up. "John wouldn't shoot either of us."

"Unless he had a good reason." Hank's voice was cyncal.

"Hank!"

"Who else?" He ignored her censure.

She shook her head. "That's it."

"Shadoe, other than the wolves, has anything else been going on around Lakota County?"

"Like what?"

"Land prices going up or down. Development interests.

Someone has something to gain here, and I'm not so certain
the wolves are the central issue at all."

Realization struck Shadoe. "Kathy Lemon! She lied to
me about you, showed up here all of a sudden, and then
asked me about ranches being put on the market for rock-
bottom prices. Said she was interested."

Hank's fists curled. "How could I not have seen this!"
He put his fist to his forehead. "That's it! The threat of the
wolves is used to drive the land prices down. The ranchers
panic and sell out. An anonymous concern buys the land
and…in a year this place is a subdivision and someone has
made a killing."

Shadoe stood up, her own fists clenched. "What can we
do?"

Hank looked at her, then smiled. "They never intended
to allow the wolves to be released. That's why they set
Thor free. He was supposed to panic the ranchers and the
residents. Then, after an appropriate time, during which
hearings would be held again and the ranchers would sell,
it would be decided not to release the wolves. Of course,
after such a long stretch in captivity, they wouldn't be able
to fend for themselves and they would have to be destroyed." Hank spoke with more anger with each sentence.
"It's a perfect plan. All they needed was to get me out of
the way. And they did. I played right into their hands."

"They?"

"Kathy Lemon and whoever is working with her. Someone with access to the wolves, to my tent, to my belong-
ings. Someone who could set me up as a murderer with my
own weapon. Someone who doesn't give a damn about the
wilderness or the wolves or anything except money and
appearances." He looked at Shadoe, fury bubbling in his
eyes. "It has to be Harry Code."

For some reason Shadoe was not surprised. Code's behavior toward Hank all along had been too aggressive. Now

it made sense. Hank had to be painted as a killer, as a man over the edge. "And Jim Larson was just a scapegoat." She hadn't realized she'd spoken out loud until Hank answered.

"That's right. When they didn't kill you with the clothesline, which they were going to blame on me, then they had to have a body. Jim was the man who walked out of the tent."

"We can't let them get away with this," Shadoe almost whispered.

"We won't."

"But that still doesn't solve the mystery of who was riding Ray? Harry Code or Kathy Lemon couldn't have walked into my barn and taken a horse. Curly would have stopped them. Or Jill."

"They wouldn't have given it a second thought if it was John Carpenter, bravely going out to look for you."

Shadoe didn't answer. She'd known John for a long time. Was it possible he'd do such a thing? But wasn't it a little strange that he'd suddenly turned up in Lakota County, buying a ranch, ready to settle down when before he'd been as free as the wind?

"Look, John could have been used by them. Maybe he's innocent. Let's drop that. For now." Hank put his hand on Shadoe's shoulder, his fingers gently massaging the tense muscles.

She was only too willing to drop that particular train of thought. Someone had tried to kill her, or Hank, but she didn't believe it was John. Could she be so wrong about a person? Hank had been that wrong about Kathy Lemon.

She felt Hank's gaze on her and looked up with a defiant glint. "I'm not going home."

"Someone needs to call Billy and get him up here."

"I'm not leaving you. If you're going to free those wolves, you'll need my help."

He couldn't take his eyes off her. She was so stubborn. And she was so beautiful, he wanted to kiss her. His hand slid down her shoulder, moving to her back as he drew her closer to him.

"You're not going to be able to make me go. And you can't persuade me." Even as she said the words she heard the catch in her voice. Hank's look had nothing to do with force, it was all heat.

"We don't have to make this decision for a little while." He looked up at the sun. It was only midmorning. "We can't do anything about the wolves until dark. The only thing we can do is stay here and wait. Whoever shot at us is gone now, but he may be back."

Shadoe's knees weakened at the feel of his hand sliding down her back, moving lower with a gentle pressure that brought her up against him and held her firm. Just when she thought he was going to kiss her, she opened her eyes to find him looking at her.

"What?" she asked.

"Why are you suddenly so determined to free the wolves?"

Shadoe had given her change of heart absolutely no thought. But she knew the answer. Just as she knew that for twenty years and better she'd loved Hank, though she'd run as hard and fast from that knowledge as was humanly possible. "Because it's the right thing to do."

"What about your horses?"

"If what you say is true, the wolves will stay up in the higher elevations."

"And if they don't?"

That was something she didn't really want to consider. "Don't you remember the time we were fishing and you asked Dad what we would do if we caught the Loch Ness monster?"

Hank's brow furrowed, then suddenly brightened. "He told me not to borrow trouble."

"Well, that's sounds like good, sound Scottish advice to me." Shadoe kissed him on the lips, savoring the thrill that ran through her at even the slightest movement of his mouth.

Hank let her kiss him, relishing her initiative, knowing that they'd come a long, long way toward repairing a lot of hurt between them. Finally, he believed, he and Shadoe had turned the corner on the past and were squarely in the present.

Lifting her into his arms, he carried her away from the hard rock where they'd hidden and over to a bed of tender green grass that had sprung up in the shade of a silver birch. Very gently he laid her in the grass, then bent to kiss her.

Her arms circled his neck, pulling him down to her with an urgency that sent a bolt of desire through him. Hank knew that whatever else he'd lost in the Montana mountains, he'd finally found the one woman that he would always love—if he could keep them both alive to enjoy it.

Chapter Seventeen

Shadoe had not believed it possible that she could drift int
such a deep sleep, but the passion Hank kindled in her ha
burned away all of her barriers, and she had fallen into
sleep as sound as that of a child. She awoke with the fee
of the sun on her body, his arm around her waist. Even i
his sleep his fingers stroked her skin.

For a long time she remained still, her eyes closed, a
lowing herself the simple pleasure of lying close to the ma
she loved. The sense of hope and serenity that came wit
that admission made her feel as if she had stepped out c
a skin too small for her. She did love Hank. Had loved hi
for years. Fear had made her deny that fact, to herself an
to him. Fear had made her run from Montana, from th
place where her heart had learned the meaning of love. An
fear had made her run from everything that reminded h
of her father. That terrible, terrifying pain of loss that ha
overwhelmed her. For twenty years she had avoided thinl
ing about Jimmy Deerman, had denied all of the things he'
taught her. Now, that was over.

She opened her eyes and turned to find that Hank wa
also awake. Like her, he'd been savoring the moment, lyin
perfectly still.

"It's time to move," he said, shifting into a sitting pe
sition.

With two fingers, Shadoe traced the shadows the sun cast against his muscled back. He'd been good-looking as a boy. As a man, he was more than handsome. She didn't speak because she didn't want to argue with him, not after the last few hours. No matter what he said, she wasn't going down the mountain without him.

"Shadoe, I can't risk the chance of losing you." He spoke with raw emotion.

"And I can't risk the chance of losing you." She was calm, determined. "With both of us working, we'll have twice the chance of getting them free and gone. Our exposure will be cut in half. We can sneak in and fade out." She finally looked him in the eye. "I'm as good at this as you are. Jimmy taught me, too." Her smile was sad. "I tried so damn hard to forget everything he ever taught me, but I couldn't. I've held it all in my heart."

He leaned over and kissed her cheek, tickling her neck lightly as he knew she liked. More than anything he wanted her safe.

"Hank, there's no guarantee whoever shot at us isn't down the mountain waiting for us to try to get home. He might have set up an ambush. It's as dangerous to go back to the Double S as it is to go after the wolves."

Hank considered that possibility. It was true. Harry Code wouldn't think twice about ambushing a woman.

"I'm not going home." She rose, brushing the tender shoots of grass from her back and legs. "I'm going to put on my boots and find that little stream west of here. I'm going to soak my thoroughly satisfied bones, and then we're going to saddle up and head for the wolves."

Hank stood up and began slipping into his boots, gathering his clothes in his arms.

"What are you doing?" Shadoe could barely suppress her grin at the picture he made.

"I'm going with you," he said. "Sounds like the best plan I've heard today."

Within an hour they had packed the horses, checked the guns and Hank had drawn out the placement of the pens so she had an idea what to do. She would release the pregnant wolf and her mate, then start to work on the females, while he dealt with the males. With her help, Hank hoped the more timely release would result in the wolves packing up and fleeing together. He did need her, but he still did not like the risk she was taking.

They spoke softly during the first part of the ride, but as the sun began to set and they drew closer to the wolves, they fell silent. Hank had been scouting the area for Thor, but to his bitter disappointment, the wolf was nowhere in sight. He'd been there in the early morning when Shadoe had arrived. He could only hope the big wolf was tailing them, out of sight.

He had selected a high, craggy point to leave the horses. When they arrived, Shadoe felt the first tremor of fear. She had committed to a course of action that could end her life, and Hank's too, all for a pack of creatures she had once feared and despised, the very animal that had taken her little brother's life and led to her father's death.

As she slid from her horse, she saw Thor between two pines. The wolf was staring at her, demanding that she return his gaze. Transfixed, Shadoe looked into his golden eyes. Dusk was falling and in the fading light of day the wolf gleamed silver.

Hank was lifting the saddle from Winston's back when he saw the wolf, and Shadoe. The tableau held him frozen. Some communication he could not fathom was taking place between the woman he loved and the animal he had fought so hard to protect. As he watched, Thor turned and trotted back into the deepening shadows of the forest.

Shadoe turned to him, tears on her cheeks. "All of this time I've blamed the wolf. For Joey, and for my father. In my heart I knew the wolf acted instinctively. She killed to protect her cubs. But I had to hate the animal, because I couldn't hate my father for rushing out and getting himself killed.'' She brushed her tears away with the back of her hand. ''Now I think I can forgive them both.''

Hank eased the saddle onto the ground and went to her, pulling her into his arms. There was no need for words. It was enough to hold her.

Sitting together, they watched the stars appear in the sky and waited. When the moon rode high, they set off through the woods on foot. Hank had not been lucky enough to get a cloudy night for his second attempt to free the wolves.

Moving to the spot where he'd been the night before, they hunkered down to watch the camp. With Jim Larson's death, the guard duties had been intensified, and to Hank's dismay he saw that Fred Barnes carried a gun—drawn and ready. There was no card playing in the tent, no casual camaraderie. Fred was alone, and alert. It was going to be a tricky business, and he realized that success hinged on Shadoe's help.

''No matter what happens to me,'' he whispered to her, ''continue with the release. I'll be okay.''

''The same applies to me,'' she answered.

As Fred returned to the tent, Hank nodded and they crept over the remaining ground to the cages.

Shadoe approached the first cage and was stricken with an unexpected feeling of dread. Inside the cage the female growled at her, warning her away, and Shadoe wanted to run, to turn tail and beat it to safety. She had come to terms with her brother's death, and her father's, but she feared the wolves, feared the fangs that could tear her throat out with one powerful snap. The terror of her nightmares threatened to immobilize her. She could hear Hank levering off the locks, but she couldn't move.

A sliver of moonlight sifted through the boughs of a fir and struck the ground at her feet. It was exactly the color of Thor's coat. At that thought, Shadoe unfroze. She hustled toward the cage and used the key Hank had given her.

Stepping far back, she opened the cage and went on to the male. To her surprise, the wolves lingered in their cages, unwilling to leave the space that was both haven and prison. She had four doors open when she heard the flap of the tent explode outward.

"Who's there?" Cal Oberton stepped out of the tent, his automatic pistol drawn and clearly visible as he stood in the tent opening.

"What's going on there?" His voice was edgy with fear. He did not intend to become the second murdered agent.

Before Shadoe could duck, a flashlight beam caught her squarely in the face, blinding her.

"What are you doing here?" Cal demanded.

Shadoe calmly turned to the next cage. She had to delay him so Hank could complete the work.

"I'm turning the wolves out," she answered. "They deserve to be free."

She was totally unprepared for the incredible sound of a gun being fired. The blow to her shoulder was like a hammer, so hard that she spun around in a circle before falling to the ground. It took her a moment to understand she'd been shot.

"What the hell?" Cal shouted. "Who's shooting? Put down that gun, you idiot," he shouted as he ran toward Shadoe, dropping and rolling as if he, too, might be a target. When he got to her he flashed the light in her face, and then her shoulder. "What are you trying to do?" he asked. "Where's Hank?"

Before she could answer, she felt Hank's arms around her.

"Shadoe!" He snatched the light from Cal's hand and immediately found the bullet wound. He scooped her into his arms and ran with her to the tree line.

When he deposited her on the ground, she pushed him away. "The wolves! You have to save them, Hank. Now! I'll be okay."

Hank hesitated, gauging the placement of the wound, Shadoe's safety, and the fate of the wolves. Cal materialized out of the darkness beside him.

"I searched around, but I couldn't find anyone out there. I don't know who in the hell shot her." Cal still had his gun drawn. "Is she bad?"

"No." Shadoe answered. "Shoulder wound. I'll be fine, but you can't stand around here gawking. Go!" Seeing his indecision, Shadoe held up the key. "Go now. For once in your life, Hank, don't argue."

He took the key from her. "Watch her for me, Cal." He disappeared into the night.

Left alone with the other agent, Shadoe forced herself into a sitting position. The wound hurt like hell, but she knew it wasn't life-threatening.

"Help him, Cal," she said. The pain was beginning to kick in and she thought she might faint, but she gritted her teeth. "This is our only chance. Set them free," she said. "Help Hank."

Cal placed the heel of his hand on Shadoe's shoulder and pressed. "You're losing a lot of blood," he said.

She shook her head. "I'm okay. Really. Hank didn't hurt anyone. This is our only chance to do what's right."

"Your shoulder... There's someone out there trying to kill us."

"The wolves," she said. "I won't die in three minutes' time."

Cal pulled a set of keys from his own pocket. He weighed them in his hand, then turned to the cages. "Hank?"

"Yeah?"

"Let's do it."

Shadoe felt a sense of total relief as she closed her eyes and concentrated on surrendering to the pain as her father had taught her. Go with it, don't fight. Save your strength to live, don't fight. Visualize the blood stopping. The wound was worse than she'd let on, but Hank had to free the wolves. She could take the pain. With the pain, there was no room for fear, not even when one of the wolves finally made a break for freedom and leaped across her, taking off for the woods. The others followed, tearing away from the cages in a pack, just as Hank had hoped.

From a long distance, she heard Hank's voice. "That's it, Cal. They're gone." She felt his hands on her body, assessing the damage, applying pressure to her shoulder.

"Cal, it's worse than I thought. Is Doc anywhere around here?" Hank asked. "She's losing blood too fast. There's not time to get her down the mountain and there's no place here for a chopper to land and pick her up."

"Who the hell shot her?" Cal asked. "I never saw another person."

Hank kept the pressure on her shoulder. He felt his panic rising. He could feel Shadoe weakening beneath his hands. Nothing mattered except they stop the bleeding and save her.

"Get some help," Hank said between clenched teeth. "Run, Cal!"

Cal took off, moving down to the campsite where the other agents were undoubtedly scrambling up at the sound of the gunshot.

Feeling desperately helpless, Hank exerted more force against Shadoe's shoulder, as if he could press the blood back into her by sheer will. Even in the moonlight he could see the pallor of her skin. "Oh, Shadoe, I love you," he said. He'd been unable to say those words to her that afternoon. Now he couldn't stop himself.

She didn't open her eyes, but she smiled. "I know." Her voice was a whisper. "I love you, Hank. I always have."

"How touching."

The angry voice cut through the darkness. Hank looked up. Standing at the edge of the clearing was Jill Amberly. She held a rifle pointed at Hank's chest.

"So, the two lovers finally come to terms, just at the moment of their death. Rather Shakespearean, don't you think?" Her laugh was filled with hatred.

At the sound of her friend's voice, Shadoe turned to her. "Jill?" Her voice held disbelief. "Jill, is that you? Thank goodness you've come. How did you know where to find me?"

"You followed the bait. I followed you." Jill's voice was matter-of-fact. "You've been the perfect foil, Shadoe. Egging Hank on, speaking for the ranchers. You'll be shot with his weapon, just like that other agent. And then I'll have to kill Hank."

Weak from the loss of blood, Shadoe didn't believe what she was hearing. "Jill?" Her voice almost broke. "This must be a nightmare. Like the wolf. But it never happened." She was rambling, but she couldn't stop herself.

Hank kept the pressure on Shadoe's shoulder, holding her steady. "Put the gun away, Jill."

"Not on your life."

"The wolves are gone," he said softly, shifting so that he was between Shadoe and the gun.

"So they are," Jill said. "It won't take much to hunt them down and kill them. After the ranchers have panicked, of course." She stepped closer, the gun held steady. "It was always in my plan to release them. In fact, that's what I came up here to do. You just saved me the effort."

"You wanted them released?" Hank had to keep her talking.

"Absolutely. Just the threat wouldn't push landowners to sell. I tried to make Harry see that, but he didn't believe me. It had to be an accomplished fact. Then a few neatly arranged livestock slaughters, more ranchers sell out. After a few months of panic, we turn the tide of public opinion against the wolves and kill them. By then I'll own thousands of acres. Land which will sell at a premium if it's divided into those lovely little ranchettes."

"Why?" Hank's question was softly put.

"I hate this life. I hate everything about it. Shadoe escaped. You left. I couldn't. My folks depend on me to send them money to live on. They left me here to do what they couldn't stomach anymore, and I had no choice. I couldn't sell. I couldn't get dirt for my ranch, it's too small. So when I heard that you were up here two years ago scouting out a place to release those wolves, I came up with a plan where I could make enough money to get the hell out of here and buy myself a new life. No cows. No parents. No schedule of work from sunup to sundown."

"You could have left, Jill." Hank's statement was softly put. "I did. I made a life for myself somewhere else. You could, too."

"I couldn't!" She almost screamed the words. *"I* was the one my parents counted on. *I* was the one who could do it and make it work. I could scrimp and save and slave. No one else would have worked the way I have for the past twenty years. No life, no family. Just work. Just trying to make ends meet so I could support everyone who counted on me."

Hank thought of a million plans, but none would work. Jill would kill him if he moved. He could hear the bitterness in her voice. How had he failed to see it before? She'd always been so perky, so much Shadoe's friend. How had she shot her?

"Stand up, Hank," Jill ordered.

"I can't. She'll bleed to death."

"Exactly." She waved the gun, motioning him up. "Do it or I'll shoot you there and watch her bleed after you're dead."

"Why, Jill?"

"It's not personal. It's just expedient. You two were bound to figure it out. Harry and I can't risk such loose ends dangling."

"Harry and you. I never would have thought." Hank had to keep her talking.

"I have a right to a life. We want the same things. Harry understands. And he knows how to get what he wants."

Hank shifted a tiny bit away from Shadoe. When he made his move, he didn't want her to get caught with the bullet. "They'll catch you."

She shook her head. "No. They won't. You'll be dead. They'll hunt for a few days for Shadoe's killer, but they'll give it up. Harry will see to it."

"Not Billy. He won't ever give up. He knows I'd never harm Shadoe. And Cal, too."

Jill shrugged. "We'll see. We're in this so deep now that Billy won't be much of an obstacle. Neither will Cal Oberton. If they are..." She waved the gun. "Now stand."

Hank knew that his time for stalling was up. Jill had gone completely over the edge. Greed, heartbreak, stress, he didn't know exactly the ingredients that had destroyed her. Maybe she'd fallen victim to one of Harry's schemes. Hank didn't know—or care. All he knew was that she was a dangerous woman. One who meant to kill him. There was no sound of reinforcements coming up the trail. No cavalry to the rescue. If he stood, Shadoe would die. If he didn't, they'd die together. He shifted, starting up easily. Maybe he could take a dive at her. It was his only chance.

As he rose, he saw a gleam of silver darting through the trees. Without a sound of warning, Thor burst into the clearing, a streak of white fang and silver body as he rose in a giant leap, flying through the air until his jaws locked around Jill's arm that held the gun.

Her shot went wild, and her scream followed the blast of the rifle. Thor knocked her to the ground, wrestling her arm back and forth in his jaws. Her screams of pain and terror filled the night.

Hank moved swiftly to the wolf. He had little time. "Thor," he said, placing a hand on the wolf's back. At his touch, Thor dropped Jill's arm and turned away. He ran to the edge of the woods, gave one look back, then ran. Hank picked up the rifle and rushed back to Shadoe. To his surprise she was up on one elbow, watching the scene with amazement.

"He saved you," she said.

"Are you surprised?" He eased her back and applied pressure once again to the wound.

She looked up into Hank's face. "No. I'm not surprised at Thor." Her voice faltered. "How bad is Jill hurt?"

"Rest, Shadoe," Hank said. Several feet away Jill was moaning and he knew he had to see about her, but not before help arrived for Shadoe. Even as he thought it, he heard the sound of the men coming. They broke into the clearing, guns at the ready.

"Doc!" Hank recognized the rotund veterinarian and called him to Shadoe. Doc paused, looking at Jill as she thrashed on the ground, holding her bitten arm.

"Shadoe first," Hank said. "Jill just tried to kill both of us."

Doc hurried over and knelt down. As one of the other agents held a flashlight, he probed the wound. "Well, Shadoe, that bullet has to come out. Do you trust an old horse doctor?"

Shadoe's grin was weak. "Do it, Doc. I couldn't be in better hands."

HANK ADJUSTED the shoulder of Shadoe's dress, the beaded buckskin warm in his hands.

"The bandage doesn't show, does it?" she asked.

"I've never known you to worry so much about your appearance," he said, brushing a silky strand of her hair from her cheek. "You look beautiful."

"I've never been married before," she answered, her voice breaking despite her best efforts. She turned away, afraid if she didn't she'd cry from happiness. Instead, she glanced down at the spectacular vista that spread below her—meadow, mountain, the June beauty of Montana. They had chosen Stag's Horn as the place for the ceremony.

"Are we ready?"

They both turned to find Billy standing, hands clasped in front of him, silver hair blowing in the gentle breeze. Doc Adams was there, too, and the preacher. They had invited no one else.

Doc stepped forward and kissed Shadoe's cheek. "I've never seen a lovelier bride. Especially not one with a hole in her shoulder," he teased. He bent lower. "Your father would be so proud of you."

Once again Shadoe felt the threat of tears, but the pressure of Hank's hand on her back made her straighten her spine and smile.

She looked around her, missing the woman who had been her best friend, and worst enemy. Jill's wounds from the wolf bite had been minimal. Thor could have torn off her arm, but he had barely bitten her. She was in jail, along with Harry Code, who had also been charged with the murder of Jim Larson. Kathy Lemon, though she had not been a part of Jill's scheme, had once again been fired when the WSTU news director had learned about her lies.

And the wolves were free. For better or for worse.

"They're out there, somewhere. Maybe watching us," Hank said, rubbing her back. "And they owe their freedom to you."

"To you," she corrected. "I wish Thor could be here," she added.

Hank kissed her cheek as he turned her to face the minister, Billy on one side of him and Doc beside her.

"Who says he isn't?" he whispered in her ear.

HARLEQUIN®

I N T R I G U E ®

COMING NEXT MONTH

#413 LOVER UNKNOWN by Shawna Delacorte
Lawman
When Lauren Jamison found him injured and delirious, she looked past the danger surrounding Kyle Delaney. After one encounter she'd become a prisoner of passion. But should she risk her heart on a man who could be on the wrong side of the law?

#414 THE REDEMPTION OF DEKE SUMMERS by Gayle Wilson
Hidden Identity
Loving was a luxury running-man Deke Summers couldn't afford—especially loving a woman like Becki Travers. But now his past has caught up with him, and more than their own desires have bound Deke and Becki in a race for their lives—and the life of her son.

#415 MIDNIGHT WISHES by Carla Cassidy
Cheyenne Nights
Everyone believes Abby Connor was guilty of killing her ex-husband. Now even she is uncertain of her innocence, or her sanity. Not to mention her new ranch hand, Luke Black. Just what does this stranger want from her?

#416 HIS KIND OF TROUBLE by Vivian Leiber
The last thing Austin Smith wanted was to guard a pregnant woman, especially one who'd jilted him. But he was duty bound to protect Tarini Schaskylavitch: he'd promised his buddy—and her ambassador fiancé—to watch her and her royal heir as his own. But how safe would she be when she revealed the precious secret she carried?

AVAILABLE THIS MONTH:

Look us up on-line at: http://www.romance.net

Heartbreak
RANCH

Four generations of independent women...
Four heartwarming, romantic stories of the West...
Four incredible authors...

Fern Michaels
Jill Marie Landis
Dorsey Kelley
Chelley Kitzmiller

Saddle up with Heartbreak Ranch, an outstanding
Western collection that will take you on a whirlwind
trip through four generations and the exciting,
romantic adventures of four strong women who
have inherited the ranch from Bella Duprey,
famed Barbary Coast madam.

Available in March,
wherever Harlequin books are sold.

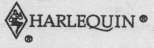

LOVE *or* MONEY?
Why not Love *and* Money!
After all, millionaires
need love, too!

How to Marry a MILLIONAIRE

**Suzanne Forster,
Muriel Jensen
and
Judith Arnold**

bring you three original stories
about finding that one-in-a million man!

Harlequin also brings you
a million-dollar sweepstakes—enter
for your chance to win a fortune!

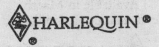

❖ HARLEQUIN ®

Look us up on-line at: http://www.romance.net

HTMM

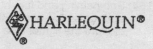

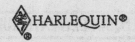

Not The Same Old Story!

 Exciting, emotionally intense romance stories that take readers around the world.

 Vibrant stories of captivating women and irresistible men experiencing the magic of falling in love!

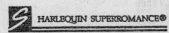 Bold and adventurous— Temptation is strong women, bad boys, great sex!

HARLEQUIN SUPERROMANCE® Provocative, passionate, contemporary stories that celebrate life and love.

 Romantic adventure where anything is possible and where dreams come true.

HARLEQUIN® **INTRIGUE®** Heart-stopping, suspenseful adventures that combine the best of romance and mystery.

 Entertaining and fun, humorous and romantic—stories that capture the lighter side of love.